ANNA FINCH

VOICELESS

A MERMAID'S TALE

ANNA FINCH

IBSN Paperback: 978-0-6489081-1-1
Published by Finch Press
finchpresspublishing.com
annafinchauthor.com

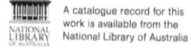

A catalogue record for this
work is available from the
National Library of Australia

For my family, who encouraged me to follow my dreams.

Never be afraid to raise your voice for honesty and truth and compassion against injustice and lying and greed. If people all over the world...would do this, it would change the earth.
- William Faulkner, 1952

Our lives begin to end the day we become silent about the things that matter.
- Martin Luther King Jr, 1963

Prefiero morir de pie que vivir de rodillas.
I'd rather die on my feet than to live on my knees.
- Emiliano Zapata, 1919

Glossary

	Hebrew	Pronunciation	English
1.	לעקוף את ההגנות	la'akof et hahaganott	bypass the protection
2.	להסיר את הכתם	lehassir et haketem	remove the stain
3.	להסיר את האצות	lehassir et haatsaot	remove the algae
4.	לתקן את הנזק	letaqenn et hanezeq	repair the damage
5.	לשנות את המראה שלי	leshanott ett hamareah sheli	change the way I look
6.	תחפושת	takhepossett	disguise
7.	ליצור הסחת דעת	litzor hasahaat da'att	to create a diversion
8.	להסתיר	lehasstir	conceal
9.	להתבגר	lehitebager	to get old
10.	לשנות את השיער שלי	leshanott et hase'aar sheli	change my hair
11.	להיות אנושי באופן זמני	liheyott enoshie be'ofen zmani	to become human temporarily
12.	להיות אדם	liheyott adam	to be human
13.	מזל רע	mazal ra'	bad luck
14.	השמדה עצמית	hashemadah a'tzmit	to self-destruct
15.	לזרוק בחזרה	lizrok bahazarah	throw back
16.	להרוס	laharos	destroy
17.	לחזור אליי	lahazor elyy	return to me
18.	להתבונן	lehitebonenn	to observe
19.	לטרוף	litroff	devour
20.	לאגד אותו לקללה זו	leaged oto leklalah zo	bind him to this curse
21.	הסתר את זה מכולם	hasster ett zeh mikulam	conceal this from everyone
22.	טהר את נשמתי השחורה	taher et nishmati hashekhorah	Cleanse my blackened soul

23.	סלח לי כי חטאתי	selah li 'ki hatati	forgive me for I have sinned
24.	למחוק זיכרון	limekhoq zikaron	erase memory
25.	חסימת זיכרון	hasimat zikaronn	block memory
26.	החלף זיכרון	ahlef zikaronn	replace memory
27.	להערים את הנפש	leha'arim ett hanefesh	trick the mind
28.	אל תפקפק בי	al tefaqepeq bi	don't question me
29.	חושך, אני מזמן אותך	hosheh, ani mezamen otekha	Darkness, I summon you.
30.	עשה את ההצעות שלי	'Asseh tt hahats'ott sheli	Do my bidding.
31.	רוקן את הקסם מעצמות אלו	Roken et hakesem meatzamot elu	Drain the magic from these bones.
32.	תהפוך אותו לחסר אונים	Ta'afoh oto le-kassar onim	Make him impotent.
33.	תהפוך אותו לחסר כוחות	Ta'afoh oto le-kassar kokhott.	Make him powerless.
34.	תגרום לו להשתחוות אלי	Tigerom lo lehishtakavott elyy	Make him bow to me.
35.	ברגע שהדם נוגע בחפץ זה	Barega' shehadam noge'a bakhefets zeh	Once the blood touches this object
36.	לטרוף את הקסם שלו	Litroff ett hakessem shelo.	Devour his magic.

PROLOGUE

I'd always known I was different; I'd just never realised how peculiar I was. In most ways, I appeared to be like the other maidens that lived beneath the sea. Not that I had a choice. Mermaids were expected to be demure and to respect their betters, which were always men. Our voices within society were stolen from us because of what happened in our past.

We all learnt the story as merchildren. Zoara-Bela used to be a city like any other on the surface. People would barter on the streets to get a deal, and merchants would shout to draw attention to their stalls. Children could run and laugh freely, but not anymore.

As merchildren, we were taught better. They taught us our place within society. For the men, their place was within their station. The son of a merchant could not become a lord, and the son of a servant could only be a servant. Maidens regardless of the station they were born in could learn only what their fathers would allow. We learnt that our life, our word, was worth less than a man's. As a merchild, I never understood why maidens were treated like this, not until I heard the story of the fall. Then I knew it was our punishment for the actions of our goddess.

As merchildren, we were told that our goddess Gaea brought about the downfall of our city because we no longer wished to follow her strict rules. Abaddon, my grandfather, wanted to rule the kingdom based on his values and not the values of a goddess who rarely made appearances before us. He ordered the death of a criminal favoured by her, leading to our curse. And so, upon our fall, he ensured that no maiden would ever have the power to cause such damage again.

None of my tutors ever went into more detail. I would always ask, what did the criminal do? Why did Gaea care so much about a criminal? Every time I asked those questions, I was told that it didn't matter and that maidens shouldn't ask questions. But I had so many questions.

My curiosity led me to Father's private archives, which contained memory orbs that recorded our history. Only the record keepers and those with Father's permission could enter. But by that age, I had already learnt how to bypass the passive perimeter wards without notifying Father through sneaking into the lessons of magic that sons of nobles had.

The spell la'akof et hahaganott (bypass the protection) was simple to cast as it didn't alter the wards, just allowed someone to slip past them without activating the defences. And in those archives, I learnt that our curse was the punishment for failing her test.

The criminal in the story was a legacy and a high priestess from a temple in Athens. Chava was a weary traveller. She had broken one of our laws and was sentenced to death. What I saw and felt within that orb terrified me. I experienced everything they did at the moment the curse was cast. The magic that stifled their breath. The bones that broke and twisted into a new shape. Their legs being joined to form a fishtail. The weight of the curse that suppressed our ability to feel. I felt it all as a merchild.

The love they felt for their children and their wives that was once all-consuming became muted to the point their connections became a duty. I felt their pain and horror at what they had become. These were things that I had never known but were taken from me by this curse. As the memory ended, I felt an itching and warmth welling up in my eyes that escaped upon blinking. Tears.

Merfolk could not cry, but somehow, I did.

CHAPTER 1

As I woke up, I uncurled myself from the strange shape I had formed within my shell. My shell was cold. It always was. Everything here was cold. My shell, the palace, even the people were cold.

Coldness is in our nature, my grandfather told me once, during one of the few times they allowed me to interact with him without my father present. My father, the crown prince Abdiel, didn't like it when I spoke with grandfather alone. It was like Father didn't trust him. Why wouldn't he trust grandfather? He was our king, the king of Zoara-Bela. And—he was almost kind. At least, I thought that was the human word for the way he treated me. Grandfather was a good—no, great—ruler. He'd been the king of Zoara-Bela since the beginning, since our transformation into merfolk.

"Moriah!"

I heard someone shout my name from the other side of my bedroom door. I groaned, trying to pull up my blankets and keep my shell closed to feign sleep. The servant who shouted my name knocked. Sleep was beyond me now. I sat up, eyelids heavy, as I told her to enter. She was new. I'd never seen her before, not that I really paid attention to the servants within my father's employ. She appeared young, but with merfolk, it was hard to tell. A mermaid could look like a middle-aged human but in reality, be thousands of years old. Like Father and Grandfather. Both were present when our people were transformed into merfolk. Grandfather was the king when it happened.

When Gaea cursed us.

The servant tried to grab my attention by reminding me that today was my sixteenth birthday. As was custom, I was to go through the same rite of passage as most children. The rite. They allowed most noble children of the sea, on their sixteenth birthday, to go to the surface world and experience what humans were like.

The only exception to the rite of passage was those considered to be unimportant. The children of servants, who would also be required to work as servants. Those who lacked beauty. Those who were weak of mind, magic, and body.

Maidens were forbidden from ever going to the human world and completing this rite unless their fathers allowed them. They considered us unimportant.

We were rarely allowed to study the ancient arts or even learn the basics of reading, writing, or numbers. This was because maidens—at least in Zoara-Bela—need not know this unless our fathers believed we should. For most maidens in Zoara-Bela, there was no choice, no power. Their lives were based on the whims of their male relatives.

I was one of the lucky ones. My father was a good merman. He allowed—well, encouraged—me to learn anything I wanted. He ensured that I could learn to read, write, my numbers, and even the basics of the ancient arts. I had every opportunity to excel, to be curious. That curiosity often got me in trouble. Father said that I reminded him of a creature that lived on the surface, one that we used to keep as companions when we had legs instead of fins.

A cat, he called it, because my curiosity could kill me one day. I had to be careful—I could be curious, I could ask questions, but I could only ask those questions with him. Not the servants, and certainly not grandfather.

I dismissed the servant so I could get ready for the day. I made myself presentable, so I could leave my home to explore Zoara-Bela once I had completed my duties. If I was lucky, I'd have a chance to explore the ruins.

As I swam towards the exit, I heard my father chuckle, "Excited, are we?"

"About what?" I said, trying to hide my intentions.

"Today is your rite of passage," he said, "You'll be a young woman soon."

"It won't be until sunset tonight. I still have time to complete my duties before wandering around the city and—"

"Visit the ruins?" he asked.

"What? Of course not, I know not to go there," I said, avoiding his eyes.

"I know you, Moriah. You're my daughter. Just promise me something."

"What, Father?"

"Don't go beyond the ruins of the ancient port. It is dangerous. Sharks are often hiding in areas near the port, waiting at the edge of our borders, warded off by the magic that protects us."

"All right," I said, rolling my eyes.

I wasn't stupid. I could sense the boundary and I knew the risks. But, as I turned to leave, my father said one more thing.

"Remember to return before dinner. You need that time to get ready for the rite."

CHAPTER 2

Zoara-Bela was an enormous city before the fall, but our population was decimated in the aftermath of the curse. Some people didn't survive the sinking of the city as they were crushed beneath debris or drowned before they could be transformed. Some were killed because of the severe damage done to the island as it sank. More died because of the transformation failing to take hold both as it fell and in the years afterwards.

The census prior to the fall was clear. As a direct consequence of the fall, we lost 60 percent of our population, reducing it to 10,000. Since then our population had only recently reached 20,000 as we were slow to reproduce due to our long life span. There had been a recent spike in births that had continued over the last thirty years (a mere blink to a mermaid) which was why I had been assigned duties within my father's palace. More than what a maiden of the royal family would normally be assigned.

According to my grandfather, this was meant to prepare me for my duties as a wife upon marriage to a merman of noble blood (whether I wished it or not).

As a result, I was expected to manage my father's estate

(under supervision). I had to ensure that the rosters for each servant were displayed ahead of time, that each task was delegated to the appropriate servant, take stock of supplies, and order more if we were low. Occasionally I had to supervise the new servants to ensure that proper procedure was followed.

Things like laundry duty or repairs in my father's personal palace were two of the things that I often had to supervise as I was one of the few in the palace that was trusted to use magic. I was one of the few who had knowledge of magic and the ability to fix any damage caused by the servants when they used magic to complete their tasks. Servants had to use their magic to remove stains caused by magic or algae growth from our clothes and repair any damage done to the clothes or building itself.

"Lehassir et haketem," I heard a servant mutter while attempting to remove a large stain from the shirt.

While another servant was attempting to fix the spell damage on the flooring in the corridor by casting a spell repeatedly because they lacked the power to do it instantly, "letaqenn et hanezeq."

However, servants were not trusted to use magic independently without the supervision of a noble or royal even if they were a maiden. Not that I agreed with it. I had seen them perform these same tasks for years and they never made a mistake.

Despite this, I was meant to supervise them even though all I wanted was to leave the palace to explore Zoara-Bela. Today though, instead of actively supervising them (like I was supposed to), I spent the time staring out the window in boredom. From my position in the laundry room, I could see the entire city. The water was tinged a light bluish-green, as the orbs of light placed strategically around the city gave off a bright glow that allowed us to separate the day and night. The light reflected off the smooth stone and coral that was used to build the homes and walls of the citadel. Despite the beauty of the city, there was a darkness hidden within that made me feel uneasy.

But before I could ponder on this further, the servant I was meant to be supervising said, "My lady, I completed the laundry and repairs of the articles of clothing as well spell damage on the flooring in the corridor."

"Excellent. Dismissed."

"Yes, my lady!"

A chime rang through the palace signalling the noon break which meant that my duties for the day were finished and I could finally wander around the city.

CHAPTER 3

D ay in. Day out. On repeat. Every day was the same. There was only so much to see in Zoara-Bela. Nothing changed. Ever. Every day I swam down the same streets. Saw the same people. The stone-mason yelled at his apprentice. The jeweller showed a customer a pearl necklace. The grocer screamed at his wife because, like always, she forgot to weigh the items for sale *before* bagging them. And, like always, he hit her across the face in front of customers. I froze, knowing that something was not right about it. But I couldn't do anything. It didn't matter that I was the Crown Princess. I was a maiden therefore, my voice didn't matter.

The only one who thought differently was my father. He was the only one who asked *me* what I preferred to do or what I wished to learn. Grandfather said that Father was giving me ideas above my station, above my place. Because he was the king, I could not tell him I disagreed or that I adored father for the *freedom* he gave me.

I shook my head to snap myself out of a daze and continued making my way across the city. The noise stopped; I could no longer hear the merchants selling their wares or even just the general hustle and bustle of the city. My world was silent. Then I realised why. I'd gone further than I was supposed to. I had reached the ruins. I should turn around and head back home. But something within me cried out. There was something I needed to see. It felt important. So I decided against my better judgement, to explore the ruins. Something I'd never done.

Spinning around, I tried to take in the sites of the ruins. They were amazing structures. Buildings made of stone, the walls partially fallen. Pillars on their sides touching the weak walls, edges buried in the sand as if trying to stop themselves from destroying the building they leaned on. A beam of light reached a crystal lying in the middle of the building, untouched by the debris around it. The buildings, covered in algae, glowed bright green in response to the light. It lasted only for a brief moment but it was beautiful.

I continued exploring the ruins. There was a statue of a human man in what looked like the city square. Strong and handsome, he looked like my grandfather with legs instead of a tail. Looking past the sculpture I saw a wall made from an unusual material. It was hard as stone but smooth to the touch. I'd seen nothing like this before. I looked closer.

"Etchings?" I muttered as I examined the strange shapes on the smooth stone.

It looked like writing. But not the writing of the merfolk. It wasn't in our language. There were some similarities. Some words that seemed *almost* familiar to me. I was so enthralled by the writing on the stone that the voice of an old woman startled me when she said, "Interesting isn't it?"

"What?"

"The writing on the stone. It's in the old language. The language from before the curse."

"Before the curse? Do you know what it says?"

The old woman shook her head at me.

"The stone has been worn by time and exposure to the salt in the water. While I can read the old language, there is too much damage and algae on it for me to read and understand it."

"What can you read from it?"

"It speaks of how intrinsic the ancient arts are to our people's way of life. It is the basis of our culture. Our way of life. It talks of *honouring* our mother creator—the earth—Gaea. We honour her through our prayers. And through *honest and heartfelt* worship. We give sacrifice to *our mother creator* through offering a portion of our meal, an object of some worth to us, so long as the sacrifice comes from the heart, from love, our mother will accept it and honour us in return."

From love? Sacrifice from the heart to honour *our mother creator*? I never knew that we had a creator that we worshipped as our mother. The closest thing we had to worship was the offerings our people gave to my grandfather, Abaddon, but that was due to tradition not love. Our ability to feel emotions was stifled and suppressed, leaving it a mere shadow of what was. To feel deeply like that was nearly impossible. It was something that, according to Grandfather, placed us above the land dwellers, the humans. But this woman was telling me that we once gave offerings to a creator, out of love and not tradition—to a maiden. If this was true, then why did our people spurn maidens? Why did we lack choice? Freedom?

"—a curse."

Wait. What?

"What about it?" I asked in confusion.

"The etchings speak of a curse that would consume the land and its peoples if they forgot to obey the rules of hospitality and rejected her love. For the creator, the mother is known to test her children. To see if they are still worthy of her love and protection. These tests had occurred twice before the fall of our city and our transformation into the merfolk we are today. Both times we passed due to the strength and kindness of our people. However, the last time that test occurred we failed. Why? I do not know. But for us to be cursed the way we are. Our bodies transformed. Unable to live among humans without them screaming in horror for our reflections in the human world are horrifying. But for our emotions to be suppressed the way they are. To be denied love, hope, and true joy. That means we did more than fail our creator's test or just deny her love. For the punishment to be this extreme. To fall further than our sister cities, Sodom and Gomorrah, we must have committed a true act of horror and unnatural cruelty—"

"Like what?"

"I don't know. I wasn't around when the test occurred. Most merfolk live only 300 years, maybe 400. Since our transformation, there have been at least ten generations to have been born. The only exception seems to be the royal line and a few noble families."

That must be why both Grandfather and Father look the same in the old carvings at the palace as they did now. Why though? Why make it so the royal and noble families lived for eternity? Was it a reward or a punishment? What did we do to be punished this way?

'Something is odd about this woman,' I thought to myself as I turned to look at her. Her face was lined and her wrinkles looked like they were carved into stone. Despite this, she was beautiful. The same way statues and carvings were beautiful. Ancient, full of meaning, with a hint of danger.

She must not have known who I was, if she was speaking with me like this, telling me about our history. A history Grandfather most likely wished to be buried, probably by burying her alive. Father, on the other hand, I was not sure about. Sometimes it was like he wanted me to learn whatever I could; other times, he wanted me to stop learning about something. Things like the ancient arts. Officially, I only knew the basics. Some minor spells and potions, nothing of power or worthy of notice as far as my father knew.

My curiosity was probably going to get me killed. But I couldn't help it. I had to ask.

"Do you know why the royals and nobles live longer than the other merfolk?"

"I know not. That is something that you will need to ask your father, Moriah."

"You know who I am?"

"Yes."

"Then why? Why talk to me if you know who I am? If Grandfather finds out that you know this history, know why we were cursed, he will kill you. You will be turned into sea foam."

"I know. However, you will not tell him yourself either. Because if you do you will have to admit to listening to my interpretation and knowledge of the history of our people. And that is something you would never do."

"I wouldn't tell him anyway. Even without the threat. I just ... I just want you to be careful. But could you tell me your name? Since you know mine," I asked nervously.

"Of course. I am Amari. It means eternal. I'm curious. Which meaning of your name did your father give you? She who is chosen by the lord or she who has the lord as her teacher?"

I froze. I didn't expect that question. In my shock, I muttered, "the lord is my teacher is the name meaning my father gave me."

Upon hearing my name meaning, the old woman Amari laughed. I felt my cheeks warm as I turned my head to look back at the etchings. As I looked at the etchings, I realised that there was something odd about her laugh. It was more than gentle humour. It sounded like cruelty and smugness with a touch of irony. Which was odd. Why would she be expressing such depth of feeling? And how? Merfolk were unable to feel true deep emotions not as easily as this. I turned back towards her to ask why she laughed when she heard my name to find that she disappeared. There was no time for me to ponder how she disappeared as I heard the toll of the bell. It was five o'clock in the afternoon. I was going to be late for my preparation for the rite.

As I swam away, I felt uneasy, on edge. It felt like someone was watching me. I could feel their eyes follow me as I left. I didn't know it then, but I was right to be so on edge because the old woman smiled within the shadows and muttered, "you will come to me in time child. They all do."

CHAPTER 4

The rite. The most important moment in the life of mermen and mermaids (those allowed to take part anyway). This tradition had existed since the sinking of our city and our transformation into what we were now.

Most merfolk, mainly maids, in the beginning of our existence as mermaids would, during their rite, go to the surface to seduce sailors who entered our waters through our song. Our song, our voices, had hypnotic qualities capable of ensnaring all who heard us. Once they fell under our power, there was no escape. No human could free those captured by our voices. It was only once they were dragged into the water by the mermaids—who were angered by their transformation—that they would remove their spell moments after they saw their reflections. Mermaids weren't the only ones to do this—mermen did it too—but the human world only ever spread tales of what our maids did.

Sirens, la sirenita, merrow, naiads, nereids. We were known by many names in the human world in ancient times. We were the inspiration for their legends. That's all we can be now. Legends and myths. According to our records, humans came close to discovering a way to find and enter our city to destroy us, which was something that we couldn't allow. So we created the boundary that surrounded our kingdom. No humans or their vessels could enter. We were invisible to their technology —sonar, radar, scanner—and anything that allowed them to explore the deep could not detect us.

Which meant that once we went through the rite of passage, we could not return to the human world ever again unless our job was to study the humans, their technology and their languages to ensure that if we were ever discovered we would not be caught off guard. Know thy enemy.

"Ouch!" I yelped.

"Don't complain, my lady!" snapped the royal dressmaker.

The royal dressmaker, Azalea, was a stern old woman who lacked a sense of humour. She always took her job seriously. Completed all the tasks demanded of her to the letter, no more, no less. If she didn't and the king or the other nobles found out, well, to put it politely *off with her head.*

"But it hurts!"

Azalea rolled her eyes as she spoke, "Beauty comes from enduring pain. You must endure the pain for the sake of your rite."

She clamped another oyster and clam to the golden frill of my fin that went from hip to the tip of my light blue tail. Azalea continued ignoring my agitation and pain to ensure all the clams, oysters and pearls required for my station adorned my tail.

"Done. Go look in your sea glass mirror."

I drifted to the sea glass mirror that went from roof to floor near my desk. My eyes avoided looking at the image, expecting to see the reflection of my soul, which wouldn't happen as that only happened on the surface, not under the sea. Azalea, losing her patience shouted, "Well. Are you going to actually look in the sea glass to see my work or not?"

Reluctantly, my eyes move towards sea glass. I gasped in amazement. I looked beautiful.

My copper brown hair had been gently pulled back from my face, a fringe and two curly bangs framed my face gently. The back of my hair was styled in a half bun, half-down style. The bun was made of little braids that had been transformed into a flower. A golden flower was placed above my ear, my crown above it. A golden necklace, forming a collar, had golden rings attached in a way that created a pattern like scales. A beautiful yellow top with sleeves like yellow jellyfish, adorned with cream-coloured jewels and pearls. A shiny yellow paint had been used to shade my brown eyes. Another golden substance, like what the humans called glitter, had been dusted across my shoulders, my back and down my arms like shimmering scales upon my olive skin. My mother's pearl and sapphire bracelet, as always, was on my wrist.

"Well?" asked Azalea.

"Thank you so much! This is perfect. I look beautiful. You do fantastic work, Azalea!"

Her lips turned upwards slightly as if attempting to smile before thinking better of it.

"Right. My lady, you need to make your way to the gardens, your father will be waiting for you there to escort you to the boundary that leads to the nearest human settlement. Once there your father will hand you the spirit gem necklace which will allow you to take human form temporarily and the cloth that will transform into a dress that will allow you to blend in when in the human world. He will also perform traditional rites that will declare you of age among our people before you enter the human world. Understand?"

"Yes, Azalea. You may leave now. Thank you for your service." I say while rolling my eyes.

As I moved to leave I glanced at the sea glass mirror. For

some strange reason whenever I looked at my tail I felt uneasy. I didn't know why.

~

Not long after I arrived at the garden my father quickly escorted me to the boundary that I would leave from, to enter the human world. At the boundary, there was a raised altar, made of orichalcum and adorned with pearls and jade containing golden script within a cave that contains a portal to the human world. Waiting there were other mermaids and mermen, chosen by my father, who undertook the rite to stand witness while he performed the ceremony. This was one of the duties assigned to my father.

"We have gathered here today to celebrate the sixteenth birthday of Princess Moriah, daughter of Abdiel, son of Abaddon. Step forward, daughter of the sea."

My father, standing behind the altar, directed me to kneel at the foot of the altar with my head bowed and my hands clasped together, as if in prayer.

"Does anyone here believe that Moriah should be denied this rite of passage?"

"Nay!" replied the witnesses.

"Let us begin. Once we walked freely on the surface but now are limited to the sea," my father droned on.

He began the traditional rites. His voice was monotone, emotionless, as he spoke about our history, our traditions.

"Princess Moriah, as is tradition you will, upon completing the rite, have taken the first step to become of age among our people. This means that you will be required to undertake certain responsibilities as a member of the royal household. Do you comply with this demand?"

"Yes, my lord," I murmured with my head still bowed.

"You know our laws. You must not let any humans observe your transformation nor move close to or around mirrored surfaces. For if a human sees your reflection be it in a mirror, a glass window, or a puddle of water they will know instantly that you are not one of them. For our reflections above the surface reflect our souls. They will see a grotesque creature that is vaguely human-shaped; your flesh may be mangled, webbed fingers, eyes sunken, muscle visible, your body covered in scales and more. Do you understand what is expected of you, Princess Moriah?"

"I do my lord."

"Very well. Take this spirit gem. This shall allow you to take human form for twenty-four hours exactly. Not twenty-four and a half hours. Not even twenty-four hours and a minute. It will last for twenty-four hours exactly."

I took hold of the necklace containing the gem but before I could put it on, my father told me sharply, "Do not put that necklace on until I instruct you. Place it on the altar until instructed."

"Yes, my lord."

He then handed me a beaded pouch and a light blue cloth that shimmered in the altar's light before saying, "The pouch contains the currency of the local human city and a gem that will lead you back to us in Zoara-Bela. The light blue cloth will transform into an appropriate set of clothing for a young human woman, allowing you to blend in. The cloth, once trans-formed, will dry instantly when arriving on the surface. It will turn back to cloth if you are in the water for over fifteen minutes. Now place the cloth in the pouch and use the pouch as a handbag. Lastly, do you agree to follow our laws regarding interaction with the human world while there, ensuring that the secrecy is maintained?"

"Yes, my lord."

"You may now put the spirit gem necklace on. As soon as the

transformation ends, you must swim straight up towards the surface. Now I warn you this will be painful. Good luck."

My hands trembled as I grasped the necklace and put it around my neck. For a moment nothing happened but then pain. I screamed in agony as a sickly green light surrounded me. Swirling like a vortex, forming a bubble around me. My tail glowed, sparks flying from it. My tail was torn in two. Bones bent and broke. My spine twisted into a different shape. The thin webs between my fingers tore, separating them. I could feel my inner organs shifting and changing into that of a human. Every breath was a struggle as my body was transformed into something that could not live underneath the sea. Everything about me was changing. My skin, eyes, organs, bones. Every cell in my body was changing.

'I want to die. I want this to be over', I screamed in my mind.

I could not form words because of the unrelenting pain from the transformation. No wonder no one wanted to find a way to permanently reverse the curse if it hurt this much when we were initially transformed. I continued screaming until I couldn't anymore. My vocal cords were being ripped and changed into something more akin to a human. I looked around me, wanting to beg for help, but the witnesses and my father stood silently and made no move to help me. My eyes became blurry, my ability to see under the water was disappearing, my eyes stung and burned from the saltwater.

My hands grasped my throat, I started to blackout from the pain and lack of oxygen. I tried to take a deep breath when suddenly the bubble surrounding me popped. My newly created legs and arms move uselessly in the water as I struggled to move towards the opening above the altar containing the portal. The witnesses and my father watched but did not interfere. I pushed myself to move through the pain of the transformation, to reach the portal that then pushed me directly to the surface.

I broke through the surface of the water, my head thrown

back, gasping for air as I looked towards the sky for the first time. The light was harsh against my eyes, making it hard to see. But then my eyes cleared, adjusting to the light and to my amazement I saw the sunrise for the first time. The sky looked as if an artist had painted it. Magnificent shades of blues, purples, oranges and yellows stretched across the horizon.

In the distance, I saw the beach and the buildings of the human world. I tried to swim towards it, my arms and legs felt like sludge but I ignored that to reach the shore. At that moment I did not know that the pain I experienced during the transformation was unusual for those who undertook the rite. There was always meant to be pain, but for most, it would last only a moment before passing. I wouldn't realise this until I was told by another but even then I wouldn't know why I felt such pain in my transformation or the rightness I felt looking at the legs that I had been given until many years later. Because at that moment, all I cared about was reaching the shore and the freedom to explore a whole new world.

CHAPTER 5

I laid flat on the sand, running my fingers through it in amazement. My eyes were closed as I breathed in the air and let it wash over me. I forgot about my worries, my pain, my secret desires for more. More than the cold, unforgiving ocean and the underlying cruelty of our society. The wind brushed gently over my skin, leaving a slight smell of salt, like a lover secretly whispering prayers into another's ear.

'*It feels warm,*' I thought to myself.

I'd never felt like this before. The loud honk broke the peace causing me to sit upon the sand, wiggling my toes. I stared at my feet in amazement. I tried to stand on my wobbly legs, but my control over these new limbs was subpar and I lost my balance quickly, falling back onto the wet sand. It took me a few minutes before I could stand without collapsing (after repeated failed attempts). I placed my hand upon the large rock that was hiding me from view; I steadied myself as I took a few steps away from the water, unsure and barely balanced. I was able to walk, eventually without its support.

I heard the loud honking noise again before I remembered the cloth, that would allow me to blend in among the humans, appear as they do. Grasping the cloth, I placed it around my shoulders, glowing brightly. The glow covered me completely, creating a light blue dress and a pair of sandals that covered my new, unsteady feet. I went to look at my reflection in the water, but then I remembered that on the surface it would reflect my soul. Even still, I pushed past my fear and looked into the water.

It confused me. My reflection, it was still me. I could still recognise myself. The water distorted my image, but I was still me with my copper coloured hair and brown eyes. There was a slight green tinge to my skin which had light green and yellow scales (my cheeks and neck mainly), webbed ears and fingers, small fangs in my mouth. But still recognisably me.

I mean I probably looked monstrous to the humans but I don't think it looks bad. Not as bad as what others have described their reflections as being. Even though I probably looked like a monster to the humans, for the first time in a long time I was comfortable in my skin. I didn't know why. I just did. Shaking my head, I looked back towards the sky with its beautiful purple and orange hues before making my way to the human city.

I explored the human city, stopping occasionally with every unfamiliar sight. Things like flowers, trees and animals that lived above the surface were so very different from what we had in the ocean. The flowers we had in the sea had no smell, the animals that lived in the ocean were all slimy or they wanted to eat us. We had coral instead of trees, which didn't even give us food like the plants here do. I was meant to blend in among the humans but my expression, which probably looked like a cross between a stunned mullet and a pufferfish, wasn't exactly helping me achieve that.

I dashed between different market stalls that contained the most wondrous objects. This world was full of things I had never seen before. In one stall I saw a colourful object in the shape of a human that felt rough to the touch, it wasn't made of stone or coral.

In curiosity, I asked the merchant that was selling the object, "Excuse me sir, what is this?"

"Seriously? You don't know what this is?" He looked at me as if I was stupid.

I shook my head in response. I probably should have just kept my mouth shut, but I wanted to know what it was.

He sighed but answered my question anyway, "It's a toy. A babushka doll. It contains multiple dolls within each shell that shrinks each time you remove a layer."

I was bouncing up and down as I asked, "What about this?"

I was pointing to a small chest with beautiful patterns.

"That is a music box."

When he saw my confusion, he turned a key that was in the box and the lid opened. In the box were figurines that were moving in a circle to the music. I had seen nothing like this before in Zoara-Bela. It must be a new invention of humans. I spent minutes at the stall asking about the various objects before I noticed that the merchant was getting impatient, so I purchased the babushka doll and the music box before I continued exploring the city.

There was a lot of noise and fast-moving objects on the street with people inside them. Why were they in those objects? I wanted to ask someone on the street but I didn't want to be laughed at or called stupid so I held in my questions. I eventually made my way across the city before pausing at the city square.

The buildings surrounding the square were made of a beautiful white stone decorated with colourful signs and vines that crawled up the pillars containing pink flowers. Objects containing a light or flame hang above the entrance to the different buildings. In the middle, there was a stone statue of a person, probably their leader, as in Zoara-Bela only the royal family could have statues. But then I noticed the people. To my amazement, people were standing around talking, laughing or eating in the square.

There were no guards pulling people away for causing such a disturbance. In fact, some guards, who were carrying weapons, were talking and laughing with other people.

The city square in Zoara-Bela was made of grey stone and dead coral. There were no decorations or laughter in the square. It was as silent as a grave. No one dared talk in the square in Zoara-Bela—most avoided it. If you loitered in the square or made conversation with another you would be questioned by the guards if you were lucky, or dragged to the palace dungeons if they believed you were 'acting with treasonous intent'.

I turned to leave, as there was still so much to explore when I heard the most beautiful sound. Music. There was a human man playing music and people were moving strangely to the music. Music in Zoara-Bela was a solemn affair. Music was only used for funerals, to announce an execution or at the very rare balls held at the king's palace. And it was always dull, as they always played the same tunes on a harp. The music of Zoara-Bela was quiet, slow, dull and had no words. But the music the human man was playing was fast, loud and had a unique tune. And the people were laughing and singing along, I'd never seen so many people so happy like these humans were.

My curiosity got the better of me, I did something that I wasn't supposed to, have a conversation with a human beyond purchasing something from them. There was a young human, possibly my age, who was talking to other teens that I tapped on the shoulder. I gasped as he turned towards me. He was tall, nearly a head taller than me. He had wavy golden-brown hair that went to his chin and gentle green eyes that contrasted beautifully against his lightly tanned skin. His looks were different to those who lived under the sea. Most merfolk had dark skin, not because of the sun, but because of our heritage, my olive skin was an oddity among them.

He asked me gently what I needed. But I noticed as he spoke that there was a shadow in his eyes, a darkness I could not name. His eyes, while gentle, seemed almost sad, like life had been drained from them. A look that I had seen in the eyes of the slaves within the Citadel. I wanted to distract him, to bring the light back into his eyes, but I didn't know how.

So with courage, I didn't know that I possessed, I tried to distract him with my question as I pointed towards the crowd, "What are those people doing?"

"The ones in the square? They're dancing."

"What's dancing?"

His friends laughed in the background, but this young man didn't. He continued to smile, his eyes warm. A glimmer of light seemed to flicker in his eyes. At his look, my stomach felt funny, a tingly sort of feeling. It felt nice.

"Seriously? How do you not know what dancing is? Were you never allowed to leave the house or something?" he asked with a smile.

"Or something."

"I'm sorry. I didn't know," he stuttered before continuing, "Well, it's a type of exercise that people do for fun or when they're happy. There doesn't need to be music. Some people dance in the rain or on the sand at the beach."

I thanked him, planning to go explore some more before he grabbed my hand gently. And asked, "It's a shame that a beautiful girl like you has never had a chance to dance. Would you like me to show you how?"

I was surprised. I thought that maybe he thought I was stupid with the questions I asked; his friends certainly did. At my lack of response, the darkness in his eyes crept back, the light in his eyes began to disappear. I didn't want to make the light go from his eyes, but I didn't know what to do. Did I follow mermaid law or did I take his hand?

Before I could decide he let go of my hand, stepping back and telling me it was all right if I didn't want to. No one ever gave me a choice like that. Unthinkingly, I smiled back at him and took his hand, that he held out towards me, I let him pull me into the square where the other humans were dancing. His eyes seemed to glow with happiness at my simple act and my chest felt warm.

He held me gently, a hand against my back, slowly explaining each movement in the dance for me, talking me through it. As he held me close and whispered in my ear the steps to the dance, the funny feeling in my chest grew as I noticed the warmth of his hands on my arm and back. I didn't understand the feeling, but it was nice. It felt warm and nice like the sun on my skin as laid on the sand, but nicer. Soon enough, I was smiling and laughing alongside him, as he twirled me around the dance floor.

At the end of the song, he dipped me low before pulling me upwards to his chest, holding me close. Both of us were breathless by the end. I could feel his heart beating, while my head lay on his chest. I felt him chuckle; I looked back up at him, questioningly. He asked me, "What do you think?"

I looked at him, beaming as I replied, "That was amazing. I wish we had something like this back home. What else do you do for fun around here?"

"Well... we could play some games at the arcade. There's also a basketball court nearby, I usually go there to shoot some hoops. There's a party at the beach tonight that I'm going to. You could come with me, beautiful?"

The funny feeling came back as I replied breathlessly, "I ... I would love to."

"What's your name, beautiful?" he said teasingly.

"Moriah. My name is Moriah. And yours?" I stammered.

I could feel a warmth in my cheeks and there was a funny feeling in my chest. I had never felt like this before. I didn't understand what it meant, but I knew that I wanted to feel like this again.

I was left slightly off-balance as I caught myself before I gave my name meaning, as I remembered that humans didn't place importance on the meaning of names like we do.

He gave a slight bow, making me giggle, before he said, "A beautiful name for a beautiful lady. My name is Michael Adams. Why don't you join me? I was going to head to the arcade before getting some lunch."

"What about your friends?"

"They already knew that I would leave early. I'll just say goodbye before we go."

"Are you sure?"

"Definitely. Your company has already made my day much more enjoyable. Besides, it'll be fun."

He held out his hand for me to take, which I did without thinking about the mermaid laws regarding the human world because at that moment all I cared about was his kindness and willingness to show me his world.

CHAPTER 6

Walking alongside Michael and seeing the world through his eyes, his smile and laugh had pushed all my worries from my mind. With him, I didn't care that I was breaking mermaid law, just that he made me feel warm and happy. I had glimpses of feelings that could have become emotions that were strangled by Zoara-Belan ideals. Feelings were fleeting, a mere flash or spark that fizzles out. I was starting to understand that emotions went beyond the surface. Emotions were deeper, ever-present and lingered long after the moment was gone.

I didn't understand what I was feeling as I held Michael's hand in mine, shoulders touching, while we walked down the streets of this city. His crooked smile made my stomach flutter —it felt warm and pleasant like a hug. His eyes had become lighter; life had returned to him. I wanted to keep the darkness, the sadness, away. Someone as kind as him shouldn't have a shadow hidden in his eyes like an executioner's axe being held over his head. It was still present, just not as obvious.

"We're here," he said softly.

I looked around; he had taken me to a building full of brightly coloured machines filled with people.

'I wish I had another pair of eyes. This is amazing,' I thought before pulling on Michael's hand to examine the large machine with a wheel and a bright red seat.

"Mario Kart?" I muttered as I tried to work out how this machine was meant to be used.

"Want to play?" he asked.

"I would love to. But I don't know how."

"It's easy, let me show you. Just sit down in the chair. See those pedals. The one on the right makes the cart go faster and the one on the left slows it down. Here just let me put some money in."

I tried to protest as he had done so much for me already. But he put the correct amount of coins in and talked me through each step of choosing my character and kart. The machine counted down until it reached zero. I did what he told me. I pushed my foot down on the right pedal. As I did that I felt his hands on top of mine moving the wheel, helping me reach the finish line.

"I did it!" I cheered as I reached the finish line in the game.

"Yeah you did," he said quietly with a strange smile on his face.

We stared at each other for a moment before I looked away with a warmth in my cheeks.

"Want to play again?" he asked me a moment later.

"Yes!"

"How about we verse each other this time? Think you can win against me?" he asked with a cheeky grin.

"Definitely."

"Ok then. Bring it."

I didn't understand what he meant by that, but I placed my coins in the machine, eager to play against him. We played multiple rounds of Mario Kart, both of us eager to win. I won the most rounds, but I did think he lost those rounds on purpose. When I asked him he denied it.

The mermen in Zoara-Bela didn't like to lose anything, let alone to a maiden. And they'd never purposely lose to one either.

Before I could think more on this, another brightly coloured machine drew my attention. It played music and people were dancing on it. I tried to pay attention to the way they were moving to the music to work out how to play it. Follow the steps on screen. Seems easy enough.

"Could we play DDR next Michael?"

He laughed as he followed me to the machine, "You sure?"

"Yes. Afraid you will lose?"

"Never."

It was harder than I thought. But playing this machine, competing against Michael, made my heart beat faster than ever before. After completing the last stage, we both collapsed on the floor of the machine laughing. I looked at him closely; the shadows had been chased from his mind for a single moment. He had slight crinkles next to his eyes as he laughed. He saw me staring at him as he said, "Like what you see?"

My cheeks felt like they were on fire as I looked away in embarrassment, "Yes actually."

"I always liked a girl that knows what she wants," he said, winking at me.

We looked at each other again before bursting out into laughter.

He stood up and held out his hand as he said, "Come on. Let's go get something to eat. There's a burger joint close to here that is pretty good."

"I'd like that," I said as he helped me up.

The strange feeling in my chest had returned. Happiness— this must be what happiness felt like.

CHAPTER 7

The hours I spent in the human world with Michael made me forget for a moment that I wasn't one of them, that I wasn't human. I liked the ocean and being a mermaid just like any other, but the ability to choose, to explore beyond our city, to walk on land or enter the sea was something that I longed for. I knew that it could not last beyond these few hours before I turned back into a mermaid and had to return to the ocean's depths, continuing to live among the heartlessness of my people and their unforgiving, unbending nature.

But still, these few hours with Michael, dancing in the square, going to the arcade, and now the party. I thought it was worth the pain of the transformation. I was almost *happy*. It wasn't an emotion that mermaids felt, but when I thought of happiness, I thought it felt like this. I thought this was what having friends was like. I wished there was something I could take with me, something physical to remember this moment, but memories were all I would have. I couldn't take him with me, for he wouldn't survive; he was of land and I of the sea.

Our friendship could not last beyond this moment. But I wouldn't regret this, even though I knew that I was in breach of mermaid law with my interaction with humans beyond the purchase of food or other goods.

Suddenly, I heard a shout; a woman on the pier was telling another person to stop kissing her and to leave her alone. To see this in the human world, when I believed that this place was better than home, shocked me. Even here, no one would do anything to help or to tell the man off. I couldn't intervene even if I wanted to. I didn't know the human laws; I didn't know what they considered acceptable or not. The night sky had turned an unforgiving grey as thunder boomed in the background, droplets of water beginning to fall from the sky; a storm was brewing. I turned back towards Michael, noticing that he was missing, but I could still hear his voice.

I swirled around, trying to find him, before realising that he was heading towards the pier where the woman was trying to fend off the man who wouldn't take no for an answer. I followed him, wanting to know what he would do. To my surprise, he told the man off for not listening to the woman's request to stop and to leave her alone. He began to escort the woman from the pier back onto the shore, but the man was beyond reasoning. He began pushing Michael, wanting to start a fight. Michael, however, wasn't responding to the man's taunts and kept on trying to leave peacefully. Upon seeing this, others intervened and backed him up in his attempt to help the woman.

The storm was stronger now; the waves crashed heavily onto the shore and the pier shook. The man's anger rose with the storm. He punched Michael in the head while his back was turned. Michael lost his balance; my hand reached out towards him instinctively, but it was like I was moving in slow motion. I failed to grab hold of him as he fell into the ocean; the waves dragged him further offshore. I knelt on the edge of the pier in shock, frozen; I didn't know what to do.

'I can't just jump in to save him. I'll be breaking every law that my

kind has. We are not allowed to reveal ourselves. And saving him will do just that. If I enter the water I turn back into a mermaid. But Michael, he was kind to me. He didn't have to let me join him or invite me to the party. Why did he have to be so kind to strangers? I know that mermaids were not supposed to feel a true depth of emotions, but I don't want to lose him or his friendship. What should I do? Please, if we mermaids have a mother creator, please just give me a sign. Show me what I'm supposed to do. Please,' I thought to myself.

Tears fell down my face, my hands clenched my dress and head bowed, I stood as I knew that was what I was supposed to do. I couldn't break mermaid law. If I did and Grandfather found out, I'd be executed. Suddenly I heard a person shout, "Someone get a lifeguard or something, he'll die if no one gets him out."

Once I heard that all thoughts of leaving and following mermaid law escaped my mind. I made my choice. I helped the one person who has ever shown me kindness. I couldn't leave him to die. I won't. With that, I took a running leap off the pier into the ocean below. I heard the other humans screaming, telling me it's too dangerous, but I ignored them. I entered the water with a splash; it hurt my skin and I had barely remembered to hold my breath before jumping. I swam out towards where Michael had been dragged underwater; I tried to force myself to swim further down against the strength of the waves. I reached out my hand, trying to grab hold of him as my vision began to blur. My legs glowed and my body hurt.

'I'm turning back into a mermaid,' I thought to myself.

I ignored the pain of the transformation. I finally reached him, pulling him up above the waves. I looked around, noticing that we were too far from the shore. I couldn't go back to the pier or that beach, otherwise, I'd reveal mermaids to the humans. Suddenly, I remembered the rock where I arrived in the human world. The humans won't be able to see us from there.

When I reached the shore, I tried to make sure he laid on his side as I slapped his back to make him cough out the water that he swallowed. I laid by his side, now turned back into a mermaid, and sang softly to him throughout the night. I sang a song of healing, one of the few higher-level spells I could sneak out of the palace library. I stayed with him for hours. The sun had begun to rise, the sky turning a magnificent orange and purple hue, just singing to him and keeping him safe. I heard him groan; his eyes began to open.

So I reluctantly returned to the sea, and I heard him call out to me, "Will I see you again, Moriah?"

I ignored him. It was the only thing I could do. Because if I acknowledged him, I would admit that yes, I wanted to see him again—but I couldn't, because it was forbidden. At least by ignoring him, he would think I couldn't hear him, and he may still have some hope that we can see each other again. At least that was my hope, but for some reason I felt like I had allowed the darkness in his heart to return.

I pushed that thought out of my head as I dived into the waves, making my way back to Zoara-Bela.

CHAPTER 8

Upon returning to the palace, I noticed that Grandfather was present in my father's receiving room when I attempted to return the spirit gem necklace. Any positive emotion was drained from me, fear smothered my curiosity and joy. I knew Grandfather didn't like humans; were I to talk about how I liked their world and their freedoms while he was there, being his only granddaughter wouldn't save me.

My father, ignoring my grandfather Abaddon, asked me, "How was your passage to the human world?"

"It was pleasant, Father."

"What did you do?"

"I mainly just walked around the human city, observing them."

"That better have been all you were doing," Abaddon said, interrupting my conversation with Father.

He turned towards Father, ignoring me and saying to him, "I don't know why you even let her undergo the rite. She should be focused on preparing herself for marriage; she is nearly of the right age to marry after all."

His eyes narrowed as he looked at me before turning back to

my father, "I know a noble who is looking for a wife. He is quite a close friend of mine. If you don't organise her engagement to a suitable merman, then I will have to do so for you."

"Marriage? But I'm only sixteen. Even the other maidens wouldn't have marriage prospects considered until they're at least twenty-one. I'm not ready to be married!"

"You will be ready to marry when I say you should be married." His expression became colder before he continued, "Control her Abdiel—"

My father stood up in anger shouting, "Do not tell me how to raise my daughter!"

Grandfather repeated, "You wouldn't want a repeat of what happened last time, Abdiel. So control her or I will."

My father shrunk into himself, his anger and righteousness draining from him, all his fight gone before replying, "Yes, Father, I haven't forgotten. I already have someone in mind. I'm in negotiations with them regarding this matter."

"Good. Otherwise, she'll forget her place and think she can act like a human," Grandfather replied before swimming out of the door, knocking me out of the way.

We stood in silence for a few minutes until the wards surrounding our home sent Father a signal that Grandfather had completely left the palace. My father looked older than I had ever seen him; dealing with the king, my grandfather, seemed to do that to him.

I sat down at the table to eat breakfast with him. I knew that I was near the age to marry, but I never thought Father would arrange my marriage for me without asking. I thought he was different. Guess he was just like the other merman of Zoara-Bela.

"Now that your grandfather is gone, why don't you tell me what you thought about the human world?" he asked, breaking the silence.

"I explored the city."

"Go on, what else did you do?"

He seemed genuinely interested in what I did during my exploration of the human world. Which was all I needed to know before I let my excitement and joy take over, I shared everything that I saw and did, conveniently forgetting to mention anything Michael-related. I blurted out everything, mostly, before pausing mid-conversation.

"What is it? What's wrong?"

"It's nothing."

"Moriah, you can ask me anything," he told me as he placed his hand above mine, squeezing it gently.

"What happens to humans when they die?"

"What makes you ask that?"

"It's just ... I saw a human pushed into the ocean towards the end of my trip. They said that he would die. I was ... never mind."

"Moriah?"

"I was just curious."

He looked up at the roof before replying, "When humans die, it's their bodies that perish and remain within the physical world but not their souls. Their souls are everlasting. They are capable of moving on to another plane of existence to spend eternity with their ancestors in peace. That is if they pass the test their creator gives them when judged. If they fail they go either to nothingness or to a pit of horror."

"What about us? Merfolk. What happens when we die?"

"Why do you want to know all of a sudden?"

"I'm just curious. I want to understand what I saw."

"Well, merfolk turn into sea foam upon our deaths, as our bodies disintegrate because we are beings of magic, held together only by the curse."

"What about our souls?" I asked eagerly.

He raised an eyebrow questioningly before replying, "We don't have souls. At least not ones like what humans have. Our souls don't grow or change, not really, not with this curse. We are creatures frozen in a moment in time. Our souls are mere mockeries of the human form and spirit. This is our punishment until the curse is broken, we are denied peace and closure, denied access to the afterlife—"

"How can the curse be broken?"

"Acceptance and love. Which is why it will never be broken, for we are nearly incapable of expressing this."

"Is there any way for a mermaid to become human?"

"Of course not."

"Hasn't anyone ever found a way to become human without using the spirit gem? Is there anyone that knows how?"

"Well, a sorcerer could—" he cut himself off before he finished his sentence. "There will be no more discussion regarding this matter. Is that understood?"

"Yes, Father."

But there wasn't a need for any more discussion because he had already given me what I wanted. A clue about the identity of the being capable of transforming into a human. There hadn't been many sorcerers in Zoara-Bela, which made it easier for me to find a record of them. The only sorcerer with the power to transform me into a human, that was still alive, was the maid that was referred to only as the 'sea-witch' in the records. All other sorcerers on the list were dead or had never specialised in that type of magic before. She may be able to give me legs. Walking on legs felt more comfortable than swimming with fins.

Hours later, I sneaked out of my father's palace to make my way to the sea-witch's tower.

CHAPTER 9

According to the records, the sea-witch lived on the edge of the boundary, past the ruins. I looked at my device, a watch orb, that we use to contact others. I brought up the copy of the notes I stole from our library and read it again, hoping for some more information about the sea-witch. But information was scarce; most of our records—the orbs or stone tablets—contained no information or mention of the sea-witch. Except for that one record orb. The only piece of information about the sea-witch, even then it was not detailed, just a map with directions to get to her tower and a brief mention of her being powerful, and vague mentions of a deal. It was as if someone purposely put that information there in a spot where I could find it easily after some searching.

Why they would do that, I did not know. Frankly, at this moment, as I was slowly making my way across Zoara-Bela while avoiding the soldiers' patrols and the spotlights as best I could, the only thing I cared about was not getting caught. If any of the soldiers caught me outside after curfew I would be dragged before my father and questioned about why I was breaking the law, before being punished harshly by being publicly whipped in the town square.

The worst-case scenario was the most likely outcome as most of the soldiers were completely loyal to the king and only showed the minimal required loyalty towards my father as was owed to him due to his position as Crown Prince. My grandfather would most likely have me tortured by his best interrogators to find out why I was outside after curfew before sentencing me to death because as a daughter I had less value than a male heir.

As I made my way around the city, about to turn a corner I glimpsed soldiers swimming towards me. I froze in horror.

'I'm going to get caught. He will kill me. Come on. Think! There has to be some hiding spot around here,' I thought, panicking.

Then I saw a small crevice between two buildings that had some crates that could hide me from view. I quickly swam over to the crevice, diving into the slight gap, barely squeezing through and ducking down behind the crates half-hidden in shadow. My hands reached upwards to cover my mouth, hoping to block the vibrations in the water caused by my breathing. I could feel my eyes widening in horror, at the possibility of being caught, my body was shaking. The light from their torches created a beam that shone near my tail; I barely had time to move my fins before it created a shadow and revealed me. I heard one soldier demand, "Well, is there anything there Arael?"

The soldier named Arael replied, "I thought there was. But it looks like it's a false alarm."

The other soldier said, "Good. Let's go. Our shift is nearly over, I'm exhausted and I just want to go home and sleep."

"Me too," replied Arael, yawning.

I could feel the vibrations in the water and heard them as they left. Their voices became more distant as time went on. My body slowly relaxed in relief at their leaving. But I waited a few more minutes before slowly swimming out of the crevice after double-checking that there weren't any more soldiers. I pulled the hood of my cloak over my head once again before swimming around the ruins to reach the sea-witch's tower.

The sea-witch's tower stood tall, nestled behind the ruins and the mountains that surrounded the edges of our city. The darkness of the sea seemed to make the building more ominous. You could almost feel the energy of the ancient arts emanating from it.

'There is something about the wards of this building. It's as if the energy is designed to make people ignore its existence, which is probably why I didn't notice this place before now,' I thought.

Straightening my back and taking in a deep breath, I attempted to summon up as much courage as I could, forcing myself to enter the cavern leading to the entrance of the tower. As soon as I swam into the opening, I heard the movement of heavy rocks behind me; I turned to look and realised that the exit had been sealed shut. I tried my best in the darkness to force the boulder to move, but I was unsuccessful.

"Damn it!" I shouted, banging my fist against the boulder before sliding down to the floor.

As I did so the marks that I had barely noticed etched onto the walls glowed, filling the cavern with light. I pushed myself up and swam towards the other end of the cavern. There was a door with no handle, that opened suddenly without a touch. It was as if she was expecting me. As if she knew that I would be coming. But how? I told no one of my plans.

I reluctantly made my way into the room before I heard the door slam shut. I heard a cackle that emanated from the shadows, echoing around the room.

I heard a voice call out in a high-pitched giggle, "Well, well, well. What do we have here? A little mermaid. Why have you come all this way? Don't you know what the punishment is for breaking curfew, child? Or do you not care?"

"I ... I came to see you, witch."

"Witch. How rude little fish. Maybe I should send you on your way if you're going to address me like that," she replied, still speaking in that high-pitched giggle.

'Her voice. I've heard it before, but where?' I thought to myself.

"I'm sorry. But I only know your title as the sea-witch. If I knew your name, I would call you that."

She laughed again, "But you do know it, little fish. I told you not so long ago."

"But I've never seen you before in my life."

The sea-witch swam out of the shadows into the light as she said, "Recognise me now, little fish?"

I gasped as her face was revealed to me. The sea-witch was a beautiful mermaid. Her golden blonde hair contrasted beautifully against the dark tan of her skin and her lilac eyes. The upper half of her body was dressed in a dark pink wrap that covered her breasts before wrapping itself around the top of her abdomen. A gold and pink necklace hung around her neck, rings branching out like scales down her neck and across her shoulders before joining the golden shoulder armour and loose sleeves made from a lighter pink cloth. A gold and pink belt with a triquetra pendant attached hung above her waist complimenting her light purple tail.

And I did recognise her. Her face and appearance were younger, her clothes different, but her voice was unchanged.

"Everyone comes to me in the end, little fish. Everyone," she said with a haughty laugh.

It was her. The old woman from the ruins. Amari.

CHAPTER 10

"**Y**ou! You're the woman from the ruins!" I shouted.

"Did you honestly think an ordinary mermaid would know so much about the actual history of this kingdom? They told me you were intelligent little fish. I guess they were wrong. If it took you this long to recognise me. Now. Let's get down to business. Why have you come to see me?" The sea-witch, who I now knew to be Amari, replied.

"I came because—" I attempted to answer her question but she cut me off mid-response.

"Ah! You are here to find a way to be with your darling prince, Michael, wasn't it? That's what you want, isn't it? To be with your human," Amari said in a sarcastic tone, slightly dragging the sounds of certain words to emphasise her point.

I was taken aback '*Where the hell did she get that idea?*'

Amari continued, "Well, the solution to your problem is simple. You need to become human yourself. With a little magic, giving you a pair of legs is not that difficult. I'm quite willing to do so."

"Why would you do this for me? And how do you know so much about me?" I said suspiciously.

"Not important, dearie. What is important is that I am always willing to help merfolk like yourself. So long as you agree to give me my rightful payment, of course."

"Right. You would turn me human. In return for what exactly?" I replied reluctantly.

'Might as well humour her. Besides, she's not wrong about me wanting to become human. To get human legs. But she is completely off regarding why I want human legs.'

"Well, it's not worth much. A mere trifle. My payment is your voice. Well, little fish? Nothing is free in life. If you want something, you need to either take it yourself or be willing to pay the price in return for what you want," she replied with a slight giggle in her voice.

"My voice. Why would you want my voice? There is nothing special about it. You are a mermaid yourself. Your voice is capable of doing the same thing as mine."

"It doesn't matter why I want your voice. This payment is a mere equivalent exchange. The intrinsic value of your voice, the fact it is a large part of your life, means that it is of equal value to me casting the enchantment that will turn you into a human. Besides, you don't need it. You can communicate without it. Well, do we have a deal, little fish?"

"No. There is something you're not telling me. You'll turn me into a human in return for my voice. No. It's not that simple. What's the catch?" I demanded.

"Oh! I guess they were right, you are intelligent after all. Good. Never sign a deal without knowing the conditions. Not that the others who came to me ever did. They should have read the fine print."

"So, what's the catch?"

"Nothing so terrible. I will turn you into a human in return for your voice. That much is true. But—"

'There it is. The fine print.'

"The enchantment will only last for three days. Got that?

Three days. By the time the sun sets on the third day of your life as a human, you need to get your human, Michael to kiss you. Not just any kiss, it has to be one fuelled by love. If that happens you will stay human permanently. If he doesn't kiss you by the end of the third day, you will turn back into a mermaid. Any other methods of transformation including the spirit gem will never work for you again. You will never be able to turn into a human again, trapped forever beneath the sea as my servant. And you will stay voiceless for eternity," she said.

"That's why you want to make a deal with me. You want a member of the royal household as a slave to get back at either my father or grandfather," I said angrily.

"Your grandfather has caused a lot of pain. To me especially. I do not forget nor forgive the wrongs done against me."

"You honestly think that if I fail to uphold my end of the bargain which, let's face it, is the most likely outcome, that my grandfather would care about me being a slave? He doesn't care about me. I'm just a tool for him to use to further his control."

"Do you want the deal or not little fish? I don't have all night," Amari interrupted me.

"No—"

"Well, I guess you'll have to live as a mermaid."

"Let me finish. I don't want you to turn me into a human. I never did. I just let you explain the deal to see what you were willing to offer. Besides, your guess about why I was here was off."

"Oh, really, dearie?"

"I don't want love. I want freedom. I want what humans have. The ability to choose what they want to do with their life."

"Huh. I never expected that."

"What I came here to ask was if you could teach me the ancient arts, to make me your disciple."

"Why would you want that little fish? It would be much

simpler for me to give you human legs and send you to the human world if you desperately desire freedom," she looked at me strangely as she spoke.

"I know it would be. But I want to learn the ancient arts from you for the exact reason I told you I came. Freedom. Choice. Power over my own life. If need be, the ability in the future to stand up to my grandfather or to escape his wrath, especially if he finds out I interacted with a human. But I especially want to learn how to transform into a human or to give myself legs whenever I want to. Not permanently or for three days only. I want to be able to choose how and when I transform."

"Oh, that is interesting. I've never had someone ask me to teach them before. Most merfolk who come to see me are so desperate to get what they want they don't think about the consequences or the long-term effects. They just want what they came for. Nothing more. Nothing less. They never even think about how they can get what they want themselves."

"But I did. Before I came, I thought about how I could become human and whether you could give me that. But I'd rather be in control of the transformation myself. And as a witch, you are not only capable of magic but the teaching of it. And if you are as old as I think you are, then you know a lot more than what is in our records about the ancient arts."

"You want me to make you my apprentice. To teach you the ancient arts?"

"Yes."

"And what will you give me in exchange for my teaching little fish?"

"What do you want?"

"I assume that your voice is out of the question?"

"Yes. I need my voice to cast most spells that are a part of the ancient arts."

"Well then, how about your mother's bracelet?"

"My mother's bracelet?"

"Yes. That one on your wrist right now."

I brought my arm up to my chest, my other hand grasped my wrist, "This is the only thing I have of her."

"Oh, you poor little thing. Did you honestly think I'd teach you and ask my payment to be something that wasn't important to you? The payment has to be of equal value to the product or service dearie. You want training. And I have to give up my valuable time to do it."

I looked at my mother's pearl bracelet, *This is the only thing I have to remember her by. There are no statues or holograms saved in a memory orb. My father never talks about her.*

She continued, "Now I'm not so cruel as to take it from you right now. I will accept a payment of 50 orichalcum coins a month for the lessons you undertake, and once I declare your training complete ... let's say, the passing of the journeyman stage at the end of your training ... I will collect your mother's bracelet then. If after the journeyman stage you wish to continue learning under me then, you will only need to pay me 50 orichalcum coins a month from that point on. Now, if you decide at any point before completing the journeyman stage to stop the lessons, you forfeit the bracelet immediately along with 200 orichalcum coins for wasting my time. Do we have a deal, little fish?"

"Why offer me such a good deal?"

"Maybe you interest me? I had hoped you would be different from the others that came begging for my help. But you were the only one to ever ask for another offer or to even ask for the conditions of my deal. Most just accept it without thinking about it. But you ... you're different. More different than you know. It should be interesting, seeing you grow," she said with a weird smile on her face.

"What do you mean?"

"Not important. Now, do you want this deal or not little fish?"

'I don't want to give up my mothers' bracelet. It's all I have left of her. But training. The training could mean that if grandfather tries to force me to marry one of his friends, then I'll have a way out or a way to stand up against him. I'll be able to transform into a human when I feel uncomfortable in my own skin or when I need an escape.'

My eyes closed shut, my hand grasped the bracelet.

'Power. The freedom to choose that this training will give me. I'm sorry, mother. I can't let myself be weak when I have the opportunity to have more. Forgive me.'

I nodded in reply to Amari's question.

"Little fish, you need to say it out loud. I haven't taken your voice. Now, do we have a deal?" she asked me, handing out a contract and a quill.

"Yes," I said as I reached for the contract to read it before signing.

Everything she said regarding payment, both of our responsibilities were clearly outlined in the text. There was no hidden loophole or extra clauses in the fine print. Everything was as it should be.

Despite this, I felt like there was something off with this deal. She wanted something from me. Something she wasn't telling me. Hopefully, nothing bad. Even then I still didn't trust her. I was probably right not to.

With that, I grabbed the quill and shut my eyes as I signed the contract as if I was a human signing my soul away. The document glowed an ominous green colour before Amari rolled the contract back up.

"I hope you're happy with your deal, little fish. I know I am," she said to me in a smug voice.

For some reason, I thought that she got the better end of the deal. And she probably did; after all, she held most of the power in this situation.

As I headed back home to the palace and the danger lurking in the streets in the form of soldiers, I heard Amari cackling with utter glee at the price she could extract from me. The sound seemed to follow me back to the city.

CHAPTER 11

I n the month following my deal with the sea-witch Amari, I
   would sneak out of the palace at different times of the day.
My training routine was inconsistent as I had completed my
rite of passage, being declared mostly of age. Not an adult yet,
though. That was why the rite existed. It was the start of the
transition period from child to adult. Those who could go
through the rite started taking on more duties and responsibilities. Royalty was no exception.

As one who had passed the rite, I was now required to
ensure that all complaints and requests for assistance by our
tenants were dealt with in an orderly manner. I was also
required to ensure that the supplies required for the running of
the household were ordered and delivered to the right people.
Within the next year I would also need to attend court to learn
more about how our nation was run. Not that I'd ever be
allowed to use those skills.

Whack!

"Ow! Why did you do that?"

"Because I could see your brain starting to drift off. Magic is a beautiful, complex and temperamental thing," Amari scolded me.

"You realise you just described yourself, right? You're telling me that magic is just like you."

Whack!

I flinched at the sharp pain. I deserved that one. Me and my smart mouth.

"Moriah, you cannot let your mind wander when casting magic. It can backfire in weird and dangerous ways."

"But still I already have some knowledge of magic and even you said I'm not a complete beginner. So why make me learn this basic spell and not teach me how to transform into a human, which you promised to do."

"You need to learn the basics of transformation before you tackle something as complex as transforming into a human. That's why you are learning this first. It will get your magic and body gets used to transforming into something different. Slowly building up your tolerance and resistance, so once you reach the stage where transforming into a human is possible, you will have better control over the magic. You will have control over how long it lasts and what mermaid abilities transfer over to your human form. If you try to cast a spell like transforming into a human right now, it could kill you."

I rolled my eyes and mimed along with Amari's words, which wasn't something new to me.

"You could at least teach me a more difficult transformation spell. I'm not a beginner."

"Fine. If you can cast this spell properly, without it back-firing then I will teach you more complex magic. But fail, you stop whining about the level of the magic and you will learn what I teach you at the level I believe you to be at. Deal?"

"Yes."

Finally, I would learn something better than the basic spell for changing my hair colour. Amari reluctantly explained the ageing spell, which was a transformation spell and how it worked and how to cast it. She also explained how the magic should feel as the transformation spell was cast.

"Remember, you must stay focused. If you lose focus for a moment it will backfire on you."

"I got it, Amari. I'm not a child anymore," I said, practically bouncing in excitement.

"That's debatable."

I closed my eyes and took a deep breath, *'Right. I need to channel my magic and let it slowly build up within me. Let it move throughout my body slowly. My skin wrinkles. My hair is turning grey.'*

I could feel my skin shift as the magic had begun to work as I muttered, "Lehitebager (to get old)."

'Hah! Told her I could—'

With that my concentration broke as I had stopped focusing on what I needed to look like and all I felt was pain. Bang! The force of the magic blasted me across the tower and into the wall, leaving a crack that webbed out on it.

I lay on the floor, dazed, *'Didn't expect that.'*

"Now you see why it's important that we start small before moving to complex magic—"

"I almost had it. I could feel it working. Let me try again."

"No. We made a deal. If you failed to cast the magic, then you agreed to stop whining and learn what I told you, when I think you are ready to learn it. You attempted to cast it and failed. Almost succeeding doesn't matter. What matters is that you failed, and it backfired on you."

"But—"

She cut me off "But nothing. If this was the spell to transform you into a human and it backfired because of your arrogance, then you wouldn't have been blasted into a wall by the backfire. No, no, no. You would have exploded. And I would have fish guts covering my walls."

She looked at me before sliding down the wall next to me. She reached over to grab my face, turning it to face her "I've been doing this for a long time. I've taught others how to use magic before. And I've seen some of my students ignore my warnings and blow themselves up because they didn't listen to my warning or read the warning labels on the spell books that they learnt the spell from. I don't want that to happen to you. Besides, you were the one to come to me to learn magic, not the other way round."

"I just thought I could be capable of so much more than basic spells."

"You are. You're just not ready for it yet. These things take time. You'll get to the stage where you'll be able to cast magic like the one you attempted with ease. Just not yet."

"Just let me have another go. I'm certain that I can cast the ageing spell if I just try again," I told her desperately.

"This is serious, Moriah. Losing focus can lead to a spell backfiring, as what happened with this spell. Even though the hair changing spell is relatively basic, it is still a transformation spell. The more difficult the magic, the more serious the consequences of it backfiring. The ageing spell backfiring sent you into the wall. Intent means everything with magic like this. Your brain drifts off, you think about something else, the next thing you know you're a pufferfish."

"Pufferfish? That's a bit specific, don't you think? Who do you know that turned into a pufferfish when they lost focus?"

"Never mind. You get my point."

"No, really, who was it that turned into a pufferfish? Was it you?"

"No, it was your father."

"Wait, really? He learnt magic from you?"

She rolled her eyes before sighing "He didn't learn from me. Andromeda, his wife, learned magic from me and your father thought it was so easy to use transformation magic. And she gave him the spell and the warning about staying focused. He thought she was exaggerating the difficulty of the magic and he lost focus when she stretched, paying more attention to her breasts instead of the magic he was trying to cast. Then poof! Instant pufferfish. Andromeda laughed so much at him, she never let him forget it."

I twirled my hair nervously as I attempted to ask her, "Did you know my mother?"

"Your mother? I take it you mean Andromeda and not—" she cut herself off before she could finish her sentence.

'What does she mean? My mother was Andromeda. My father's wife,' I thought to myself.

"Who else would I be talking about? My mother's name was Andromeda."

"Of course," she replied, her eyes avoiding my face.

'She's lying. Why is she lying?'

"You said 'not'. Who did you believe was my mother?"

"No one. I sometimes get confused. Never mind."

'Why is she still lying? What's so bad about telling me the truth? If Andromeda is not my mother then who is? No. She has to be my mother. But what if she's not? Who am I? I need to know, but I can't ask her. I need to ask my father. He's the one with the answers,' I thought.

Amari seemed almost sad and lonely at that moment. Even if Andromeda wasn't my mother, I still knew nothing about her. Which was why to distract her (and to get some answers) I asked, "Could you tell me about her, Andromeda? What was she like?"

She looked at me, "What do you know about her?"

"Nothing. I know her name. I know what she looked like from her statue and the carvings in the palace. That I look like her. Father doesn't talk about her. It's almost like remembering hurts him."

She looked at me as she spoke, "You remind me of her. She

was kind and loyal beyond measure. She would never hesitate to help someone in need. Curious about everything. Her curiosity led her to me. She wanted to learn magic. She never wanted to be helpless again."

"What do you mean?"

"Andromeda wasn't of noble blood. In fact, she was a servant of a noble household that no longer exists. The noble who ran the household treated his servants as slaves. This was before the fall when slavery was outlawed in Zoara-Bela. She was silenced and abused horribly through magic. Which is why when she learnt of my existence, she came to me. She wanted to learn how to free herself from magic like what was used to keep her prisoner for years before your father noticed it and freed her. She never wanted to be helpless again. She was probably my best student. Eager to learn, but she also wanted to learn more complex magic in the beginning, thinking her progress was too slow. She begged and begged to learn a more complex spell before I gave in. I gave her the ageing spell as I did you but she was further along in the spell when it backfired on her. It nearly killed her. If I wasn't there, then it would have. That's why I'm so hard on you. I don't want to see you hurt. You are so eager to learn enough magic to stand up for yourself or protect yourself just like she was. Not that it helped her in the end."

'Why does she care so much about my wellbeing? I might like her, but I still can't trust her. She wants something from me. I have to hope it isn't too bad,' I thought.

"What do you mean?" I asked her gently.

"Nothing. Now do you want to learn more complex magic despite my warning?"

I shook my head.

"I'm sorry for not listening to you."

Amari laughed. Her laughter was warm; I could see flowers bloom around her.

'How did she do that? That wasn't normal merfolk magic.'

"You are young. It was bound to happen eventually."

"Now how do I cast the hair changing spell?"

She smiled at me before talking me through each step slowly until I could cast the spell perfectly, according to her standards.

"Leshanott et hase'aar sheli (change my hair)," I chanted repeatedly until I cast the spell perfectly.

It took me hours, but I eventually succeeded in turning my hair a beautiful sky blue.

CHAPTER 12

I had been training with Amari for nearly two months, but we never once touched on curses. Curses were the one topic that I had no knowledge of despite my attempts to learn whatever I could when I snuck into my father's private archives and library. My knowledge of curses began and ended with the fact they existed and they were dangerous. For some strange reason, Amari seemed reluctant to teach me anything about curses.

Despite this, I would constantly ask her questions about this topic. Eventually I irritated her enough that she cancelled my lessons for the next two days. And in my boredom I went exploring within my father's palace. I had explored most of Zoara-Bela, but not my father's palace. So for a lack of something better to do, I went exploring in some lesser-used areas of the palace. It was only when I went past my mother's garden that I felt a shock go up my spine. Magic. There was magic near here.

I closed my eyes and let my magic guide me to the magic hidden within the garden. Upon opening my eyes I realised I stood before a stone wall that held engravings of a disaster carved on it. The engraving was of the fall of Zoara-Bela. But why put an engraving in an out of the way corner of a garden that no one comes to?

I placed my hand on the engraving to work out where the magic was coming from. As my hand moved along the engraving, I felt one of the engravings was raised higher than the others.

'Why is this higher than the rest?' I thought.

I looked behind me nervously as I checked if the gardens were still empty. No one was watching as I pressed down on the slightly raised engraving. For a moment nothing happened, but before I could remove my hand, I felt the stone beginning to shift. The wall moved back in on itself before sliding to the left, revealing a passageway.

'A secret door in my mother's garden. Why would this be here?' I thought as I looked at the dark entry.

Sound carried through the water, I heard my father calling for me. In my panic, I swam into the entry that the engraving created. Upon entering, the wall sealed shut behind me before I could change my mind. It was too late for me to change my mind so I swam forward slowly in the darkness. There was another door at the end of the passage that I opened after a few minutes of searching for the handle. As the door opened, orbs of light glowed along the walls to reveal a room.

The frames and pillars were made of orichalcum with feminine decorations, containing the magic within the room. Furniture was made of orichalcum, coral and stone. But along the walls were shelves containing orbs and sheets of orichalcum behind a desk. The desk was messy as if the merfolk that used this room had left in a hurry but never came back. I moved closer to the shelves to examine the objects on there. Algae covered many of the objects and labels.

"Lehassir et haatsaot (remove the algae)," I muttered.

I used the spell to clear the algae off the orichalcum sheets so

I could read what was written on them. Spells. They contained spells.

At random, I selected one sheet to read. The spell inscribed on it was a jinx. According to this when cast it will cause the person to experience bad luck. Nothing too serious, according to the instructions. There was a warning written underneath it, but it was too worn out and faded to read. I shrugged it off as I believed that it was something minor and continued reading.

It was only when I heard the chime of the bell that I realised I had been in the room for over an hour. I placed the spell sheet back on the shelf before I left the room. But as I swam past the desk, I recognised the decorations on the box that was on the desk. Those decorations were only ever used on containers that held a crown. My hands shook as I opened the box to see a crown within it. I recognised the crown instantly. It was my mother's.

CHAPTER 13

I spent hours in a daze after finding her crown. I knew that my mother, Andromeda, learnt magic from Amari. But I never expected to find her study hidden in a garden. Father must not have known about it, otherwise he would have destroyed it by now. I finally had something that belonged to my mother. Something no one could take away from me as long as I was careful. I would learn every spell in her study. I wanted to feel closer to her. Maybe this would help.

I knew that I wasn't supposed to try new spells without supervision. So, out of curiosity, I memorised the theory of the spell that could cause bad luck out of curiosity. I never intended to cast it until I learnt more theory connected to this spell, as I had never cast a jinx before.

But the next morning when I went to the marketplace I saw something that angered me greatly. I had seen similar sights before today and had done nothing. But since meeting Michael during my rite, I'd felt off. Seeing the grocer hitting his wife and berating her in front of his customers, something that was a common sight in the market, angered me greatly. I wanted to do something. He had to pay for what he had done.

I wanted him to suffer. I wanted him to feel the same pain as his wife. My magic seemed to move on its own, twisting into an unfamiliar shape.

'*Maybe a bit of poor luck will get him to stop,*' I thought as I began casting the jinx in the middle of the marketplace.

Just as I was about to cast the jinx on the grocer, I felt a hand around my throat before it pulled back me into the shadows. Someone disrupted my spell. I turned my head to yell at the merfolk who'd grabbed me but stopped when I saw Amari's face.

"We are going back to the tower. Now," she whispered coldly into my ear before teleporting us away from the market.

My heart felt like it had stopped upon hearing her voice before it began beating rapidly. It felt like fear.

As soon as the spell teleporting us was released I collapsed on the floor nauseous and dizzy. As soon as I tried to move upright, a body pushed me into the stone wall. I tried to talk, but the hand on my throat squeezed tighter. Amari was furious. Her face looked like Grandfather's whenever someone disobeyed him.

"You stupid fish! What were you thinking? Trying to cast that spell in the marketplace. The king has eyes everywhere. Do you really think he wouldn't find out it was you who cast that curse?"

I tried to speak, to tell her it wasn't a curse, and that I was sorry. I was willing to say anything to get her to stop, but her hand just squeezed tighter. I tried to push her hands off me, but her magic held me in place.

I couldn't breathe. My vision blurred as I couldn't get enough oxygen in my lungs. My body felt loose and floppy as I began to blackout. It was only as my eyes began to close that Amari let go of me.

I continued looking at the ground as I struggled to get

oxygen into my lungs. I could feel my eyes beginning to sting and could taste blood in my mouth.

'*Why was she so angry? She's never been angry with me when I cast a spell that I shouldn't have known before.*'

"Well, little fish. Why would you do something so stupid?"

"I … I just wanted him to stop hitting her … I wanted him to pay," I coughed out.

"So, you thought cursing him was an excellent idea? I thought you were smart little fish. Guess I was wrong. I should end your lessons right now. You promised me you would learn whatever I thought you were ready for. I don't know where you learnt that curse—"

I cut her off, "Curse? I wasn't going to cast a curse. I was going to cast a jinx. A minor jinx. It was just a bad luck jinx. It never lasts more than two hours. I'm not stupid. I read the warnings for this spell."

"Jinx? That wasn't a jinx, you stupid fish—"

"It was the jinx mazal ra'. It literally is bad luck. It was never a curse. If you had just asked me what I was doing instead of attacking me, then you would know that."

"You didn't know?"

"Know what?"

"Mazal ra'. It is a minor jinx when cast properly but the way you cast the spell it was a curse. It would have started out as minor bad luck, but it could have ended in the merman's death."

"What?"

"You told me you wanted him to pay for what he did. Well, your magic would have listened to your desire. The jinx would have transformed into a curse that would punish him. Instead of being a minor jinx, it would have turned into a curse. It would have become hashemadah a'tzmit which means to self-destruct. It would have destroyed his life."

"I … I didn't know. I swear I didn't know. I never knew that jinxes could become curses."

"I know. And I'm … sorry that I attacked you. I thought you knew," she said reluctantly.

"But I didn't. Never attack me again."

"Or what?"

"Or I'll cast that jinx on you."

She laughed at my warning. She may have more experience than me, but I won't let myself be pushed around by her.

"Oh, little fish … I'm glad that you have finally grown some spine, but you are millennia too young to harm me."

"Who said that I would cast the spell to your face?"

Her face lost its smile as she moved closer to me "Little fish, you're a lot of things but you'd never stab someone in the back. You're too honourable."

"What good is honour if it costs you the battle?"

"Honour separates you from the king. Do you want to be like him?"

"No."

But what if grandfather found out about me learning magic? I can't beat him by fighting him directly. I wouldn't stand a chance without trickery … Not going to happen. I won't let him find out about my lessons,' I thought.

"I thought not. You are too kind to cast a curse."

"Mermaids are not kind."

"Maybe not. But you are."

"Why do you think I can't cast a curse?"

"You could, but it would go against your nature. Curses are fuelled by negative feelings and emotions. Most merfolk wouldn't be able to cast even the most basic curse as their ability to feel emotion has been suppressed. But you feel too much. Which makes casting a curse dangerous."

"Why is it dangerous?"

Amari looked uncomfortable with the question but replied anyway, "Because you have to mean it. With a curse, you have to want the victim to suffer. To see them in pain. To make them pay. And you have to desire it so much that it consumes your very being. The more curses you cast, the easier it is to cast the next."

"That doesn't sound too bad."

"The darkness of each curse will create a scar, for a lack of a better word on your magic. The darkness will infect you. Slowly change you over time. For most curses, the damage is minimal. Eventually, your magic will heal and the darkness will disappear if you don't cast any more curses. But with curses that last for years or centuries or millennia like the curse on Zoara-Bela, the cost is far greater even for a god."

"What do you mean 'even for a god'?"

"Curses are unnatural. They aren't meant to exist. So the world or nature fights against it. If a condition for breaking the curse isn't specified then this causes the curse to break down over time until the right catalyst or event happens that breaks it."

"But why would it be costly for a god?"

"Even gods have to follow a set of rules, little fish. And the curse on Zoara-Bela, once cast, would have fed on the magic of the goddess who cast it as punishment. The same would have happened to you. The magic of the curse you were going to cast would have drained your magic until either he died or you did."

"How do you know this?"

"Not important. What is important is how you have been progressing so fast in our lessons and how you learnt that jinx?"

"I told you I wasn't a beginner. Maybe my study wasn't well rounded in magic, but I'm not a complete novice."

"But how did you learn?"

"I ... may have ... snuck into the magic lessons of the sons of the nobles that took lessons with the same tutors I did."

"You learnt magic through eavesdropping," she looked at me in disbelief.

"And from stealing spells that were kept in Father's personal archives and library."

"That would explain how you learnt that jinx."

I didn't bother correcting her assumption about learning the jinx from my father's archives or library. As long as she believed that, then she wouldn't go looking for my mother's study. I knew that I should feel guilty for lying to her, but I don't. That study was the only thing I had left of my mother and I won't let anyone take it away from me. Not even Amari.

CHAPTER 14

My third month of training with Amari was the turning point for my progression in the ancient arts or magic. I had finally reached the stage where my magic was mature enough to use more difficult magic such as the ageing spell and illusions. According to Amari, I had been progressing fairly quickly, mastering spells, enchantments and a variety of potions that would normally take months to master in weeks or sometimes hours.

However, Amari constantly beat it into my head that it was only because of my parents' inherent abilities with the ancient arts that made it possible for me to draw upon and use the more difficult magics—that and I already had the basics mastered and I knew what my magic felt like. She constantly warned me to not get cocky before whacking me in the head if I lost concentration for the slightest moment and bringing my ego back down to the seabed.

Like most of my visits to Amari's tower, it was filled with lessons of magic that led to me being thrown into walls and other objects. Every lesson I was constantly thrown about or whacked in the head or turned into random sea creatures as my spells backfired.

However, what I enjoyed most were the conversations we had afterwards. Sometimes we talked about magic. Other times we just talked about what we enjoyed doing. Occasionally we went out. And as time went on, I learnt more about Amari. I got to know her better than I thought I would. She was a hard taskmaster, expecting perfection in every spell and potion created, but she appeared to care deeply about the merfolk she interacted with.

She had an amazing sense of humour and took joy in making the consequences of the deals she made ironic if they failed to uphold their end of the bargain. But there was something about her. Something that separated her from the rest, and I didn't mean the fact that she lived in a tower on the edge of the kingdom. It was in her eyes and the way she moved and spoke.

Something otherworldly. Powerful and ancient. Something that made people think twice about crossing her. For she was quick to anger, slow to forgive, and her punishments *always* fit the crime. Even so, I liked her. I enjoyed learning from her in between my duties to the palace, which had been growing slowly. Despite this, the thought she wanted more from me that she hadn't told me about weighed heavily on my mind. While I liked her I knew I couldn't trust her.

Today was the day that she would teach me how to cast a full-body illusion. The base of the magic was relatively simple, however, making it so another couldn't break it was a lot more difficult. I could see Amari roll her eyes at my inability to stay still as I was practically squirming in my excitement.

She began the lesson by explaining each step of the magic, "You need to calm yourself. Close your eyes and breathe in and out slowly. Clear your mind of all distractions. Focus only on the sound of my voice. You already know how to cast illusions.

You know how each part of an illusion works together. What you will need to do today is cast each aspect of the illusion one after the other so each illusion builds upon the next. Each illusion that I cast is tightly woven into a net of magic that surrounds me. Imagine your magic building and cascading gently over you. Imagine the image you want to project. What is the colour of your hair, your skin, your eyes and your tail? Imagine each scale upon your skin, where it is placed, the colour of it. Imagine what age you want to appear as and what your voice sounds like. Let the net shape the illusion you are casting."

I could feel my magic building and covering me from head to tail tip as I listened to my teacher's instructions.

She continued, "That's it. You are doing so well. Now the illusion is a part of the net of magic surrounding you. You need to focus on attaching the loose thread of magic to a loadstone or anchor to hold your magic in place. Tie it to a ring or necklace or hairpiece. Something that will be on you even hidden behind the illusion. It needs to be something you are unlikely to remove yourself as a habit while the illusion was in place. Take that loose thread and weave it through and around the object you are using an anchor. Imagine taking that thread and creating a knot around the anchor that only you can undo."

I followed her instructions as closely as possible. I wove the thread around and underneath the ring on my right index finger and imagined tying a knot that only I could break. I could feel the magic take hold and solidify around me as I muttered, "Leshanott ett hamareah sheli (change the way I look)."

I heard the snap of fingers as I opened my eyes to look at my teacher. Amari looked proud as she asked me how I felt.

I replied, "I still feel like me. I even sound like me."

She was still smiling as she spoke, "Not to me you don't. Look in the mirror on the wall if you don't believe me."

I gasped in amazement as I stared into the sea glass mirror.

There in the reflection was a mermaid staring back at me that looked nothing like me. The general shape, facial and body features were the same. The mermaid in the mirror had blonde curly hair, lilac eyes and peach coloured skin that suited her round face. There was the odd strand of grey hair that framed her face that held slight lines and crinkles near her eyes and mouth. She wore a solid white top with a light blue fabric that covered her back and sides forming a triangle shape. Her tail was of a slightly different shape, similar to dolphins, in a light purple colour. She was plain but still lovely to look at.

My hand raised to touch the reflection in the mirror. The appearance of my illusion looked like someone I knew. The face was older, but it was familiar despite the ageing. Staring at the image in the mirror I felt like crying but I didn't know why. I knew that I had never seen the maiden whose reflection I had used as my own, but still, there was something in me that was crying out. There was something in me that thought this maiden was important, that I should care about her.

Amari's voice broke me out of my daze, "What inspired your illusion, little fish?"

"I'm sorry. What?"

"What made you think of this appearance for your illusion?"

"I... I do not know. I just thought of it, I guess."

"So you weren't thinking of a specific person when you cast the illusion."

"I don't think so. I mean ... looking at the reflection now ... this face ... it seems ... almost familiar to me. Like I should know this face. Like I should care about the person whose face I'm using. Do I look like someone you know?"

Amari's eyes looked sad and distant, "Someone I knew years ago. She was murdered. Her father still mourns her."

"Who was she?"

"Just a young mermaid who tried to change the hearts of those around her and was killed for it. Hardly anyone remembers her now besides her father, her killer and I. He never should have encouraged her the way he did. She tried to do too much too fast that it backfired on her."

"What was her name?"

Amari looked at me as if I should already know this, but I didn't. Sighing, she replied, "I will tell you so long as you never mention her name to anyone besides myself. Not your father and definitely not your grandfather. Promise me you won't tell anyone."

"I promise."

"Adalina. Her name meant little noble. It suited her well. She was young but noble of heart and blood. She deserves to be remembered."

"Who was she? To me?"

"I cannot tell you. Just that you knew her as a child and that you adored her. Just … promise me you will remember her."

"I will. Is it safe for me to use this illusion? I can change it if it's not."

Amari shook her head "You don't need to change it. It is different enough that people will dismiss the resemblance. You also made it look significantly older than she was."

Amari grabbed a light blue cloak from the rack and handed it to me saying, "Now put this on. It is time to test your illusions in the outside world. You need to keep the illusion active. It cannot waver as we head to the marketplace and interact with the merchants. If at any point someone looks at you too closely, pull the hood over your head. I enchanted it. It will make people ignore you so long as you do nothing to capture their attention."

I put the cloak around my shoulders and followed her out the door to head to the market in the Citadel.

The market within the Citadel was busy when we arrived. It was around noon, which was when the rush typically began. Merfolk during this time of day, especially on a weekend, spent their time haggling for the best prices before they headed back home for their midday meal (even though it occurred around one o'clock). Walking through the marketplace alongside my teacher, who was also in disguise, was an interesting experience. No one looked twice at us, at me.

For once, I was just an ordinary mermaid. One of the crowd. I looked to Amari wanting to begin a conversation, small talk really, to take my mind off my nerves regarding the illusion spell. My mouth opened to ask her a question when she looked harshly at me, hissing out a spell. Nothing came out of my mouth. She silenced me. My hand reaches to grasp my throat. I panicked as no sound came out. Not a word. Not a note. Not even the hiss of my breath. My eyes widened in panic.

I looked at her frantically when I heard her voice. But her mouth didn't move. She wasn't speaking out loud, but in my mind with a spell. She told me harshly, *Moriah, I know that you have been relatively sheltered by your father. But you can't have completely forgotten the way our society views women. We have little to no rights. If we speak when not spoken to or have a conversation between ourselves, we could be labelled scolds and have spiked bridles put in our mouth by the guards if we are unlucky. We may be dressed as noblewomen, but that will not protect us. Not completely. They do not allow most noblewomen to leave their households. They send slaves or servants to the marketplace to purchase what they want. Which is why we need to limit our conversation to the merchants who will sell us their goods and only haggle for the products.*

She continued, *Any conversation outside of those bounds will be looked upon negatively. If we offend them, they can call for the guards. And I doubt that your illusion will last under extreme pressure. Worse still, the king alongside his guards passes through the marketplace at this time of day. We cannot afford to draw attention to ourselves.*

Which is why my disguise is a lot older than yours. Most mermaids only show their age if they are near death or they are older than the average age of death, which is 400 years old.'

She paused to gather her thoughts. *'By looking this old there may be some leeway given to me if I speak out of turn or breach the rules of conversation. It will make it more unlikely that they will call the guards on me as they still respect the elderly, even if they are women. But you. Your disguise is still relatively young. They will not have the same consideration. Now only reply through this spell and not out loud. To reply, just concentrate on what you want to say to me and think about me receiving the message.'*

I look at her in concentration before replying telepathically, *'Why tell me this now? Why not warn me before we left your tower?'*

'I thought you knew this already. You are known for visiting the marketplace. You swim past it regularly. I thought not conversing with others beyond haggling and purchasing goods was common sense.'

'I was never told this. I mean, I knew we had practically no rights. But I didn't know that talking with others, making small talk, would get mermaids in trouble. No one ever told me. I would regularly have a conversation with the merchants about how their sales were going, about their families or about new products that they were selling. I mean the first few times they looked strangely at me but now they begin the conversation with me,' I thought in reply to Amari's comments.

'They looked strangely at you because you were breaching the rules of conversation. But they probably never reported you because you are the princess and they thought the conversations you were having were part of your royal duties. And the guards probably never punished you because you were the princess and none of the merchants complained. Or if they did, your father told them that this was part of your royal duties to protect you. You've been lucky that you have a position of power. But in this disguise, your power is gone. Because right now you are not Moriah but Muriel, meaning bright sea. Muriel is but a noblewoman. Speak only when spoken to. Keep

your answers short. And for the love of the sea, don't draw attention to yourself.'

I nodded slightly at her reply. I knew that I couldn't afford to get caught. I was not supposed to know this magic, let alone be here at this time of day. I was meant to be working in my mother's gardens. The illusion in the palace would hold unless someone caught me in the marketplace if my illusion wavered. I was not the only one in danger here. If I got caught, then Amari would be caught with me. She could be killed for encouraging rebellion. And I would be married off then.

It took us a few minutes before we arrived at the clothes merchant who had some new fabrics on display and some jewellery. I would normally speak with him, but I remembered that in my disguise I was a stranger to him. I let my teacher take the lead.

"Good merchant. I would like to purchase some pink silks. The best quality you have. I will be creating a gown for my granddaughter."

The merchant collected some beautiful light pink and magenta silks before asking, "Which of these colours do you wish to purchase, my lady?"

She pretended to examine the silks closely by touching the fabrics before turning to me, "Well, granddaughter, which colour do you think is best suited for the occasion? The light pink or magenta?"

I kept my eyes low and head bowed before replying softly, "The magenta silks with possibly light pink sheer cloth to emphasise the colour and quality of the gown would work the best, Grandmother."

She smiled "Good. You can learn granddaughter. It seems that my tutelage in fashion has paid off. Very well. I would like to purchase a roll of the magenta silk... around two metres would be best, good merchant. Now the sheer light pink cloth that you have in the corner. I would like around... a metre. Yes, a metre would be best."

The merchant, following Amari's instructions, quickly cut the required length of each cloth that she asked for and packaged it. He then asked, "Would you like anything else?"

"Ah, yes! The small roll of the golden thread you have over there. And a roll of the gold lace. The gown requires some embroidery. How much would the total cost be, good merchant?"

"For the silk, sheer cloth, thread and lace," he paused while speaking to calculate the total.

"Twenty orichalcum, fifteen silver, and ten copper coins, my lady."

"That is far too much. Reduce it to twenty orichalcum. Your quality is good but not that good," Amari replied.

With that, Amari and the merchant haggled back and forth for over ten minutes. Neither giving an inch. Before the merchant gave his last offer.

"Twenty orichalcum and fifteen silver if you also purchase the simple pearl brooch. This is my last offer."

Amari paused as if to consider the offer before replying, "Good merchant, you drive a hard bargain. Deal."

They shook hands before Amari counted out the required payment of twenty orichalcum and fifteen silver. She handed it to the merchant who recounted each coin eagerly before bowing his head slightly as he said, "Thank you for your personage, my lady. Have a pleasant day."

"I will, good merchant. Your service was excellent. I will recommend this to the other noblewomen. Now granddaughter, hold the purchases for me. That is the least you could do today, girl."

As we swam away from the merchant we passed the grocer who, like always yelled at his wife who forgot to weigh the items before bagging them. The comments that the grocer was saying towards his wife were horrible. Worse than normal. No one was doing anything. Why wasn't anyone doing anything?

Michael. A mere human boy stood up for a stranger that was being harassed and helped defend them. This grocer was yelling at his wife, shaking her and moved to slap her as he did months ago. Last time I did nothing to stop it. I attempted to move towards the woman to stop the grocer from hurting her, but Amari cast a spell that froze me in place. Stopping me from helping her. My voice and body were frozen.

I couldn't yell at her for stopping me from helping that poor woman. Then I heard her voice in my head again saying, *'I know that seeing this is upsetting. I believe that this is wrong too. But you cannot act now. Even if you were in your true form instead of a disguise, you could get into serious trouble. You have no support base. No one will back you up. They will arrest you and punish you heavily for being outspoken.'*

In my anger, I replied harshly through the telepathic link, *'Who cares? What he's doing is wrong. He needs to stop. If a human could treat a maiden with respect, why shouldn't merfolk do the same?'*

Amari's voice in my head was gentle, *'I agree with you but you need to learn patience. Don't act out of anger. If you want to change something you need to build support for change by slowly introducing new ideas and beliefs through those who hold power among the common people. Put your ideas into a perspective that the traditionalist and the average person will accept and agree with. But you can't do this today. Not here. Especially not now.'*

I replied, *'Why not now? Change can start today.'*

Amari swam closer to me before she said, *'You haven't been paying attention. Listen. Notice that the merchants are rising to attention. That means the king's carriage is headed this way. Which means we need to step aside. Keep our head bowed and eyes to the ground, our hands clasped together as if praying. Now, little fish copy what I do exactly. Do not move from your position unless I tell you to. Now!'*

I heard the panic in her telepathic message. The trumpet of

my grandfather's carriage was approaching quickly. So I followed Amari's instructions to the letter, by moving close to her side. I also put the hood of the cloak up as an extra measure of protection. I heard the carriage move past me; I glanced up to see my grandfather dressed in his finery. His copper coloured hair was plaited and hung across his shoulder with golden threads woven through it and his crown upon it. His dark skin was decorated in black patterns like waves moving across his arms, shoulder and chest. Silver and blue jewels around his neck and arms. His tail was shaped like a serpent's, yellow with orange and light green frills from hip to tail tip. His symbol of power, the trident, gleamed in the sea light. His blue eyes contrasted beautifully against his dark skin. He would be considered beautiful but you could see the cruelty, arrogance and coldness etched on his face. His very countenance screamed that if you crossed him, you would perish.

I could feel his eyes roam all over my body in suspicion. I feared that he would shout for his guards to arrest his grand-daughter and bring her to the palace. But that never happened. His eyes passed over me as his carriage moved across the marketplace. I stayed frozen in that position until sound returned to the marketplace, signalling that my grandfather had completely left the area. Amari and I left quickly after that. Any joy or further teaching experiences would have to wait until next time.

CHAPTER 15

E very day since I began training with Amari, I would always, without fail, head to the place no one would go to look for me. Every day since I completed my rite of passage since I rescued the human boy Michael, I would go to the same spot. The beach where I placed Michael after I rescued him, near the rock where I first arrived in the human world. I would go there to think. To get away from my family, my duties and my training.

Going near the shore where I left Michael was dangerous. A human could spot me at any moment. I could reveal merfolk to the human world if I was not careful. But I would still go to remember my experience in the human world and think about what I learnt and how I could try to change my people, even just a little. I would float in the crest of the waves and seafoam that glowed and shimmered in the early morning light. I would stay as hidden as possible between the foam, waves, seaweed and the rock in the ocean.

At first, I didn't notice, as lost in my thoughts as I was. But eventually, I heard the tune of the song of healing that I cast on

Michael coming from the shore. A human was playing the song on an instrument, one I didn't recognise, but I recognised the human.

Michael remembered my song. I never quite managed to gather the courage to get closer to the shore. To speak with him. But I would go to the beach, regardless. Even if it was raining or cloudy, he would always be there. This was the closest that we could be.

That was what I thought at least. Until today. I had been training for nearly four months with Amari and today was the first time that I'd had a break. The only time in the past four months that I didn't have duties to attend to or training that I need to complete. As a result, I let my guard down as I swam freely near the shore before stretching out on a smooth rock to take in the sun's warmth. My tail swinging freely in the water. The waves crashed gently against it. I was relaxed but not stupid. I made sure that the rock that I sunbathed on hid the lower half of my body from view. I positioned myself to allow a quick escape.

Despite this, the day was beautiful. The sky a clear blue with slight wisps of cloud stretching across the sky. I could hear the call of seagulls from above and the music of songbirds from the shore with the sound of the sea calling out. Everything moved in sync. The world was in harmony. I was completely at peace, drifting off with the melody of the world when the tune of the song of healing joined nature's harmony.

It was only when I heard the crack of a twig being stepped on that I awoke from my daze to sit up. Sleepily I looked towards the noise, rubbing my eyes, stretching and yawning. I was still half asleep, so it took me a few minutes to realise the melody stopped and there was a human on the shore staring at me.

It took a moment for this realisation to sink in. Once it did, I moved quickly as I was going to jump back in the ocean but paused as I heard him call out, "Wait! Don't go. It's Michael. I just want to talk. Please, just ... wait."

I knew that I should ignore him. Just jump into the ocean and never come back. I shouldn't risk exposure like this. But this was Michael. The human I'd saved, who had shown me something better than Zoara-Bela in such a small amount of time.

As I submerged myself in the water, I hissed out a spell, "Takhepossett (disguise)."

As the spell took hold, I imagined my tail to be a pair of legs and made it appear as if I was wearing a swimsuit like what I'd seen human women wear. I double-checked my illusion before I spoke.

I took a deep breath before I replied, "Hello Michael."

With that, a smile appeared on his kind face. He spoke softly, his tone warm, "I thought you were going to continue ignoring me."

"I ... I don't know what you mean, Michael. This is the first time that I've seen you since the party months ago."

"Moriah, you've been coming to this beach every day for the past few months. This is the longest you've stayed here for. And this is the closest you've come to the shore. I've seen you swimming further out at sea. You only ever stay for a few minutes. How you can swim here even in terrible weather without drowning, I'll never understand."

"I'm just ... a lot better than you when in the water. I was practically raised in it," I said in a slightly joking manner.

"I already knew that. Um ... how have you been?"

"Fine... I've been fine. Busy, you know," I said reluctantly.

"Good. That's good."

He bit his lip as he tugged his plaid shirt, "Look I just ... I just want to ask you something. Please don't ... don't disappear on me. Please. It's just a simple question."

"What's the question? Depending on what it is, I may not be able to answer."

He breathes in and out shakily before asking, "Were you the one who saved me when I fell off the pier into the ocean during a storm four months ago?"

I looked at him. I should tell him no. Make him think glimpsing me that day was a hallucination. But then I looked at his face. He was so kind to me. He helped me even when he didn't have to. He was braver than me. I could see his shoulders drop as he believed that it was his imagination. I knew that was how it should be.

But this wasn't what I wanted. I wanted to be brave. I just wanted someone to talk to. A friend. I wanted a friend like those he had. I looked closely at his eyes and I noticed that the darkness that had been in them the day we met had crept back in. I didn't want to see the light disappear forever.

He turned away and before I could change my mind; I reached out and grabbed his wrist in my hand. I bowed my head, eyes low as I quietly told him the truth.

"Yes. I was the one who saved you that night."

"Why didn't you tell me? Or even stay with me?"

"I … I couldn't. I don't come from this city, Michael. This isn't my world."

"I realised that you weren't from here when I met you. You don't have the local accent or know some basic things that people do for fun. I just thought you were sheltered. That you didn't go out much."

"Well … you are not wrong. It's hard for me to tell you this. There are … rules that I have to follow. Talking with you … letting you know even a little about me or where I'm from is dangerous. If anyone finds out that I talked with … that I hung out with you … risking exposure. I'll get in serious trouble."

He scoffed before he saw my face, "You aren't joking. Oh

god! What are you ... in some cult? If you need help to escape ... I can call the cops. They can help!"

"No! I don't need help ... what's a cult?"

"What's ... What's a cult? Um ... Ok ... ah ... A cult is like a community that has some strong religious belief and extreme devotion to something. They generally have extremely strict rules and practices that they use to control everything in their people's lives. Their practices are generally thought of as strange or too controlling according to most people."

I pondered that for a moment before cheerfully replying, "Yeah. That sounds like our community."

He laughed uneasily "That's ... not a good thing. Most people think of cults as something bad because people get hurt or killed if they try to leave."

"Oh! I didn't know. Sorry," I said, shrugging my shoulders.

"Yeah. I could tell. Although you live in a cult?"

"That's your word for it. Not mine."

"Right. How exactly did you save me?"

"I'm a *really* good swimmer."

"I got caught in a rip, dragged under the ocean towards the sea during a storm. The currents are too strong for ... anyone."

"I am a *really, really* good swimmer."

"Don't lie. How did you do it?"

"I'm not lying. I am a really good swimmer. I just ... can't tell you exactly how I saved you, especially during a storm. I *really* can't tell you."

"Right. The cult. How you could do this is *somehow* connected to the cult you're in?"

"Yeah. I can't tell you anymore."

"Ok. What can you tell me?"

"I can't tell you anything about my community. I could get in serious trouble. Talking with you is dangerous enough. But telling you about my community ..."

He laughed, "I don't mean your community. I mean you. You as a person. What do you like? What's your favourite colour? Your favourite animal or song? I just... just want to know about you? I want to get to know you more. Maybe we can become friends?"

"Friends?"

"Yeah. Friends. You have friends ... back home ... right?"

I shook my head, "No. They do not encourage us to form ... shall we say ... attachments. Friendships along with any other emotion-driven connections are heavily frowned upon. As the daughter of ... let's just say someone important, I have some leeway regarding this. But still, no one else in my community has these sorts of attachments. Trying to seek it from others would end badly for me."

"Why don't you tell me something this important in your culture? I'm not asking about specific details of your community. Just one thing that your people value. It can be a belief. Anything."

"Names are important in our culture. The name you chose or the name they give you will influence the way people treat you. It tells the community either what your parents value most or what they hope for you."

"What does your name mean?"

"Moriah. It has two meanings. But the meaning that my father gave me is 'the lord is my teacher'. Um ... I know most people don't place that much importance on this. But what does your name mean ... if you know it?"

"Michael. It's the name of an archangel in the Catholic faith. It means 'he who is like God'. And my last name, Adams, is the plural version of the name of the first man, the first human male."

This was the spark that ignited our discussion. He was so willing to accept me as I was despite the secrets I was hiding. I felt the beginning of a bond between us that would only grow and strengthen. Something connected us. We just started talking. It was as if the floodgates had opened and there was no way to stop it. I could feel the warmth in my chest grow with each question asked.

"So, Moriah, what is your favourite colour?"

"Blue. Sky blue."

"Why do you like that colour?"

"The sky is freedom. It's something impossible to touch. The sky can change its colour and hue without restriction. No one can tell it what to do or how to feel. It's pure freedom," I said as I looked upwards at the sky.

He looked at me with a sad smile on his face. It was like he knew that I was no longer talking about my favourite colour but my own desires. I wanted to avoid my problems with Zoara-Belan society, so I asked him what his favourite colour was.

"Aqua blue."

"Really?"

"Yeah," he whispered with a far off look in his eyes.

"How come?"

"Aqua blue ... for me ... it's hope. Aqua is the colour of the sea, but the sea is actually a reflection of the sky. The sea absorbs the light of the sun and sky and reflects it back to the sky above. The sky feeds the sea, and the sea feeds the sky. They're linked. The sky may be freedom, but the colour of the sea is hope. Hope is something that I haven't had for a long time. You gave me that hope."

He looked at me with a soft smile, the darkness in his eyes fading slightly as a spark of light entered them. He looked at me like I was his entire world. Like I had saved him in some way besides saving him from drowning. It was like I held his hopes and dreams.

No one had ever looked at me like that. Like I was important. Like I meant something to them beyond my position as the princess. The warmth in his gaze as he looked at me made the funny feeling in my chest grow. Is this what friendship feels like? I didn't understand this feeling, but I knew I wanted to continue feeling like this. I didn't want to lose this feeling.

I felt weird, so I diverted our conversation to a new topic, hopefully a safer topic. So I asked him, "What is your favourite food?"

"I'm sorry if I made you uncomfortable with my comment."

"You didn't. I just want to know more about you."

"Okay. So my favourite food is probably... chocolate. Which is more of a dessert than a food, really."

"Chocolate?"

"Yeah. I'd buy it from the milk bar near my home. The owner, he'd let me help with putting things on the shelves as a kid. He retired and sold the milk bar because his health declined. But as a kid he'd always give me a chocolate bar or piece of chocolate cake for helping. Not the healthiest snack, but it was better than nothing. He knew—" he cut himself off.

"Knew what?"

"Nothing important. So, what's your favourite?"

I panicked, the food in Zoara-Bela was different to those on the surface. But then I thought about it more. The day we met we went to get burgers. It was something different to what I ate daily, but it was enjoyable.

So, I said, "Burgers. The ones we had the day we met were lovely. I'd eaten nothing like it before."

"Wait ... you never ate a burger before we met?"

"No. We eat whatever we can grow, collect or catch. Most food in my community is eaten raw."

"Seriously?"

"Yeah. Which is why I liked the burger so much. It differed from what I normally ate."

"Wow. So, if I said I liked pizza, would you know what it was?"

"Nope. Never heard of it or tried it," I said cheerfully.

"Cake?"

"No. I haven't had chocolate either."

"Okay. I'll see if I can organise a picnic or something so you can try some different foods. Cause you are seriously missing out on something awesome if you haven't had chocolate or pizza."

"Picnic?"

"You don't know what a picnic is either?"

"No."

"Wow! Your community must suck the joy out of everything."

"You have no idea."

"No wonder you were so in awe of everything the day we met."

"So, what's a picnic?"

"Um… it's basically a basket of food that people eat at a park or on the beach for fun."

"I would like that but…"

"But?"

"I can't exactly leave the ocean right now. And I can't exactly tell you why."

"Is it connected to your community?"

"Yeah."

"That's okay. We can have the picnic here on the beach near the water."

My stomach started doing flips at his gentle smile. I didn't want to focus on what this meant. I just wanted to learn more about him.

"So, what do you enjoy doing for fun?"

"I love reading books and poems. I also write stories and poems for fun. And you?"

"I enjoy exploring and learning new things. I like listening to or reading the records of our histories. We don't use books though."

"What do you use then?"

"Stone for writing. But most of our histories and learning is through speech or audio recordings, not through writing. The only stories we have are those of our origins."

"Writing on stone is pretty interesting. When you say that the only stories you have are about your origins, do you mean that you only tell stories based on fact or actual events?"

"Yes. Why?"

"Cause the stories that I read are fiction, the writers' imagination and emotion, not fact. I'll bring a book with me next time to read to you."

"I'd like that a lot."

We continued talking and laughing for hours. It was like we had known each other for years rather than a few hours spread out over four months. Whenever our conversation got too close to something about Zoara-Bela, he quickly shifted it to something else. It was the most fun that I'd ever had. This feeling—it was almost like joy and hope. I'd never felt something like this before. These feelings. This friendship. It was something new.

I never wanted to lose this. To lose this connection and the joy that it brought me. With Michael, I didn't feel so alone anymore. I wanted to keep this connection with him. I knew that this was wrong. That me talking with him, getting to know him was wrong. It went against everything they'd taught me. It broke every rule. But at this moment I didn't care. I just wanted to continue feeling like this.

As I said goodbye to Michael, I promised to continue returning to this spot every morning as long as he never tried to look beyond the rock that hid my lower half from view. He agreed to my condition as like me; he didn't want to lose this connection we had.

As I dived back beneath the waves to head back home, my mind was only thinking about what we would talk about tomorrow. I didn't know it then, but this one moment, this one conversation, was the spark that ignited genuine change in me and those around me.

CHAPTER 16

I lay on the warm rock, my tail hidden by the rock and water, listening to Michael's gentle voice reading from a book with poems. Poems, he said, were created to express a person's emotions and ideas in a way like a song. His voice was light and playful as he reads a book containing some of the most popular poems in the world, according to him.

"What would you like me to read next?"

I jumped slightly before I turned to face him.

"You pick," I said cheerfully.

His beautiful green eyes met mine as he read the poem out loud. There was something about him, his voice, that drew me in like the mermaids of old. His voice was soft as he spoke each word with such emotion. I felt a warmth in my chest and in my cheeks. My heart began to beat faster. I did not know what this emotion was, but it felt nice and warm like the sun upon my skin. I wanted to continue feeling this warmth. Something this beautiful, kind and soft wouldn't last long beneath the sea, which was probably why I was so drawn to it like a squid to the light of the anglerfish.

"Shall I compare thee to a summer's day?
Thou art more lovely and more temperate:
Rough winds do shake the darling buds of May,
And summer's lease hath all too short a date:
Sometime too hot the eye of heaven shines,
And often is his gold complexion dimm'd;
And every fair from fair sometime declines,
By chance, or nature's changing course, untrimm'd;
But thy eternal summer shall not fade
Nor lose possession of that fair thou ow'st;
Nor shall Death brag thou wander'st in his shade,
When in eternal lines to time thou grow'st;
So long as men can breathe or eyes can see,
So long lives this, and this gives life to thee."
- Sonnet 18, William Shakespeare.

The moment the last word left his lips I said, "beautiful."

"Yeah it is," he replied.

I wasn't talking about the poem, but I let him believe that. And to distract myself from what I was feeling I asked, "What was it about?"

"Love. It's about love. How it's like the summer, beautiful and dangerous. Life is short, which is why we need to hold on to love for as long as we can. He hoped that by writing this poem his love would last forever, even if neither of them were still alive. As long as this poem exists their love will be eternal."

Love? Was what I felt love?

No, it couldn't be. How could I feel something like this? No. It must be something else.

I felt uneasy and off-balance at the thought of feeling something that was believed to be impossible for all merfolk. So, to distract myself I asked Michael more about poetry because there was no poetry underneath the sea, not unless it was to honour and praise Grandfather.

"Michael, why do they write poetry about love? There are more interesting things they can write about. Why focus on love? I don't understand. It's not logical."

"Of course it isn't logical. Poetry is about emotion, not logic. People write for many reasons. To express love, grief, joy or pain. To preserve memory or history or to even express what their day was like."

"Why do the poems you read to me mainly focus on love?"

"Because love is something that everyone wants or hopes for. Love isn't an emotion, it's a promise. A promise to care about someone. To be there for someone. To remember them even when they're gone. And people want to honour that promise, to show them they care because love keeps people going."

"I still don't understand."

"Ok. Name one thing that you care about."

"Um ... I don't know ... the sky," I said uneasily.

I don't want to tell him he's probably the person I care about most. I don't want to scare him off because honestly, he's probably my only friend,' I thought.

"The sky ... give me a minute to think of a poem," he said.

He took a deep breath before he spoke.

"I once looked at the sky,
and only saw in greys.
The light of the sun cast monochrome rays,
that blended and fused
with the cold dead stone
and the fractured concrete paths that I walked along.
With each step that I took
it shattered further.
The walls closed around me
until I could no longer see
the difference between the walls, the floor and me.
Trapped within a never-ending cycle,

a life that was no longer mine
but theirs to command and consume.
Suddenly, a glimpse of light appeared
a hand stretched out of the dark
and pulled me out of the shadows.
And through their eyes
I could see
the colours of the sky
and a future in front of me."

I felt an itching and warmth welling up in my eyes. My sight had become blurry. As I blinked, I felt something warm escape my eyes. Before I could think about what it meant I felt warm hands on my cheeks. Startled, I looked in Michael's warm green eyes as his thumbs gently brushed away the tears that escaped me. The warmth that I felt in my chest earlier returned and spread throughout my entire body, making it tingle.

"Are you ok?"

I could barely think straight, all I could concentrate on was the warmth of his hands and the calluses on his fingertips that were lightly touching the corners of my eyes.

No one had ever been this gentle with me before. The only touch that I ever received with any regularity were the sharp taps of a stick used to reinforce my behaviour. Hugs or gentle touches that showed affection were rare. Father hardly ever hugged me or asked if I was all right unless it directly related to a problem he was focusing on. I was used to the occasional slight smile or a positive comment about my achievements from Father which was still rare.

Michael had only known me, truly known me for two months. Our first meeting five months ago was a brief flicker of light in a sea of darkness that would have been swept away if Michael hadn't chosen to confront me and I hadn't given in to his questions. He'd known me for such a small amount of time, a mere drop in the ocean for a mermaid, and yet he had shown me more kindness, gentleness and warmth than I had ever known.

"Sorry. What?" I asked, forcing myself to concentrate on his question.

"Are you all right? You were crying," he asked again, looking more concerned.

"Yes. I'm fine. I don't even know why I'm crying," I said.

He smiled, "I hope it wasn't too terrible."

"No, it was beautiful. And... I can't think of a better word than... heart-breaking. It was so sad."

"Yeah."

"Who wrote it? The poem."

"I did."

"What made you write it?" I asked curiously.

At my question he removed his hands from my cheeks and placed them on the lap in front of me, his fingers moved oddly as he replied quickly, "No reason."

"What really made you write that poem?"

"I don't know. It may have been the depressing movie that I watched last night," he said.

He's lying. Why is he lying? I thought to myself.

"Michael are you all right?" I said as I placed my hand on top of his.

"Fine. I'm fine."

He looked at his watch before standing up suddenly, "I've gotta go. My shift at the cafe starts in half an hour."

"Michael, you don't normally start work for another two hours. What's wrong?"

"Nothing's wrong. The cafe is short-staffed today. There's like ... two workers away, so they asked me to come in a couple of hours earlier. I just forgot to tell you."

"Have I done something wrong?"

"No, of course you haven't. I was just asked to come in earlier than normal for work, that's all."

"Promise?"

"I promise. I'll see you tomorrow Moriah," he said as he gave me a quick kiss on the cheek before running back towards the town.

Without even realising it, my hands moved to touch the spot where he kissed me. He had never done that before. I knew it was just a distraction, but it felt tingly and warm.

Was that what love felt like? I didn't know. But I don't want to lose this feeling, this friendship.

With a smile on my lips, I dived back down into the waves. It was only when I reached the border of Zoara-Bela that I realised why he left so quickly and tried his best to distract me. He didn't want me to realise that he was talking about his own mental state. As I returned to the palace, I made myself a promise. I promised that I would always support him and help him get the help he needed to get better. I knew that it would be difficult but he was my friend, my only friend, just like I was his.

CHAPTER 17

F or the first time, I had a friend. Someone I trusted. Someone that I could talk with about anything. Well, almost everything.

He still didn't know what I was. I wished I could tell him, but it was forbidden. No matter how much I wished I could tell him my secret, I couldn't risk either of our lives. Despite this obvious secret between us, our friendship had grown as had our trust. I hoped this secret wouldn't come between us, but somehow, I knew that it would. Maybe not now, but at some point, it would.

Even though there were a lot of differences between humans and merfolk, we'd been able to become friends, get along, in spite of it. Michael had been unbelievably kind and understanding to me, gently telling me about the world above. He thought I grew up in a cult. I let him believe that because it was easier to believe than me being a mermaid. Until now, the differences between our kind had been small or unimportant. Nothing that could cause any actual anger or conflict. I should've known it would not last.

I laid half in the pool of water against the warm rock, sunning myself and using an illusion to hide my tail, as Michael talked about his day. He never talked about his family. I didn't know why. I was afraid to ask him. But I asked anyway, to my own surprise "Michael why don't you talk about your family?"

"Why do you ask?"

"Because you never mention them. You avoid talking about your family. I don't understand why?"

He sighed before replying, "I don't talk about them because I don't enjoy thinking about them."

I looked at him patiently, waiting for him to continue which he did reluctantly.

"You're like a dog with a bone, you know that?"

"A what?"

"Never mind," he said before laughing. "My parents don't care about me. They can't wait to get rid of me. They're waiting until I turn eighteen so they can throw me out without getting into legal trouble. I want to get away, but there's no escaping them. If I run away, I will get sent back. I tell my teachers and in the worst-case scenario, I get put into foster care, moving from home to home because hardly anyone would want to adopt someone my age until I turn eighteen before I'm left on the streets, anyway. They don't physically harm me, so there's no escaping them. And they've become worse over time. You saved my life, you know that?"

"I know... I pulled you out of the water and saved you from drowning."

"That's not what I meant," he replied softly.

But I didn't understand what he meant, so I asked him to explain it to me.

"Nothing important. What about your family?"

I knew that he was trying to divert my attention, but I could see he was uncomfortable with where our conversation was going. So I told him, "There's just my father, grandfather and I. My mother died when I was young. I don't even remember her. Father never talks about her. My father … is different from most people in our community. He always encouraged me to learn. He let me learn whatever I wanted as long as it didn't go against our laws. Because of him, I was lucky enough to learn how to read, write and do mathematics. Things like the basics of business management and budgeting. Normally, only boys may learn this because they have to take over the family business."

"Wait. Girls aren't allowed to learn basic literacy and math skills."

"No. Unless their fathers or male relatives let them or think they need them. Girls rarely learn anything beyond basic crafts or housekeeping duties."

"That's illegal here. And in most places in the world. Everyone has the right to an education. The community you live in can get into legal trouble for doing that."

"Not in our community. Our laws are different. It's not against our laws."

"You live in the same area as me. The police could be called on them at any time. All the adults could be arrested."

"Maybe in your world. But you don't know where I live. Besides, no one would be able to stop it. My grandfather's rule is absolute. No one can go against him. He's too powerful. He's killed plenty of people who have disobeyed him."

"Moriah there has to be someone who could change what is happening in your community. Even if you don't call the police."

"There is no one, Michael. Most men follow Grandfather's way of thinking. Those that don't agree with it follow it anyway because they're afraid of him or his guards."

"What about the women? Maybe if enough women protest you could get changes pushed through."

"Don't you get it? Women are voiceless in our community. We have practically no rights. Women who speak out in public are often labelled scolds and have spiked bridles put in their mouths. Some are beaten in the streets—" I shouted before Michael cut me off.

"That's barbaric!"

"Yeah. Well, it's the law. I've been lucky, Michael. The only reason this has never been done to me is because I'm the ruler's granddaughter," I shouted back at him in frustration.

"That's it. If you convince people, get them to change their minds. If you spoke up, maybe things could change?"

'It might work. If I can convince enough people, maybe... no it wouldn't work. Who would listen to me?' I thought to myself.

"No. No way. Even being the leader's granddaughter won't save me. I could still be executed. In fact, he would do it on principle alone," I replied.

"The way your people treat women is wrong. You understand that, right? Things need to change in your community. Can't you think of anything?"

"No."

"Moriah—"

"No Michael. I don't want to talk about this anymore. Can we talk about something else? Last time I visited you mentioned something called... a theatre. What is a theatre?" I spoke quickly to divert his attention.

"Fine. We'll talk about this later."

"Thank you. Now, what is a theatre?"

As he explained the concept of a theatre to me, the thought of changing Zoara-Bela circled my mind. I couldn't get the thought of changing my home from my mind. Amari's suggestion had merit. Maybe if I tried to influence some powerful merchants into changing their minds by twisting their traditionalist views into my favour, things would start to change. Maybe Michael's idea could work. If enough people supported my ideas, then Grandfather would have to listen to them. It could work.

A smile stretched across my face. Hope for a better future ignited in me. For change to happen, people needed to want it. I wanted this change. There must be others who wanted it too. I could do this. I could change Zoara-Bela.

CHAPTER 18

I t had been nearly four months since I began visiting Michael on the surface and yet I was still bound to the ocean. The sea felt like a prison with my father and grandfather as my wardens. With each passing day, my desire for more, for a life outside of the sea has grown significantly. But I was unsure of my own skills in transformation. I didn't know if I was skilled enough to transform into a human. I didn't want to ask Amari about it, only to find out I wasn't skilled enough for it.

These brief stolen moments with Michael needed to be enough, but I knew it wouldn't be. Eventually, I would get more and more reckless in my desire to be with Michael, to walk the earth alongside him.

I turned my head slightly to look at Michael as he read scenes from *Romeo and Juliet*. He spoke each word with such passion and longing, giving each character their own unique voice. It was his passion that made me enjoy the story because instantly falling in love with someone with a glance wasn't possible. Even I didn't fall in love with Michael instantly. I felt a powerful connection, the possibility of friendship, with him, but it wasn't love. What I felt for Michael had grown in intensity over four months. There was nothing instant about it.

But as I looked at Michael, I realised that for me to feel so strongly about him with the curse still in place was strange. The love I felt for Michael shouldn't be possible. A mermaid's ability to feel love and other positive emotions was limited to the point our society became emotionless as a whole.

The words that left Michael's lips echoed in my mind and sent a shiver down my spine.

> "My life were better ended by their hate,
> Than death prorogued, wanting of thy love."
> - *Romeo and Juliet, Act II, Scene 2, Shakespeare*

Was this love? To desire instant death over the suffering of life if love was denied. I did not know. But as I thought about grandfather's potential reaction to my friendship with Michael, my blood ran cold and my heart froze. I realised that, yes, I would rather die than live a life without him. Life without his smile, his love and joy would shatter me. Life without him would be a living nightmare. I would become a shadow, a mere spectre in my life.

As I closed my eyes, listening to Michael's voice, I realised that what I felt for Michael was love ... and he could never know.

CHAPTER 19

In between the training and responsibilities that I held, I would find small moments of peace in my friendship with Michael. Even though I could not share my genuine history, my reality with him we could still find many things to talk about. I did my best to talk in general terms, but sometimes hints of my true nature slipped out. He never held this against me. I could tell that he had held some things back, but I didn't hold it against him. I couldn't. He didn't expect me to tell him everything about me, so I didn't expect him to tell me everything either.

Those moments with him mean everything to me. Which was why I had come to Amari to learn the spell that would turn me into a human. I wanted to see the human world with Michael. To explore. To learn all about them. At the very least I wanted a spell that would allow me to walk on land even for a few hours so I could at least see the movie he talked about. It sounded interesting. We had nothing like it under the sea.

Besides, learning this spell would be a stepping stone into learning the more complex magics. If I could transform into a human temporarily, then the complex rituals and spells regarding environment manipulation would be possible for me to cast.

Today was the one day this week I had no duties to perform as the princess of Zoara-Bela. Over the past few weeks, I'd been mastering the manipulation of magic for transformation to prepare for learning the spell to turn me human. It would be very difficult, but I knew that I could do it. I'd been researching human anatomy. I knew what each part of the human body did. I knew its function and purpose.

However, there was also no training scheduled for today. This meant convincing Amari to teach me the spell would be difficult. Which was why I took a detour through the market-place within the Citadel. I purchased some potion ingredients that I knew she was low on but could not stock up on recently and some good quality cloth so she could make herself a new cloak as hers looked old and worn. I really hoped this would work.

I didn't use an illusion when purchasing what I needed as I wanted to converse with the merchants beyond general purchasing of products. Since meeting Michael again on the shore, I'd been visiting the market and talking with the merchants. Trying to slowly change their perceptions of me and maybe, just maybe getting them to change their beliefs or even their treatment of women in just some small way would be a win for me. This was something that Michael suggested to me a few weeks ago when I asked him for some ideas on how to change the perceptions or beliefs of some stubborn and stuck in the past mermen. And you know what? It seemed to be working.

For example, every time I spoke to the grocer, I would try to suggest methods of improving business that I learnt through my research into my father's private archives. The first few times he ignored it but when he noticed that other merchants used the same method that I mentioned to him and had increased sales then he listened closely to what I was telling him.

I focused on other things connected to his business, things he would have no trouble with agreeing to, not on the main issue (the way he treated his wife). Mermen were stubborn and arrogant. I needed to prove to him that what I was saying had value, that it was better for him to listen to me.

Two days ago, he came to me to ask for another method of 'fixing the problem' of his wife constantly forgetting to weigh the items. The only reason he did this was because he knew that what I had to say would improve business.

"My Lady, your advice has helped improve my business to a height that I would not have achieved without your assistance. I wished to ask if you had any advice on how to deal with my wife's forgetfulness. Nothing that I have done so far has worked," he said to me with his head bowed.

"Of course, Ramiel. One strategy that I have found that has worked with the slower servants in the palace are reminders in their direct line of sight while working. I have noticed that it has reduced the mistakes made by newer servants and gently reminding those with more experience. If reminded gently or through written reminders carved in stone, they are more productive and willing to do the work," I replied.

Yesterday I noticed that Ramiel, the grocer, implemented my ideas. He normally yelled or slapped his wife for forgetting to weigh the goods before bagging them, but he didn't yesterday. He was calm and spoke to her softly before putting little reminders on their side of the table in front of their products and next to the wrapping for the goods to help remind her of weighing the goods before bagging them. Today, he even told me that because of my strategy he'd had fewer issues with her forgetting to weigh the goods. She still forgot sometimes, but she could correct herself now. She was smiling today. Unlike most days, there were no bruises on her cheek or arms. She was content and unharmed.

***

By the time I reached Amari's tower, it was nearly time for the midday meal. As I entered the tower, I heard Amari making a deal with another mermaid. From what I could see, as I hid in the shadows of her spell room, the mermaid wanted something to get rid of her husband. Permanently. I could see that she ignored all of Amari's warnings about the consequences of the potion if she didn't follow through with her payment or if she was caught or if she tried to use the potion on someone it wasn't intended for. She just signed on the dotted line before grabbing the potion and swimming away from Amari's tower, muttering about what she would do with her husband's estate once she tricked him into drinking the potion.

I rolled my eyes at the mermaid's stupidity. I couldn't believe that some could be so stupid as to sign a contract enforced and bound by magic without reading the terms or negotiating. Once she had left, I slid out of the shadows to alert Amari about my presence.

"Good afternoon, teacher!" I said cheerfully.

Amari jolted upwards in surprise.

'I can't believe that I caught her off guard with my illusion and silencing spell,' I thought gleefully.

"Did I scare you?" I asked her cheekily.

She straightened up before slowly turning to face me "No you didn't."

My lips twitched as I struggled to hold in my laughter as she tried to pretend that I didn't startle her.

"Really?"

I couldn't help prodding at her embarrassment. What? I had to get amusement somehow.

She finally lost patience with me as she said, "What do you

want? Today is your today off. There is no training today. So why are you here?"

I held up my purchases of cloth and potion ingredients with a smile.

"I came to bring you a gift teacher. I found this beautiful silk cloth in the market today and it is of excellent quality. The stretch of the fabric makes it a lot more versatile than normal so you can use it to make anything."

I placed the cloth on the table as I began telling her of my purchases. The cloth was shimmering lilac silk that was expensive for the average mermaid to purchase.

I continued, "I also noticed that you were running out of some potion ingredients. You were low on mugwort, ragweed, thistle and some other herbs. Oh! I also found squid ink from a Kraken in the apothecary. This can be used in a lot of interesting potions—"

Amari seemed amused as she cut me off, "such as the one that turns you into a human."

"Yes, including the one that—"

She sighed, "You didn't need to bribe me. You could just ask me what you wanted me to teach you."

"So ... you don't want the cloth and ingredients?"

"I didn't say that. You offered. And I gladly accept the offering because I planned on buying new cloth for a cloak and the ingredients you bought for me. You've saved me time and effort. Now ask me what you want while I put these ingredients away."

She turned around after she gathered the ingredients to place them in her cupboard.

"I ... ah ... wanted to ... well, ask you ... um ... if you could teach me the spell that will allow me to turn human even just for a few hours. I've been studying the human anatomy and the potential side effects of the spell and practising those meditation exercises and other transformation spells that you gave me. And—"

Amari cut me off, "Why?"

"Why what?"

She rolled her eyes at me, "Why do you want to learn this spell so much? The fact that you are only six months into your training makes learning this spell dangerous enough. It's possible to learn it, but I don't advise that you learn it so soon. So what is the actual reason for becoming more motivated and focused over the past two months? You've been so focused and determined that your recent progress has startled me. Depending on your reason for wanting to learn this spell, if I find it good enough then I may teach you how to become human very soon."

"Could we start today?"

"If the reason is good enough. Just … don't lie about it."

I looked towards the floor as I had planned to give my original reason behind wanting to learn magic from her, which was freedom. I knew that she would accept my answer. But she knew me well enough that she would realise that it was not the genuine reason I wanted to learn this. I didn't want her to be disappointed with me.

I twirled my hair in nervousness as I explained that I wanted to learn the spell so I could spend time on land with my friend Michael, a human. The boy I saved months ago during my rite of passage. I told her that over the past two months that I'd been visiting him at the shore where I originally arrived in the human world and where I left him to be found by other humans after I saved him.

I explained that I had been talking to him face to face, with my inhuman features hidden from view with illusion spells and the water. I'd been learning so much from him about the human world. That being around him made me feel happy, even though that was not an emotion that mermaids were supposed to feel.

He had supported me and encouraged me. I just wanted to be a good friend to him, like he was with me. As long as I was unable to become human, I wouldn't be able to be the friend he needed.

I attempted to continue blabbing about why I wanted to learn how to become human when Amari raised her hand to tell me to stop talking.

'Oh no! She's going to stop teaching me magic because I've broken mermaid law regarding human interaction. If she does I won't be able to continue being friends with Michael. He'll eventually stop talking to me because he won't understand why I can't leave the water. Why didn't I say that I wanted freedom? That I wanted to feel comfortable in my skin. Which is true, but I wouldn't be as pushy as I am now because it is not my key motivation,' I thought to myself.

Amari said, "You've broken mermaid law to hang out with a human. And you've used the magic that I have taught you to do it."

'Here we go,' I thought.

She sighed, "Well at least it is for a good reason. What? Did you think I would yell at you about making friends and getting support from someone else? Or yell at you because you needed someone to talk to? It doesn't matter that he is human. What matters is this. Does he care about your friendship? And do you feel the same way?"

'Why is she so understanding and accepting of this? I thought she would have been angrier because if I'm caught I could accidentally bring my grandfather's attention to her. What does she want from me?' I thought.

"Yes, teacher. I ... I don't know what I'd do without his friendship."

Amari smiled as she replied, "Good. I will teach you a spell that will allow you to become human at a surface level. Which means you'll be a mermaid with human legs and with your inhuman features removed. Biologically you will still be a mermaid, able to breathe underwater and possessing an

enchanting voice. This spell is the easiest of the human transformations but also the weakest. It will last for twelve hours at
most before you will have to return to the water because the
spell will break down. If it does so on land it will be excruciating. My condition for teaching you this spell is that you will not
use it on the surface until I tell you you've mastered it to the
point you won't kill yourself the first time you use it for real.
Talented students are hard to come by."

"Really?" My voice quivered slightly.

"Yes."

I squealed in joy as I leapt towards Amari to hug her tightly
in response, "Thank you! Thank you so much, teacher."

"Yeah, yeah, yeah. Just remember that you need to master it
to where you won't kill yourself using it on the surface."

She took me to a cave above the surface with an entrance
that led to the sea. I worked my way through the spell slowly to
make no mistakes. This was one of the most difficult spells that
I had ever cast. I made mistake after mistake. The spell
constantly backfired on me. On one notable occasion, I ended
up turning into a pufferfish, stingray and a dolphin in no
specific order. Despite these setbacks, I constantly pushed
myself until I achieved my goal. It was only after a week of
learning this that I made significant progress in my goal.

The transformation spell wasn't the only spell I had to learn
and master. Because even though she agreed to teach it to me, I
still had to work on the other spells that I was supposed to work
on during that time as if I wasn't learning this. By the end of
two weeks, I could stay in human form for an hour. After three
weeks, I could hold my transformation spell for over five hours
and reverse it when I wanted to. By the end of the month,
Amari declared that I had mastered the spell to her satisfaction
and declared that it was now safe to use it to walk the earth.

Which was exactly what I planned to do.

CHAPTER 20

It was the morning before the day I would walk the earth alongside Michael for the first time. I was going to head to the surface after completing my duties, to do some last-minute preparations—like making sure that my fake identity papers will pass inspection and everything else. Like always, my servant needed to yell at me to wake up as I tried to stay curled up in my shell for as long as possible.

As I ate breakfast with my father, I gathered up the courage to ask him a question that has been on my mind for some time. I asked him about my mother.

"Father?"

"Yes, Moriah?"

"What was Mother like?"

He choked and hit his chest as his food went down the wrong way.

"Why are you asking me?"

"Because ... you never talk about her. If it wasn't for the sculptures in the palace, I wouldn't even know what she looked like."

"Why ask me now?"

"I don't know. I'm just curious. I just wanted to know more about her ... never mind."

"Your mother ... was beautiful. The first time I saw her, she was dancing next to a fire. Its light made her glow. The sheer joy I could see on her face from dancing to the music drew me to her. She was kind. Adventurous. A free spirit. Like you."

'What? That doesn't make sense? Amari said that my mother was a servant bound by magic to obey her abusive lord and that Father freed her from it. It was before the fall so the dancing thing makes sense but ... he doesn't look like he's lying. If Andromeda isn't my mother, then who is? Amari refuses to tell me and I know that if I ask Father about it he will stop talking about my mother,' I thought.

Instead, I asked, "Did she ... love me?"

"She did, Moriah. She loved you so much. She did everything she could to keep you safe. She wanted to see you grow up. She would have been so proud of you. Of who you've become."

"Really?"

"Really. She loved you with all her heart."

"I thought mermaids couldn't feel love or deep emotions father?"

"That's not true. Not completely. We can love. Feel positive emotions. Maybe not as quickly as a human. But it can happen. It's just ... more difficult. But when it happens ... it consumes us. When we love ... we love deeply and fully with everything we have. To lose it ... was worse than dying ... it haunts our days ... shatters us. We become mere shadows of who we were. For love is the only thing that can change us to any degree."

"Is that what happened to you? Why are you different?"

"Yes. She was the only one who ever got me to think about the way I treated the people around me. She pushed me. Challenged me. Changed my mind. You have her gift. You light up the world around you. You make the people around you better people," he said softly.

"I doubt that. I don't have that ability."

"Yes, you do. It is a gift that is hard for a person to see within themselves. But you make my world better Moriah," he said before reaching over the table quickly to hug me tight.

I froze in surprise. He never initiated hugs for as long as I could remember. But just as I moved to hug him back, he let go of me.

"Moriah, will you be alright to complete your duties today?" he asked me abruptly.

"Yes, Father. But I wanted to ask you some more questions about Mother."

"Not now, Moriah. I've answered enough questions about her today. I need to attend court just as you need to complete your duties."

"Father—"

"No. Go do your duties."

"But—"

"Goodbye Moriah," he said as he swam out of the room.

I sat by myself at the kitchen table wondering why he abruptly stopped the conversation. He seemed almost happy to talk about her. So why did he stop?

We had plenty of time before we needed to complete our duties. But as I raised my head and looked out the glass window, I caught a glimpse of a servant from my grandfather's palace swimming away from the window. It was then I realised why Father never talked about Mother most of my life. It wasn't safe to. We were being spied on by my grandfather at random times of the day. Which was why my fathers' behaviour towards me would change randomly.

I needed to be more careful about my visits to the human world, otherwise I could get us all killed.

CHAPTER 21

The water had bubbled and glowed as I slowly raised out of the ocean casting the spell—liheyott enoshie be'ofen zmani (to become human temporarily)—which would allow me to become human for twelve hours only. I wished that the limit of this spell didn't exist, but I didn't have enough control over my magic to make a transformation last longer than twelve hours. Despite this, I was finally ready to walk the earth alongside Michael for the first time. He will be so shocked when he sees me waiting for him on the sand, ready to explore the human world.

Since I began visiting Michael I had sneaked into the palace library to steal the spells I needed if I wanted to live on the surface without drawing unnecessary attention. I felt guilty about asking Michael about things people needed to live in a new place. I knew that Michael wanted to move away from his parents' home and I took advantage of that to get the answers I wanted. But if I wanted to live in his world I needed to blend in, which meant that I needed documents that verified my existence.

I had gone to the surface a few weeks ago to buy one of the

beach houses that had been abandoned and left empty for years to store some supplies for when I travel to the human world. I had to do a mixture of location spells and mind magics such as compulsion and memory manipulation to get what I wanted. Which was why I overcompensated the people involved. I knew that it wasn't right even though it was necessary for me if I ever lived on the surface full time.

Anyway, I had the beach house renovated slightly, so it contained a bathroom, a compact kitchen (fully stocked of course) and a large bed. I may have cheated a little. Just a little bit. I only did it so that the beach house was expanded through magic and so it didn't look like a wreck. Fresh paint and floorboards. I even enchanted some orbs, so it mimicked those fascinating objects, light bulbs, so if I ever spent the night I could read as long as I wanted.

I stood in front of my sea glass mirror that I bought from the Zoara-Bela marketplace in disguise as I remembered that human reflective surfaces reflected our souls. The image in the sea glass kept flickering between my soul and body's reflection, irritating my eyes. It seemed that the curse affected even mirrors made under the sea if it was above the surface. Because of the flickering, it took me some time before I could get ready for my day out with Michael. I chose a floral dress with blue flowers against a white background and light blue frilly coat. I pulled my curly hair back into a half bun and half down style with a simple pearl clip holding my hair in place.

The chime of the clock in the beach house rang causing me to quickly cover the sea glass mirror with a cloth before I grabbed my handbag and ran out the door. As I waited behind a tree for Michael to turn up, I looked up at the sky which was thankfully clear. The sun and wind were warm against my skin; the salt of the sea was calming.

In the distance, I heard Michael's voice calling for me. He's staring out at the sea while calling for me. After a minute of no reply, his face became disappointed. He probably thought I would not turn up today.

Before he could leave, I stepped out from behind the tree and called out to him, "Michael! Wait! I'm right here!"

He froze for a moment before he turned towards my voice. His jaw dropped in surprise as he saw that I was on land and not in the sea. It was only when I laughed that he snapped out of his daze and ran towards me. To my surprise, he picked me up and swung me around before pulling me close.

"You're here. I thought you finally got sick of me," he said.

"Never. You're my friend."

His laugh was bright and full of pure joy as he asked, "I thought you weren't ever going to leave the ocean because your father could find out."

"Well. What he doesn't know won't hurt him. Besides, I found a way around his … shall we say reach. Neither Father nor Grandfather will ever find out unless someone tells them I was here. This means that I can hang out with you in the city, not just talk with you in the sea. Now I can only stay here today for a few hours because my cover will only last so long. Eventually, I'll find a way to stay longer."

"Just not today," he said.

"Just not today. But someday soon."

I took a deep breath before asking, "So what do you want to do today. I'm yours for the next … oh … twelve hours at most."

"Well, I've never been to the museum here in the city. We could go there first, then maybe see a movie at the cinema. If you want?"

"I'd like that. I'd like that a lot, Michael."

The museum that Michael took me to was one of art. Mermaids did not understand art. It was a human concept. I mean we have statues but they're only ever made as a show of power that royalty has over the common merfolk. They were never created for beauty or for the joy of creating something. The art museum contained paintings, carvings, statues and other objects of beauty. Michael and I went on one tour they had of the museum where they talked about specific artists and certain artworks that they created.

There was one painting in the museum on loan from another that was created by a human who struggled with mental illness, went in and out of mental institutions before he killed himself. The painting was beautiful with swirls of colour and vaguely present buildings. Starry Night, they called it. The painter's story nearly brought me to tears as I wondered why no one helped him with his illness.

We never ended up going to the cinema that day as we got distracted by the musicians playing music in the square. I let him lead me onto the makeshift dance floor in the square. Music had a way of pushing all our worries and concerns aside as we danced the day away. It was after dinner that I found the tingle of my magic warning me that the spell would run out in about an hour.

I reluctantly told Michael that I needed to return home as the cover that allowed me to visit for a longer period than normal would run out soon.

Neither of us wanted tonight to end. We were two lonely people, isolated and treated differently because of who we were. This connection meant everything to me. I liked to believe that Michael thought the same. I didn't know why we are so drawn to each other, but I didn't care.

It was not long before I waved Michael off, watching him leave before I quickly changed into my normal mermaid top and entered the water. I let the spell unravel around me as I dived into the ocean with a bright glow against the night sky.

CHAPTER 22

I t was one of our rare days off, so Michael took me on the picnic he promised me many months ago. Luckily, I had mastered the transformation spell to where the incantation was shorter and quicker to cast, liheyott adam (to be human). This meant that I could stay on the surface longer without having to return to the sea.

I had walked toward the park where we were supposed to meet when I spotted Michael walking ahead of me with a basket. Instead of calling out to him, I decided to quietly come out from behind him and shouted, "Hello!"

He jumped so high as he shouted, "What the hell did you do that for?"

I just laughed in response.

"Seriously, why?"

"I don't know … It just seemed like a brilliant idea."

"Seemed like a brilliant idea … come here you," he said leaping forward to grab me.

I twirled out of the way and said, "Catch me if you can!"

As soon as I said that I sprinted across the park as he chased after me, twirling away every time he came close to catching me.

"Gotcha," he said as he wrapped his arms around me and lifted me up slightly.

Instead of asking him to let me go, I used one of my legs to hit his ankle and knock him down to the ground. We both fell on the grass laughing. I turned my head to face Michael who was still laughing and smiled. The shadows I saw in his eyes the day we met were gone, at least for the moment.

His gentle green eyes, which normally contained a glimmer of darkness, were warm and filled with light and joy. He looked so carefree that I didn't want this moment to end. Suddenly, he stood up and removed a blanket that was tied to the basket that he then laid on the ground next to a tree.

"What are you doing?"

"Setting up the picnic. You can't have a picnic without a picnic blanket. Come sit on the blanket while I set up everything."

"What's that?" I said while pointing to a specific food.

"That would be pizza. I just got a basic pizza because I wasn't sure whether you were allergic to anything."

"What else did you bring?"

He just smiled as he handed me a cup filled with a clear liquid and said, "Try this."

"It looks like water."

"It's not."

"Then what is it?"

"Just try it."

I took a small sip of the drink but as soon as the sweetness touched my tongue, I ended up drinking the entire thing at once.

"What do you think?"

"It's sweet and bubbly. I like it. What was it?"

"Lemonade soda. Want to try something else?"

We ended up spending the next half an hour just talking and trying new foods. I liked the pizza and the apple pie, but not the liquorice lollies. He laughed at my reaction to those. Apparently, the face I made was hilarious. Liquorice tasted terrible. It was worse than the squid ink candy we ate in Zoara-Bela.

"I will bring some squid ink candy for you to eat next time. It tastes a lot better than these lollies you gave me."

"I look forward to it," he said cheerfully.

"Seriously, I'll make you eat it and the kelp and squid ink cakes too."

"Kelp and squid ink cakes. Do you seriously only get your food from the ocean?" he said while laughing.

"Yes."

"How do these kelp and squid ink cakes taste?" he asked cheekily.

"Better than liquorice."

"Well, I have something that is a lot better than liquorice for you to try."

"Better according to who?"

"The world."

"I doubt that."

"I'll prove it to you. Close your eyes."

"No way. I want to know what I'm trying."

"Guessing is half the fun. Come on. Close your eyes for a moment."

"But—"

"You trust me, don't you?"

"Well, yes—"

"Then close your eyes."

Not long after I closed my eyes, he asked me to open my mouth so I could try something new. It was sweet and fresh as I chewed on it.

"What was it?" I asked.

"Chocolate covered strawberries. What did you think?"

"I loved it. I can see why you like chocolate."

"So is it better than your kelp and squid ink cakes?"

"A lot better than those cakes."

"I bet."

"What are we going to do now?"

"What do you want to do?" he asked.

I paused for a moment, "Could you read *Romeo and Juliet* to me?"

"You always want me to read to you."

"That's because you make it interesting. Please."

"You're lucky that I have my copy of the play with me," he said while rolling his eyes.

He rested his back against the tree trunk as he opened the book and read from the play. Without thinking, I sat next to him and rested my head on his chest. Just as my eyes had closed as I listened to him read the play to me I felt an arm wrap around my arm and a hand lay flat on my stomach. Startled, I looked up and realised that Michael had put his arms around me as he was reading. I didn't like being touched most of the time, but Michael made me feel safe and happy. With him, I felt safe and loved.

His every action showed me he cared for me deeply, even if it was based on friendship and not romantic love. I knew that I loved him more than anything, but we came from two different worlds and we couldn't be anything more than friends. Our friendship was dangerous enough, but romantic love was deadly.

If anyone ever found out I loved a human, whether he loved me in return didn't matter, they would order my death or re-education. Re-education could break the strongest or bravest person into a million pieces and reform them into a shallow crystal doll that obeyed every order and request asked of them. I wouldn't be my own mermaid anymore. I'd be an extension of the merman they would force me to marry. At least with friendship, the threat of re-education no longer existed.

I had to hope that this friendship was enough. But I knew it wouldn't be.

CHAPTER 23

According to Amari, my progress regarding the ancient arts had been fast compared to most students that she had taught in the past. However, she also said that I needed to make sure that my understanding and practice of the ancient arts were, in her words, 'fine-tuned'. Apparently, I lacked finesse. I mean, come on, I'd only been seriously learning and practising the ancient arts for a year, unlike her centuries of experience. Of course, I lacked finesse.

I had reached the journeyman stage of my learning of the ancient arts. Which meant that today was the day I had to hand over my mother's pearl bracelet. I had promised Amari this when I made the deal for training. I could not break the deal. I had seen what happened to those who broke their deals with Amari. Let's just say—it was often humiliating, ironic and violent. I did not want to be one of those who broke their deal. Even though I was reluctant to part with the only thing that I had left of my mother I wouldn't break my promise. I wouldn't.

I thought my father could see something of my reluctance, sadness and guilt on my face that morning during breakfast as he was kinder than normal. He asked me if I felt all right or if someone was threatening me. I had to reassure him I was just stressed. As a result, he gave me the entire day off from my duties in the palace. While it was kind of him to do so, it meant that I would have to head to Amari's tower earlier than planned. Which meant that I would have to pass the test earlier than planned. It was not like I could pretend to fail it. Amari would see straight through me and realise that I was doing it to keep the bracelet for longer. She may refuse to train me anymore and take the bracelet anyway.

I tried to delay going to the tower as much as I could by lingering in the ruins that morning before the test. I was procrastinating. Okay. I could freely admit that. It was not like anyone else didn't procrastinate to avoid doing something unpleasant but necessary. It was during my procrastination that I noticed that the writing on the stone wall, the etchings in the old language, had become clearer for me. My progress with learning the ancient language wasn't as fast as my progress with the ancient arts, but it was still progress. I reached out to touch the stone-like wall with my finger as the pointer to slowly read the etching upon it. Some of the writing was no longer covered by algae and seaweed.

It was as if the magic in the stone slowly cleared away the debris and algae the more someone understood the ancient language. Which was smart. It meant that only the most knowledgeable in the ancient arts could even read the writing on the stone. I knew for a fact that both my father and grandfather had practised the ancient arts and could understand the ancient language. I pretended to ignore the rumours of both my father and the king being present when our city sunk to the bottom of the ocean floor. If that was true then they could read the entire tablet. But the fact it was still intact meant they didn't know that it was here.

Suddenly I heard a creak in the background. Someone else was here. I quickly searched for a place to hide when a beam of light touched the abandoned crystal in the middle of the ruined building. The crystal shone, lighting up all the buildings in the area making the algae glow an ominous green. The sound grew closer, leading me to swim towards the crystal to dive behind it. As I was hiding behind the crystal, my hand touched a loose stone which then lowered as a result, acting as a key to a door. Beneath my tail was a narrow staircase.

Between the creepy staircase and the potential guard of my grandfather, I chose the creepy staircase. Quickly, I slid down the staircase as the stone doorway moved to cover it. Breathing heavily, I closed my eyes and wrapped my arms around the joint of my tail to calm myself down.

'I should have gone straight to Amari's tower. What the hell was I thinking? Coming to the ruins? Actually, besides me and Amari, who would want to come to the ruins?'

The voice above my head snapped me out of my thoughts. I needed to find a way out of here. I spun around the room and spotted a cupboard near a pillar. I hid within the cupboard as quickly as I could. Not a moment too soon because as soon as I entered the cupboard and closed its doors, I heard the stone entry moving open.

I muttered the spell lehasstir (conceal) to obscure my presence by bending the light around me to, not make me invisible exactly, just unnoticeable as long as I didn't draw attention to myself. I also cast a spell that created a viewing orb, allowing me to see outside of this cupboard.

I tried to suppress my gasp at the image in the viewing orb. It was my father. My father was in the room. If he found me here, he would be required to drag me before my grandfather. They would question me about my reason for being at the ruins and use all manners of enchantment to drag every secret from my throat. I could feel my magic waver in my panic.

'No! I can't let it fall. If my magic falls, then I am doomed.'

Before I could be dragged further into my thoughts, I

noticed something strange. My father had moved to the front of the room and pulled down a dark cloth. Underneath that cloth was a statue of a woman dressed in armour, holding a sword and an orb that looked like the image of the Earth that Michael showed me once.

I attempted to zoom in on the plaque on the bottom of the pillar which contained a name. Just a single name. Gaea. My father then lit a fire, ethereal fire, the only thing that could burn underwater, within the orb of the statue. The entire room lit up in response. The beauty of the room amazed me.

The insides were made of marble, orichalcum and with Zoara-Belan silver and gold leaf wrapped around the pillars. Gems of topaz, citrine, moonstone and almandine garnet. The light of the ethereal fire bounced off each gem, making the room appear to be above the surface. It looked like a sunset beneath the sea. It was then that I realised the purpose of this room as each gemstone had a meaning in magic.

Topaz symbolised wealth, health and happiness and drawing on the power of the sun to warm, to heal and bring life. Citrine represented personal will, free-thinking and the ability to make hopes and dreams into reality. It was also connected to the comfort and warmth of the sun while encouraging creativity. Moonstone was directly connected to the moon and its effects on the earth, its rhythms and the way it ebbed and flowed. It was also connected to love, victory, and wisdom to improve the decisions made by an individual.

Almandine garnet symbolised regeneration, energy and strength. It was meant to provide balance and protection by strengthening the individual's strength of will. It had ties to the earth and its powers. This place was a temple. A secret temple to Gaea hidden beneath the ruins. Each gem paid homage to the primordial goddess Gaea, our creator. But it also strengthened and healed the individuals within its chambers. My father was praying to Gaea for guidance and support. Then I heard him mention my name in his prayers. The volume coming from the viewing orb was not very clear. I heard him mention that he didn't want me to end up like Andromeda or a person called Zeva.

'Who is Zeva? What happened to her that was so bad that you don't want me to end up like her? What happened to Mother?'

He stopped talking as he finished his prayer by leaving an offering at the foot of the altar in front of the statue's feet. He let the ethereal fire continue burning as he covered the statue with the dark cloth and left.

I stayed in my hiding spot for at least another ten minutes before leaving it, just to be sure it was safe. I attempted to examine the offering left behind the cloth when I noticed that behind the offerings were several paintings encased in a crystal. Each painting bore a name. There were seven in total. Israfil, the only boy, looked younger than me. Then there were the images of six women. Andromeda, Cassiopeia, Amina, Davida, Adalina, and Zevachya Mowrihya. I could see parts of myself in the images, all but one. The image of Adalina looked near identical to my Muriel disguise, only a lot younger.

The image of Andromeda, my mother, looked nothing like me. I could see her in the paintings of the other girls but not the boy or myself. I mean she has the same eye colour and her hair was a dull light brown but I could see nothing of myself in her. Why was it that when I looked at the image of my mother, it was as if I was staring at a stranger?

I could see more of myself in the image of Israfil and the five women besides Andromeda. The sound of the bell signalling noon drew me from my pondering. I quickly replaced the cloth over the offerings and left the temple of Gaea to head to Amari's tower for my test.

∾

Upon my arrival at Amari's tower, I was immediately dragged into the ritual room where most of my testing would take place. These tests were like the human exams that Michael told me about. I would be tested on everything that I had learnt over the year. There would only be quick breaks for snacks and brief moments of rest between tests as Amari would not only be testing my skill but my ability to work under pressure. Which was why failing was not an option. No matter how much I wished to keep my mother's bracelet.

'I'm sorry, Mother but learning magic, having power over my destiny, power over my life that this magic will give me ... It's something that I desperately need. I can live without your bracelet. But the power and over my life through magic is something that I need more than this trinket,' I thought as I tried to prepare myself.

"Are you ready for the testing to begin, Moriah?"

"Yes, teacher."

"Good. Now, remember failing this test means you will have to repeat the learning of the specific area that you have failed before being retested. This is only available to you if you fail because you genuinely do not understand how to do something. If you pretend to fail to keep the bracelet, then I will end all lessons here. You will not learn any more magic from me. And I will take that bracelet as payment, anyway. Do you wish to postpone your testing due to lacking knowledge in an area that will be tested today?"

"No teacher," I replied hesitantly.

"Very well, let's begin. We will start with potion based magics. You will be tested on your academic understanding of potion making and the practising of it. It will slowly increase in difficulty. You will also need to identify the potions with the specific vials. This will take at least two hours to complete. Let's start."

With that, the testing started in earnest. The academic test on my understanding of potion-making was completed through the use of an orb that projected the questions through a holographic screen. I had to select the correct answer (for multiple-choice questions) and use the special quill to write the answers of the extended response questions. There must have been over a hundred questions.

'How the hell this testing is supposed to take two hours in total to complete if the first part is so long, I have no idea.'

I had no time to think about my answers before moving onto the identification and creation section of the potion test. Healing poultice, cleansing potion, lust, pain-relieving potions and poison identification. The most complex potion that I had to create was the animal and human transformation potion, which physically transforms an individual into a sea creature or human depending on the one consumed.

I was given test after test that mentally, emotionally and magically drained me. Illusion magics, spiritual magics (this includes the theory of communicating with spirits and divining the future), healing magics, basic elemental magic and mind magics. Some tests were a lot longer than others due to the extent of what I learnt over the year.

But mostly, I was taught the basics of each area and depending on my aptitude up to a possible intermediate level. It was nearing sunset according to human time when I finally reached the last test.

Transformation magic. This was the area of magic that I had the most extensive training in. From minimal shape-shifting and body manipulation to the more complex transformations that caused changes on a species level.

It wasn't long after I had finished transforming into unique animals of both land and sea with varying differences in biology that I had my ultimate test. I was to completely turn myself as human as possible for magic. And I had to complete this all above the surface in the cave where I first learnt mermaid to human transformation (near water, of course).

To pass, I needed to avoid expressing any pain or discomfort in the transformation, but also maintain the transformation under heavy attack from spells designed to dissolve transformation magics. Which was something that was not my strength when it came to magic. If I panicked, my magic would waver, leaving me an easy target for Amari's magic.

My body was partially submerged as I began casting my magic to turn me human, along with the secondary spell that would create clothing for me to wear. As the magic took shape my body glowed, my tail turned into a pair of legs and a shiny dress covered my body as I took my first steps out of the water and onto the floor of the cave.

As soon as I had steadied myself on the floor of the cave Amari began blasting dissolving magics at me. She started with the most basic before progressing onto the more complex and painful of the dissolving magics. I could feel my magic waver with a sting of pain at the most complex dissolving spell which she blasted at me repeatedly to ensure that my return of control was not a fluke.

With each blast, I could feel my resolve to pass her tests waver. Because if this was just a test to become a journey-level apprentice, I didn't want to know what the test to move to mastery level would comprise of.

Amari's eyes narrowed as if reading my thoughts, which she probably was, led to the strength of each spell blasted at me doubling and my magic wavered in response.

Then she suddenly shouted, "Moriah, you are not even trying to block me. I can see your magic and will wavering. It's time for you to stop defending and start fighting back. If you do not give it your all I will assume that you are not serious about your learning. And I will ensure that you can never practice magic again as I will notify your grandfather, the king, about your learning of magic without permission. You will never be free."

"What! You—You can't do that! He'll kill me or worse, torture me! Nothing will change in Zoara-Bela ever again if you do that!" I cried out in horror.

Amari blasted me across the cave and into the stone wall with such force that I coughed up blood as I felt my very human bones break. Before I could even think about standing up Amari lifted me by my throat and pinned me against the wall before stating, "Well then, I guess we will have to get used to this regime and stagnation because if you can't muster up the energy to block against magic or against my limited physical strength in this form during a test then what use are you in changing Zoara-Bela."

She dropped me to the floor in disgust and walked back towards the water as if to end the test. I shakily stood up, my legs wobbly, and feeling as if they would collapse from under me as I continued to cough up blood. I cast a basic healing charm before I shouted, "Wait! I can still do this!"

"I doubt it. It's over."

My eyes filled with tears before anger overtook me and I shouted, "No. I won't let you do this. I refuse to be powerless ever again."

My body moved on its own as I blasted a chain of spells at Amari just as she turned to look at me. Spells of dissolving, transformation, pain and elemental magic. I threw every scrap of magic that I knew at her, whether or not I learnt it from her. I could not afford to lose. I wouldn't let myself fail. Spell after spell hit its mark. Some were more effective than others. A few did not affect her whatsoever.

My anger and frustration at the situation blinded me. It only took one hit from Amari to knock me off balance. I was completely drained of energy. My magic was heavily depleted and Amari's wasn't. I knew that I lost but I just couldn't stop myself from trying to rise to my feet, because losing meant that I would die whether it was because I pushed myself beyond my limits or my grandfather executed me or worse. If I was going to die, I would die free. So even though I was weak, bones broken, body beaten, coughing blood and wheezing, I rose to my feet unsteadily. My eyes blurred and fluttered closed as I fell back into the water, my transformation spell finally dissolving and my dreams of freedom disappearing with it.

I awoke hours later in my room with Amari floating over me. My body was sore and my magic drained, but to my amazement, most of my injuries were completely healed. I attempted to speak. To beg her for one more chance to prove myself. To pass her test. But she never changes her mind. Until today.

"Moriah, you were never supposed to pass every test, let alone the last test. I wanted to see what you could do. I wanted to see your resolve. I wanted to know exactly how much you wanted to learn what I had to teach you. To my amazement, when push came to shove, you stood your ground and fought for what you wanted. You surpassed my expectations. If you put this much effort into influencing change in Zoara-Bela as you did today in your test then change is certain to come."

"Did I pass?"

"You passed. You achieved beyond my expectations."

I slowly moved my arm to slide my mother's pearl bracelet from my wrist to hand it to her. She'd upheld her end of the bargain and I needed to do the same. With a tinge of regret, I placed the bracelet into her palm. And she smiled before replying, "You rest. Take this week to recover. I will see you at my tower for our usual lessons next week. That is if you still want to continue learning from me?"

"Yes. I still wish to learn magic from you," I coughed out weakly.

As my eyes closed a thought entered my mind, '*Amari looked like her plans had come together. What does she want from me? Why does she want Zoara-Bela to change as much as I do our laws don't affect her as she lives on the edge of the boundary? And why does that fill me with a sense of unease?'*

The decision I made to continue learning from Amari sealed my fate. All other paths had disappeared. There was only one path available to me now. Where would it lead me?

I didn't know. But it would be worth it. All things worth fighting for were.

CHAPTER 24

I knew that I was supposed to be resting my magic for a full week, but visiting Michael was important. For a couple of days, I just used the basic illusionary spells. Nothing too complex or magically taxing. Just a little illusionary spell, litzor hasahaat da'att, to divert attention so I could continue visiting Michael at the beach until I recovered enough to cast a transformation spell. It took me about three days for my magic to recover enough to cast transformative magics but I waited for five days, just to be safe.

Not long after I arrived at the shore where our visits took place and changed into a fresh set of clothes within my beach house, I just stood in the sand. I let the water gently flow over the top of my feet that lay in the squishy sand with my eyes closed. I just let myself breathe in the ocean breeze and bask in the warmth of the rising sun. Listening to the birdsong that hovered above me. I didn't know how long I stood there in the sun, water and sand, but all my worries, my fears, drained out of me.

I began stretching my body. My back bent backwards

slightly as I raised my arms towards the sky and slowly let them roll downwards until they were at chest level before pushing them out to the sides. As I was doing these movements, I felt a hand lightly touch my shoulder, startling me. I reacted without thinking. I could feel my body turn as if to block and divert an attack before retaliating in kind. My body acted before my brain. Luckily, I stopped myself in time. I just barely stopped before I hit Michael in the face.

'Maybe I should've let my magic rest more? It still feels on edge. Like I need to be alert. It feels like someone has been watching me,' I thought.

"Michael I'm so sorry! I-I didn't realise it was you. I just reacted. I'm sorry," I stammered out my apology.

"I realised."

"I'm - I'm so sorry."

"Moriah, it's okay. I should've called out to you to let you know that I was here," he replied gently.

I looked everywhere besides his eyes. I tried to avoid looking at a person's eyes if I could get away with it. I didn't know why. I just did.

As if sensing my unease, he asked, "Are you all right, Moriah?"

His hand reached out to gently move my bangs behind my ear like normal, and his eyes narrowed and his face darkened at the massive bruise near my eye and cheek.

'Damn it. Did I forget to cast the illusion over my bruises before I came here?'

I quickly turned my magic inwards so I could check that my illusion spell, litzor hasahaat da'att (to create a diversion), was still in place.

'The spell is still in place. The magic can't have wavered. I just passed my test. How? How can he see right through me?'

"What happened, Moriah?"

I did my best to avoid the question "Nothing. So what are we going to do today?"

"Moriah."

"You said that you liked history last time we talked. We could go outside the city to see that museum you've been mentioning."

His eyes closed, and he pinched the space in between his eyebrows, "Quit avoiding the question."

"Avoiding … I-I'm not avoiding. Wasn't there some festival today? We can—"

He raised his hand, stopping me in my tracks.

"Moriah. Just tell me what happened. Please. I'm worried about you," he said softly.

I turned my face away from his before I replied, "I … I can't tell you. I mean, there's nothing to say. I got hurt. I'm getting better. Can we just hang out like normal?"

"Moriah, just tell me something. Anything."

"I can't!"

He's taken aback. I'd never yelled before.

"Moriah. Please. The last few days. You've been quiet and jittery. And interested in my life. A lot more than normal. You've—you've been avoiding questions about what happened last weekend. I thought I was imagining the bruises. It was bright. You never left the water. The first time in a week you're on land you react as if you're being attacked. There's a massive bruise on your face. I mean—I know that you have to avoid speaking about your home with any specifics. Cause of some rule or law. I mean, I thought you were in a cult to begin with. Don't get me wrong. The place you come from sounds a lot like a cult or a dictatorship—"

"Dictatorship?"

"Like that. You don't know basic things like what a cult or a dictatorship or music or dancing is. You are a regular fish out of water. And I mean that literally—"

I cut him off, "What is that supposed to mean?"

"I'm your friend. I trust you. I thought you trusted me too. I've been waiting for you to tell me the truth. I've been patient. I waited a year. Spent three months thinking that I was crazy before you even spoke to me."

"Tell you what?"

"I know. Okay. I know what you are."

My eyes watered, "You know ... nothing about what I am."

"Yes. I do. I think I've always known. Your reflection told me as much."

'No. Please. No. Don't say it. Please. I know I'm a monster. But I ... can't bear to have him tell me this too.'

He continued, "I don't know how you found a way to walk on land or to look human. I just don't understand why you couldn't just tell me. I thought I was going crazy when I noticed a gold-coloured shimmer that sometimes hovered above your skin—"

"Wait. You can see it. My magic. How?"

"I don't know. Maybe I'd know if you didn't continue pretending to be normal and just told me the truth for once."

"I have told you the truth. I can't tell you everything. Sometimes I withhold stuff, but I haven't told an outright lie," I stammered out in reply.

"Yeah. You bent it. Just tell me. Just this once. What are you? Be honest."

"I can't tell you. If anyone finds out that I told you. They will kill me. Secrecy is our biggest law. And telling you ... I won't just be killed ... they'll torture me ... interrogate me. They will try to make me lead them to you. You'll die too," I told him with tears in my eyes.

"Yeah, right. I guess this friendship means more to me than it ever did to you."

"I'm not lying, Michael. That's the punishment. If I tell you my secret and he finds out ... Both of our heads, and our families' heads, if he feels vindictive enough, will be on the chopping block. And I promise … it won't be painless or quick."

"I highly doubt that. You just want to keep me as some human pet. I guess that this is goodbye, Moriah."

He turned away from me to walk back to the town.

'I can't … I won't let this happen to him. He is innocent. He doesn't deserve this. He deserves better. At least if he leaves now … then he'll be safe, right? No. He said he already knew. Just knowing is dangerous. The fact he told me he knew was dangerous. But if I stay away, then it will protect him. But … he's my friend. My only friend. I need him. And he needs me. I … I can't let this end like this. There's got to be some way around this… That's it.'

I looked back up and he was further away from me than before. And I called out, "Michael, wait! Just wait. Please."

He turned back towards me, "What? Are you going to tell me the truth now?"

I took a deep breath "Michael … I want to tell you what I am, I do, it's just … my grandfather. He has ways of finding out whatever information he's looking for. I don't know how. I just know that the last time someone even got remotely close to a human, that human was murdered. They left her body displayed on the beach where her lover would visit each day. That man was tormented heavily. That's just for starters. A young girl, a noble, rescued a human like you, many years ago. She loved him. And he paid the price. They killed him. They ruined his kingdom. They stole her voice. And they enslaved her for many years before Grandfather had her sold to a rich nobleman that wanted a wife. And she was beautiful and unable to fight back. Being the grandchild of our leader will not save me from this … it will make it worse."

He looked as if he was about to interrupt but stopped when he saw my eyes filled with tears and the look of desperation on my face.

I took a deep breath before continuing, "Michael. I can't tell you outright. But … if you tell me what you think I am … I can nod … to tell you if what you thought was true. Give you slight hints until you guess correctly. But I can't outright tell you. Will you please tell me your guess?"

His face softened and his body relaxed, "Yes."

"Thank you. Now, what do you think I am?"

"You're connected to the ocean. Obviously. You're beautiful physically. Your voice can draw people in. But your reflection only vaguely matches your outside appearance. You are some siren."

I moved my head from side to side "That's one thing that we've been known as. But that's not what we are called. Less mystic. More fairy tale."

"Fairy tale? Wait. A young girl who lost her voice as punishment for loving someone. A prince … mermaid. You're a mermaid."

I could feel my heart sink like stone as I nodded. The lines from the play *Romeo and Juliet* that he read to me that day we had a picnic in the park echoed in my mind.

'These violent delights have violent ends
And in their triumph die, like fire and powder
Which, as they kiss, consume.'

Love would destroy us all. Love destroyed Romeo and Juliet. Their love left a trail of destruction. Losing my mother's love destroyed my father, just as losing Michael's love would shatter me. I hated myself for putting him in so much danger because I was selfish. My selfishness would get him killed, and it would be my fault. I loved him and that love was dangerous.

This love has made me reckless and more than willing to take risks even though it could kill us both. But I didn't regret this because Michael was important to me. I never wanted to see the light go out of his eyes. And if I denied him the truth, I knew that light would disappear and he would be swallowed by darkness once again. I had to believe that our ending would be better than the others who fell for a human.

"You said that you're the grandchild of the leader. He's a king. Isn't he? And that makes you a princess."

"Yes."

"Wow. My childhood is a lie."

"What?"

"Nothing, just a cartoon. You're nothing like what I thought a mermaid was like." I looked back down again in shame before I heard him add, "You're better."

"Really?"

"Yeah. Could you ... tell me more about mermaids?"

"I can't tell you much. Not outright. But if you read between the lines, then you could learn a thing or two," I joked.

"What can you tell me?" he asked excitedly.

"Not here. We're too close to the ocean for me to risk telling more. This is risky enough as it is."

"Okay. There's a cafe further in the city that we can go to. They have private booths that we can book for a few hours. I know the owner. Maybe afterwards we can see that movie I've been telling you about."

For the first time since our conversation began, I smiled. Michael knew what I was. And he still wanted to know me. He still wanted to be around me. He'd mentioned my reflection, but he had said nothing bad. He hadn't called me a monster or a freak. Maybe this would turn out okay. Maybe I could keep hold of this friendship and tell him more about me and my people. I could have the best of both worlds.

We spent hours just talking about mermaids and mermaid culture, as best as I could without breaking the law more than I already have. We ended up seeing that movie he talked about. It left me hoping people could change. That Zoara-Bela could change.

As I swam back home, I felt for the first time in a long time comfortable with whom I was, whether I had feet or a tail. I felt something like the love of a friend. I pushed past my doubts and ignored the genuine possibility of my demise.

CHAPTER 25

I n the months following Michael discovering exactly who and what I was, our friendship and love only grew. There were very few secrets between us now. Michael encouraged me to find out more about my peoples' past just as I encouraged him to get the support he needed to escape his parents as he was nearly eighteen. We shared our hopes and dreams for the future.

'*A future together*,' my mind guiltily whispered.

My worries and fears of exposure, of my grandfather or my father discovering my communication with a surface dweller, still terrified me. We were being as careful as possible with our talks by making sure that any discussions regarding my nature as a mermaid occurred well away from the ocean, for the ocean had ears and could whisper our secrets into the ears of its king and prince.

Grandfather was the strongest user of the ancient arts that was still alive. He made sure that he was the strongest alive by getting rid of any competition that arose. According to the records I snuck a look at, a mermaid who had the potential to rival his power and ability with magic was 'murdered' for her magic. Grandfather had her killed slowly and painfully by ripping her magic out piece by piece.

Amari was a powerful user of the ancient arts who might rival Grandfather. But she stayed hidden in the thoughts and minds of merfolk. A mere whisper with a dash of truth to draw in the poor unfortunate soul that required the help that her magic could provide.

By living in whispers within the minds of merfolk she could create an air of mystery and intrigue, but it also ensured that most believed she was a mere legend. A myth. A fantasy. But as we all knew, every legend had a grain of truth. Only the most desperate of merfolk (and the occasional human who grabbed her attention) would even dare to sneak beyond the Citadel or the smaller city for noble folk to swim to her tower on the edge.

The boundaries surrounding the edge combined with the magic of her tower would cause most to flee in terror and fear of the unknown. Which lowered the number of idiots who came to her to make their dreams come true. I was one of the few who could push past the fear long enough to ask her for training.

Which was why I needed to be very careful when I used my magic within the Citadel. I hadn't found out how my grandfather was able to find magic users who might rival him. I didn't know what sort of magic he used. I knew nothing beyond the fact that if I was caught, I'd be dead. Simple as that.

Today I planned to explore the marketplace and talk with the merchants and lower classes some more in my Muriel disguise. I knew that I was not supposed to draw attention to myself. Especially in that form. Which was probably why I reacted in the loudest manner possible when confronted by the rudeness and violence of a guard to a member of the lower class. The poor merman was being beaten in the middle of the street by a guard for 'breathing too loudly' near him.

I haven't completely lost my mind. I didn't directly confront the guard and yell at him for treating one of our citizens like this. Nope. Not completely stupid. I just used magic to blow up a crate filled with inert ethereal fire that then exploded with a loud and bright bang.

The flames were very beautiful in the aqua water. The guards didn't seem to think so, though. I know I said that I needed to be careful using magic in the Citadel, but it was for the right reasons. They were most likely going to drag him off to the palace dungeons to make up some bogus charge where he'll be executed or enslaved. So, I gave the guards something else to worry about. By the time they came back, the poor merman would be gone and considering no one in the upper class paid attention to those lower than them, they wouldn't be able to identify who it was that they were beating.

Once the coast was clear I swam towards the poor merman to help him gather his things and said, "Are you all right, sir? Did you need some help?"

"Thank you, my lady. But you shouldn't lower yourself to help a member of the low caste like myself," he said.

"I know. But I want to. The way he treated you. Hurting you simply because you were near him was disgraceful."

"My lady, you shouldn't say such things. If anyone hears you. They could arrest you."

"There is nothing wrong with me speaking my mind. Besides, you know that I am right."

He looked around nervously to check if anyone was watching us before making a slight nod in agreement that was nearly impossible to see.

I smiled in response, "What is your name?"

His eyes didn't move from the seafloor as he responded, "Jedidiah my lady. Jedidiah means 'friend of God'."

"That's a wonderful name. The name I am going by is Muriel meaning 'bright sea'," I said.

"Is that because you are in disguise, princess?"

"W-What? I don't know what you are talking about. What princess?"

"While my talent in practising magic is fairly poor. My ability to identify magic and who it belongs to is powerful for a member of the low caste."

"Wait, you can do that?"

"Yes. It is a talent that most are born with. Those without that talent, if they learn magic, they may be able to learn enough to detect surface spells. But those born with this ability like me can see past illusions and view the reality underneath through our interpretation of the magical energy."

'That must be what Michael can do. But how can a human do that? The blood of the gods has thinned considerably since the fall.' I thought.

"But how did you know it was me?"

His eyes were soft "You've been coming to the marketplace for years to talk to the different merchants. But you also talked to me. You always spoke with kindness even though I was extremely below your level. You always asked me about my day. I got used to your magic, which was normally below the surface. But don't worry, only those with this specific talent could identify who you are. And even then, they would have to be exposed to your magic over some time. So don't worry, your illusion still holds."

"You can't tell anyone that I'm here or that I can use magic. If the guards find out they'll take me to my grandfather and—"

"Don't worry, my lady. I won't tell anyone. Besides, who would believe me? I am of the lowest caste of the free merfolk."

"You'd be surprised by what they believe. Especially if they bring me to my grandfather."

He just smiled indulgently at my response as I bent down to place his purchases into the bags before they floated away in the current.

"Thank you, my lady, for your help," he said before looking at his purchases which were of poor quality and very minimal.

"What is the matter, Jedidiah?"

"It's nothing, my lady." I continued looking at him. "It's just … the vendor … he gave me less of the kelp and grain than what I paid for. That's why I got the guard called on me. I argued about him cheating me out of my due purchase and over-charging me."

"He called the royal guard because it upset you that he cheated you out of your due purchase. That is illegal. I should go talk to him now—" I said angrily as I moved towards the vendor.

But I stopped when I felt Jedidiah's hand on my wrist. His head was still bowed "While I am thankful that you are willing to act on my behalf, but you are still a woman, even if you are disguised as a noble. They will think you are hysterical or that you are easily led like a child. They will dismiss you. You shouldn't have to be exposed to that kind of ridicule, my lady."

I had forgotten that I was in my disguise, in my anger. He was right. If I went over there as I was now, they would not listen and dismiss me. Or have me arrested at worst.

"You're right. Jedidiah, do you have enough money to purchase the rest of your groceries?"

He shook his head.

"How many do you need to feed in your home?"

"I live by myself but there are several families with young children that are homeless or are worse off than me that I help feed. That's why I buy a lot of kelp and grain as it is the longest-lasting and the most filling."

"How many do you need to feed? An estimate if you please."

"I try to supply around 30 merfolk with food. But I'm not the only one who tries to help feed the families in the poorer districts," he replied after a few moments of silence.

"That is kind of you. Right. What else did you need to purchase?"

"Why do you want to know?" he asked sceptically.

"Because I want to help. If I'm the one who purchases the goods, they won't overcharge me. That and I can have anything extra put into a cart for you to take with you."

It took me a few minutes to convince him to tell me what he needed. But I eventually wore him down and took over the purchase of his supplies. After I assisted Jedidiah purchase his goods and took them back to his home, I spent hours just helping him feed the homeless and poor families.

Their faces lit up with pure joy, something that I never thought I'd seen that expression on the face of merfolk before. They were amazed at the amount of food that we gave them and at the quality of it. I may have gone a bit overboard with my purchases. I bought enough to last a month, maybe more, if they rationed it carefully. The fact that they didn't have to worry about whether or not they would eat for the next month was a relief for them. I promised to help Jedidiah with preparing the meals for the poor once a week and to help him purchase the needed goods from the market when supplies got low.

Seeing their joy at such a simple thing like a meal made my chest feel weird. It felt almost like pain. Pain and anger at their desperation and poverty. Something felt different today. There was something different about me. I'd seen poverty and desperation like this before as I explored the marketplace. I had seen members of the lower class beaten for standing up for their rights or just because they were of the lowest caste free merfolk could be. This wasn't something new to me.

But the fact that I reacted—I got angry. I wanted to fight on behalf of Jedidiah because what happened to him was unjust. This was out of character for me. I would normally either ignore it or speak to the vendor later about it. To try and subtly change their mind. I tried to avoid confrontations like this. Something had changed about me. Why? I didn't know. But it seemed to be a good change.

At least I hoped it was.

CHAPTER 26

In the two weeks since I met Jedidiah, I had talked with other merchants about the treatment of the lowest caste of free merfolk. I had attempted to shift their thinking about the treatment of the lowest caste by positioning them to consider the potential financial benefits of treating them better. Not all were inclined to agree with my suggestions which was why I cast a combination of leha'arim ett hanefesh (trick the mind) and al tefaqepeq bi (don't question me). Both spells were designed to make people more susceptible to my manipulations.

Despite casting these spells regularly, I still had a queasy feeling in the pit of my stomach. These spells manipulated the mind, made them believe every word that I spoke as long as it didn't go against what they believed in. Every time I cast one of those spells, I hesitated. I knew that this was the best way to ensure that change happened in Zoara-Bela. It wasn't right, what I was doing to gather support, I knew that, but it was the best way to gather support quickly and with the least amount of bloodshed.

I shook my head in an attempt to focus on my task. It didn't help much, as my morals conflicted with the necessity of my actions. Today I was handing out bowls of dulse (a red leafy seaweed full of protein and antioxidants) combined with spirulina (a blue-green algae containing iron and calcium), carrageen moss (a red algae seaweed containing potassium), sea grapes and crushed shrimp. As I handed out the bowls of food to the poor, containing nutrients for healthy living, I realised upon looking at their gaunt faces and sunken eyes that were only beginning to contain a glimmer of hope that this was something we had denied them.

I tried to keep my shoulders relaxed and smile upon my face as I handed out the bowls. I couldn't let them see my anger. I didn't want them to think my anger was at them. So I pretended that everything was all right, even though it wasn't.

As I finished handing out the last bowl Jedidiah pulled me aside. He kept looking behind him, his hands were shaking and his eyes looked everywhere except my eyes. I attempted to ask him what was wrong, but he shushed me. It was only when we entered the storeroom he spoke, "Moriah, I heard you speaking with Ramiel, the grocer, about the treatment of the poor this morning. You need to be more careful."

"I am being careful."

"No, you're not. Azazel and his wife Ariel approached me the other day about you. They overheard one of your conversations with another merchant about the treatment of the poor. What were you thinking criticising the king in the open?"

"I wasn't criticising the king. I was just suggesting that the way we treat the lowest class showed a … lacking on our part. Nothing I said was about the king."

"He won't see it that way! He will see it as treason because you are suggesting that he is not fit to rule!"

"I never said that!"

"You didn't have to. You are implying that the way we do things in Zoara-Bela is wrong. By suggesting that, you are saying that you don't trust the king and that is treason."

"I ... I didn't realise."

"You need to be more careful. Don't suggest that the king is wrong... you need to be more subtle. Focus more on the individual and how treating the poor well benefits them."

"I have been—"

"It's not enough. You need to remember it's not just your life at stake."

"I know, okay! I'll cast a spell to make sure no one can say anything."

"Good. But there is one thing that I still don't understand."

"What?"

"Why help us beyond giving us food? Why take the risk?"

I paused for a moment and twirled my hair in my fingers. I didn't even understand why I cared so much or why I'd been trying to change the merfolk around me. I knew that my behaviour wasn't normal for a mermaid. Mermaids were supposed to be silent, calm and demure. Voiceless dolls that could only do what their puppeteers allowed them to. I didn't understand why I was so different.

Before I could reply the scream of a maiden echoed throughout my mind. I grasped my hair and rocked slightly from the pain. Flashes of a memory drowning in fear and horror paralysed me.

'Moriah look out!' the voice screamed.

A body collapsed in a swirl of blonde hair and lilac eyes that lost their light.

I was trapped within the memory. I could feel a body covering mine. I could taste blood turning into sea foam. I didn't know what was real—the body on top of mine or Jedidiah's hands on my shoulders asking if I was okay. My brain felt like someone cut my head open with an axe. Suddenly, I felt a jolt of lighting against my skin. Gasping, I slid down the wall, breathing heavily.

Jedidiah placed his hand on my shoulder, startling me, "Are you all right?"

"I ... I don't know."

"What happened?"

"Um ... it felt like ... a memory."

"Was it your memory?"

"I don't know. It felt real, but I remember nothing like this happening in real life. It might be from one of the memory orbs that I've watched. I'd remember if something like that happened to me."

"What was the memory about?"

"I felt her die."

"Who?"

"I don't know. I didn't recognise her. Anyway, you asked why I was taking a risk helping you, right?"

"Yes, but—"

"I want Zoara-Bela to change. I want a better life for all of us, not just the king and his men. That's why I'm putting myself at risk. I want a better life for all of us."

"Is that what you really want?"

"Yes."

He breathed in deeply and looked away from me. His hands covered his face briefly before dragging them downwards in frustration.

"All right, meet me at the boundary; there is a hidden cave system. No one goes there anymore because they think it collapsed."

"Why do you want to meet there? I can come back here tomorrow."

"Not for this."

"For what?"

"Ariel and Azazel weren't the only ones to approach me. Other merchants and lords have approached me as they heard that you might be interested in allies. I know the merchants better than the lords, but they are all well respected."

"Allies? Where did they get that idea from?"

"I don't know. But meet me at the caves tomorrow. And Moriah?"

"Yes?"

"Make sure you have a plan to convince them and to keep them quiet."

I could feel my lips tilting upwards slightly as I tried not to smile. Before I could thank him, one helper yelled out for us to go back to the front of the building as more families had arrived. I felt a mix of relief and dread as I swam back to continue handing out bowls of food. Maybe there was hope after all.

I ended up arriving early to the meeting point, so I waited in the shadows next to the cave just in case it was a trap. Not that I thought Jedidiah would betray me, as I was the only reason the health of the poor was improving. The longer I waited, the tenser I became. My head was pounding like someone was throwing blasting spells at my brain. There was a tingling in my shoulders, spreading down to my fingertips. The tingling soon changed to a fiery sensation, almost like someone had poured lava directly on my bones that then solidified. My fear and anxiety paralysed me. The water felt like rocks being rubbed against my skin and my heart felt like it was being tugged by a whirlpool that would drag me to the bottom of the sea.

"Breathe," I muttered.

Breathing was a struggle. My breath came out in brief hisses and my vision blurred. I hated feeling like this. It was like someone had used a mind-control spell on me to make me their puppet, but I knew it was my body and mind that betrayed me. Before I could spiral down further, I heard the voices of Jedidiah and some lords making their way to the cave.

I couldn't let them see me like this. I couldn't show weakness. I closed my eyes and forced myself to breathe in deeply. I needed to push my fear and anxiety aside. I couldn't have my meltdown here, not in front of the strangers I wanted the political support of. Besides, if I let these sensations overwhelm me then I may lose support because the lords would only see weakness.

I pushed forward with a fake sense of calm and control, straightening my shoulders. I knew that doing this meant that when I went home, my meltdown would be worse. It always was. Thankfully, Jedidiah gave me more time to calm down than necessary by distracting the lords and merchants that had arrived.

As I entered the cave, I noticed to my surprise that they had set it up with a table of snacks that were the quality that the lords and merchants were used to. There were only ten merfolk that came to the meeting. However, these merfolk were among the most respected and wealthy.

"Thank you for coming my lords and merchants," I said.

"Thank you for having us, Princess Moriah. I am Lord Nathaniel."

"Well met."

The greetings continued for a few more minutes before I spoke about why they have been asked to meet here. I spoke for what felt like hours about the various issues that need to be addressed in Zoara-Bela such as the treatment of the poor and maidens.

I couldn't cast the mind manipulation spells that I usually used, on them because of my high levels of anxiety which would interfere with the strength of the spells and possibly reveal my skills in mind magic. This was something that couldn't happen.

Meaning my words needed to be convincing enough on their own.

Luckily, I prepared a binding oath of silence which wouldn't need them to directly sign a physical contract the day before. By entering the cave they were automatically bound to the oath. Not that I told them that, as it is a common trick used by nobles who want to talk about things privately.

I continually looked at their faces, which were emotionless, as I spoke about the changes I wanted in Zoara-Bela, things that I believed that would improve their own lives. I tried to appeal to their own greed and vanity so they would be more agreeable with my ideas. As soon as I noticed that they had become disengaged I asked them what changes they wanted to see in our society. Like I expected, most wanted changes that would improve their financial and social standing.

Lord Nathaniel stepped forward once we finished discussing the changes we wanted to see in Zoara-Bela. They elected him to be the leader of the group, which was probably a good thing as Ramiel was known to have a temper. I could tell from the look on his face I would not like what he would say.

"My lady, while I agree that the issues you have brought up are of serious importance. And we all agree that these changes should be implemented, however, we will not stand against the king unless you already have allies capable of standing up to him. Which you don't otherwise you would have mentioned them. You are only just beginning to gather support for your rebellion."

I attempted to speak, but he cut me off, "It is a rebellion—no, it's treason. And unless we have a guarantee that you will get your ideas passed in our society, we will not actively support you in this. We will not go against you but we will not actively support you unless you get more support and alliances from other lords in Zoara-Bela."

"And if I gather more allies, will you give me your support?"

He nodded "But we will not be involved directly in any rebellion."

There it is. He doesn't want to risk anything if I'm caught. If he's not directly involved, then he can claim ignorance,' I thought.

"Very well. I'll keep that in mind when looking for allies. But at this moment there is no plan for a rebellion, just a few minor changes that will improve the quality of life for all who live here. I just thought you would be interested in having some input."

"I thank you for that."

"Please take some dulse and squid ink cakes on the way back to your homes. I look forward to discussing further ventures with you."

I had to smile while I wanted to break. Pretend to be happy when I wanted to scream and shout. My body felt like it was made of glass, fragile and inches away from shattering. But I held in my fear and anxiety until I knew that I was safe. Being in the presence of lords who could sense weakness like sharks smelling blood in the water was not a place for me to break down. The wife of the merchant Azazel paused at the entrance of the cave, hovering silently in the water. She kept biting her lips as she looked between me and her husband that was swimming back to the city.

"My lady?"

"Yes?"

"I hope that you succeed in implementing those changes you talked about. I think … that we need those changes. For what it's worth … you have my support."

"Thank you. I forgot to ask, what is your name?"

"Ariel. My name is Ariel."

She moved to leave but paused again, "If you need help with feeding the poor then I will help you."

"Thank you. Jedidiah is the one you should speak to about this as he is the one in charge of feeding the poor."

She nodded before swimming off to catch up to her husband.

"Moriah, don't lose hope. Next time will be better," Jedidiah said.

"I know. It's getting late. We both need to be home before curfew begins."

He looked at me as if he wanted to say something else, but the sound of the bell interrupted him, warning us that curfew would begin in an hour.

"Go. I'll see you next week."

With that, both of us left the cave to head back to our homes. Upon entering my room, I collapsed in my shell, curling up into a ball. I was shaking and hitting the frame of my shell, unable to speak. I wanted to scream but I couldn't let anyone hear me, so I covered my face with my spare pillow and let go. The pillow barely muffled my screams and cries. I didn't even know why I was screaming or crying. I couldn't control it. It was like I was trapped in my mind and had lost all control over my body. Every time I held in my fear and anxiety, this happened afterwards.

I hate feeling like this but I knew that I had to continue holding in my emotions until I was in the safety of my room, because breaking down like this would be a sign of weakness. And I refused to be weak.

CHAPTER 27

I n the weeks since meeting Jedidiah at the marketplace and helping him purchase food to feed the poor, I was becoming more confident in how I could change the people around me. But I must not have been as careful as I thought I was because as I was about to leave to help Jedidiah, my grandfather entered the room.

Grandfather was intimidating enough when he came to dinner occasionally, but today of all days he seemed far darker in his demeanour. He'd plaited his copper hair with golden threads like always, but his eyes were different. His glacial blue eyes seemed to glow brightly. There was a gleam in his eye. It wasn't the usual arrogance or cruelty, but something like glee. For him to feel glee when he wanted to talk to me was nothing good.

Upon seeing him, I became filled with fear as I thought, *'Did someone see me go to the surface or talk with a human? Did someone report my visits to the edge, to Amari's tower? Was I too reckless?'*

"Good morning Moriah."

"Good morning, Grandfather. How are you today?"

"I'm fine. Now where are you off to today?" he asked with a slight smile on his face.

I gulped before replying with my eyes facing the ground, "To the market Grandfather. I plan on buying some fabrics from the merchants there. I found a pattern for a cloak I liked. I plan on making it."

"Really? I thought you disliked sewing."

"It's grown on me. It's something that I can do while I'm not completing my royal duties."

"Good. It's good that you've grown to enjoy it. I expect that your father will arrange a marriage for you soon. And that will most likely be the only thing your husband will expect of you."

I bit my tongue until I felt a cut forming on it. I only stopped biting it so it didn't bleed, because merfolk could taste blood in the water. He would definitely taste it. I didn't want to anger him so I replied, "Of course, Grandfather."

"Excellent. You can be taught after all. That is if you are actually going to the market to buy the fabrics."

'He knows! Shut up brain, he doesn't know for sure.'

"What do you mean, Grandfather? I always go to the market to buy fabrics or something I think Father might like or need."

"So you haven't been talking to the merchants about anything to do with the way we treat women in Zoara-Bela?"

"Of course not, Grandfather. I know better. Besides, the treatment is *just* because you say it is so."

The words tasted like vomit in my mouth. I hated this. But I knew that saying what he wanted to hear was the only way I could stay alive and avoid his suspicions. I hated him for making me feel like this. His eyes and his smile were like a shark. Sharp and deadly. His eyes were as dark as a bottomless pit.

He spoke, "Good. Then I assume you don't mind me accompanying you. I need to visit the market today as well. And having my granddaughter accompanying me would do wonders."

"Accompanying you? Are you sure? I wouldn't want to interfere with your royal duties. You have better things to do than be with me," I blurted out as my voice squeaked at a high pitch caused by my fear.

"Only I decide what is better for me."

"Yes, Grandfather."

"And I wish that you would accompany me."

"I just need to get something from my room. I'll meet you at the gates in a few minutes."

"Very well. You have five minutes."

As he swam off, fear and dread overwhelmed me. I hurried to my room to collect a pouch, some money, an enchanted ring and an orichalcum sheet to carry a message.

Jedidiah. Can't meet you at the market today. The king is suspicious. Money for supplies is in the pouch. The ring has an illusion. Just think of what you want to look like and the magic will change you into that merman. Avoid looking like a real noble merman. May be late to the meeting. I can't let him catch on. See you tonight if all goes well.
Moriah.

After ensuring that everything was in the pouch, I cast a quick spell to teleport it to Jedidiah. I glanced around my room for a bag to carry some fabric and a money pouch to avoid further suspicions from my grandfather.

As I swam to the gate where my grandfather was waiting for me, I was terrified of being found out. He scolded me for taking longer than five minutes before we left for the market. I ended up buying fabric because of my excuse and a special pen for inscribing that I had engraved with his name on it. I hoped to pacify him. It seemed to work. When we returned to my father's palace, he ended up dismissing me and returning to his own.

I stayed, paralysed, in the corridor he left me in for almost fifteen minutes before I collapsed and fell against the wall. I stayed sitting against the wall for nearly thirty minutes, shaking in fear and relief that I could divert his attention.

"That was too close. Way too close. I need to be more careful."

Despite my fears, I still went to the low caste's living area. I should have postponed it, but I had been successful in diverting grandfather's attention. I was confident that I could get there and back without being spotted. I went a different route. I used every spell that I could think of to divert attention. I thought I did it.

But I was overconfident. I didn't realise until the next morning that Grandfather had a servant of his spy on me and they glimpsed me leaving the low caste district. I should have waited a few extra days before going instead of the hours after diverting his attention.

CHAPTER 28

I was sitting at the breakfast table thinking about my plans for the day. I wanted to bring some traditional foods from Zoara-Bela for Michael to try. I wanted to see the face he'd make when he tried a squid ink and kelp cake or maybe an oyster with dulse and sea grape paste. I would have continued daydreaming if it wasn't for the question my father asked. It snapped me out of my daze. I could feel my heart begin to pound rapidly in my chest. Because of my daydreaming, I wasn't sure if he asked me that question, so I asked him to repeat the question.

"Moriah, have you been near the ruins lately?" he repeated with a slight smile on his face.

"No, Father. Why do you ask?" I said with a slight stutter.

"Some guards have reported movement in the area recently, so I thought you may know."

"Movement near the ruins? I haven't been near them since … my rite of passage, more than a year ago now. Why? What has happened?" I said, avoiding his eyes.

"Nothing much. Just some fresh magic residue near the

statute. But I have heard that you have been going to the markets a lot lately. Find anything interesting?"

"Some new fabrics and beads to create a new dress or a cloak. I haven't decided yet."

"You must show me when you're done then. I'm amazed that you can sit down long enough to make something that detailed. Don't you heavily dislike sewing?"

I started twirling my hair before replying, "I don't … dislike it. It's not my favourite thing to do, but I need to do something during my spare time."

His lips twitched, "So you picked something that you admit is something you do not enjoy."

"Father. We're mermaids. We don't feel joy."

"Maybe not joy but we can feel pleasure or comfort from something in a moment. Oh! Before I forget to ask, have you been around the low caste compound or living area at any point during the last few months?"

"W-What? Why would you ask me that? Why would I even know where their living areas are?" I replied while twirling my hair and avoiding his eyes.

"Good. Then I can tell Father that the rumours of treason from the lower caste are just lies spread to cause chaos and upheaval by an unhappy individual who just wants to get rid of them," he said, trying to get me to react.

"W-What! Grandfather knows about it!"

Why did I say that? I just gave myself away. Only someone actively involved would react like that.

"Of course he does. Or will. It's just a matter of time before he gets a report from the royal guard. At least when he talks to me I can redirect his rage. Unless you have something to tell me?"

I looked down at my clasped hands as I replied, "No, Father."

~

I tried to go about my day as normally as I could because I didn't want to draw attention to what I was doing. I was a lot more careful than usual as I cast more concealment spells than I had in more than a year. It was only when I returned home that I felt a shiver go down my spine. I needed to know what evidence Father had about my interactions with the lowest caste.

I carefully checked the wards of the palace; it was only when I sensed that neither Father or Grandfather were in the palace that I began swimming to my father's room. Upon entering my father's room, after making sure that his wards didn't detect me, I noticed that it was sparsely decorated, beautifully designed, but containing very little furniture.

Looking around the room, I attempted to find anything that suggested that he knew what I was up to. After half an hour, I was about to leave when I noticed that one drawer in my father's desk had been sealed with magic. To my horror, the drawer contained a viewing orb linked to a recording spell focusing on me. I had hoped that my concealment spells were effective enough to hide me from the magic of the recording spell, but my hopes were shattered as I began viewing the recordings.

Gasping, my hand covered my mouth as I struggled to breathe. I could feel a pounding in my brain as my fear and panic built. Light and sound hurt my eyes and ears. The water felt like dry sand against my skin as I watched myself in the viewing orb, laughing with Michael and talking with the poor. I had hoped that this was all that was recorded, but then I saw my conversation with Amari about magic. Magic that I shouldn't know.

I could feel myself beginning to have a meltdown.

"Breathe. I need to breathe," I said, trying to calm myself down.

I closed my eyes before I took a deep breath and hissed it out.

"Right. I need to see if he's watched what was in the orb. Hopefully, he hasn't watched it yet."

I waved my hand above the viewing orb and focused on sensing the number of times that the viewing aspect had been used today, as the spell had only been actively recording since morning. To my relief, it had only been viewed once, meaning that I was the only one who watched it. Before I could think about what to do, I sensed my father passing through the gates of the palace.

In my rush, I couldn't alter the recording as much as I wanted to. So, I erased the recording of my interactions with others that could even remotely make someone believe that I was committing treason. I also altered the recording of me on the surface to suggest that I was on my own the entire time, which wasn't worthy of punishment. I could sense Father coming closer so I quickly checked that my spells worked and swam rapidly out the door, avoiding the wards meant to detect movement, not realising that my spells were weak enough to be dismantled.

CHAPTER 29

I rested my head against Michael's chest, listening to his heartbeat as he read poems out loud. I stared at the leaves of the trees that had turned red and yellow; they looked like they were on fire when touched by sunlight. Michael had placed his arm around my shoulder as he continued reading. I ended up closing my eyes as I felt safe in Michael's arms. I didn't realise that I had fallen asleep until I felt Michael's chest rumble in laughter. Looking up at his gentle green eyes I realised that I could still see some shadows in his eyes but the light drowned out the shadows.

I could feel a warmth in my cheeks, "What are you laughing at?"

"Nothing. I didn't think you'd fall asleep while I was reading."

"I'm just tired. That's all. I'm awake now."

"What's wrong?"

"Nothing is wrong."

"Moriah, you look worried about something. Did something happen at that meeting you told me about?"

"Nothing happened. That's the problem."

"What do you mean?"

"None of the lords or merchants that turned up to the meeting will support me in changing Zoara-Bela. They wanted to wait until I had other allies that would help me directly before even supporting me indirectly."

"From what you've told me, these people are used to having all the power. Following you without guarantees of maintaining their power would never happen. They wouldn't want to risk the power they have under your grandfather's reign. Unless your grandfather does something that limits their wealth or power, they won't have much reason to support you. At least this way if you rebel and win they can claim to have supported your ideas, and if you lose they lose nothing."

"I know. It's just disappointing. I hoped at the very least they would agree to support me indirectly. I just got my hopes up."

"Don't worry so much about it. They'll support you, eventually. Even if they don't you'll get other allies."

"Really?"

"Yeah. You're clever. You'll work out a way to convince them to your side, eventually. Just give it time."

"Thank you," I said.

I couldn't stop myself from smiling. When I was with him it was like all my fears disappeared. He had done so much for me, the least I could do was take him out to eat at his favourite place.

I stood up suddenly and told him, "It's nearly time for lunch. Let's go to that restaurant you like, the one in front of the square."

"I don't get paid until next week. I don't have enough money to take you there."

"Michael, don't worry about the cost. I'll pay for it. You've done so much for me the least I could do is take you out for lunch at your favourite restaurant."

"You don't need to pay."

"I know but I want to. Besides, you told me last week that they have a new autumn menu that seemed interesting."

He smiled as he took my hand, letting me pull him to his feet when I noticed him wince as I did so. I didn't let go of his hands after helping him up.

"What's wrong, Moriah?"

I said nothing as I pushed up the sleeve of his right arm and noticed purple marks on his wrist in the shape of human fingers. While looking up at his face I push up the sleeve of the other arm and see the same marks. The marks on his arms, the bruises were in the shape of large human fingers, most likely made by a man. Michael turned his head to the side, eyes facing the ground before swallowing. He seemed to become smaller as his shoulders slumped.

"Michael, what happened?"

"Nothing," he said as he pulled his hands from mine.

"There are bruises on your wrist that look like they were made only a day ago. Did I do this to you?"

His eyes looked startled as he shouted, "No!"

"If I didn't do this, then who did?"

"It's not important."

He avoided my eyes and seemed to shrink further into himself. I reached out and gently turned his face towards me, "It is to me. Michael, you're my friend. I just want to help you."

"My parents were angry that I've been staying away from the house so much and staying at other peoples' houses, especially since the neighbours found out I've been seeing a school counsellor. Apparently, they've started asking questions about my parents' behaviour towards me. Their reputation is all they care about. They can't wait until they can kick me out but have pretended in public like they actually care about me so they can save their precious reputation. I thought that maybe they had changed … that they regret treating me the way they have, but I heard them talking about their reputation."

He took a deep breath before continuing, "I got so angry. I just grabbed my bag and tried to run out the door. I couldn't stay there any longer."

"That doesn't explain the bruises," I said.

He avoided my eyes as he said, "They tried to stop me from leaving. My dad grabbed my wrists and shook me when I tried to leave."

I could feel my magic beginning to build up like a volcano about to explode, "Michael did he do anything else?"

He shook his head, "No, I was able to push him off. But—"

"But what?"

He looked to the ground as he said, "They told me that if I didn't come back, they'd report me as a runaway and claim that I have been aggressive."

"They can't do that."

"No one else knows about you or what I do when I'm not working. They could say anything and the police will believe them because no one can claim differently."

"Michael, how long did they give you before you had to return or be reported?"

"I've got until tonight."

"Are they home right now?"

"No. Why?"

"We'll go there now. I'll help you pack up your things. You can bring them to my beach house. I had it set up like the houses on the surface—it has a bed, kitchen and bathroom. You can stay there as long as you need. I know that you wanted to move out and rent your own place. You can still do that if you want. But at least this way you don't have to stay with people who have harmed you."

"Moriah, I turn eighteen in less than two months. I can handle staying there until then. Besides, doing that means they'll have evidence showing that I ran away."

"You shouldn't have to handle it. And who said anything about letting them report you as a runaway?"

"What? Moriah, you can't use magic on my parents."

"Why not? I will not harm them, just suggest that it is in their best interest to pretend that they gave you permission to move out."

"I can take care of myself."

"I know. But just let me help you just this once. Don't worry. They won't be hurt. I'll just cast a minor memory blocking spell. They will be so distracted that they won't remember to report you to the police. Let me do this, please."

"You promise you won't hurt them," he said softly.

"I promise. Now let's go get your things."

With that, both of us walked towards his parents' house. It would be the last time he willingly enters the house. I'd promised Michael that I wouldn't harm them, and I didn't.

I cast the memory blocking spell hasimat zikaronn like I promised. But I never promised that I wouldn't use magic to make them regret hurting him.

A minor bad luck jinx, mazal ra', tied directly to their reputation wouldn't physically or mentally harm them, just their reputation and social standing. Luckily, for them, I was calm enough to cast the jinx without it escalating into a curse.

Besides, magic like this would wear off eventually, which was why I also planted an orichalcum stone with runes designed to conceal a person. No matter how hard they tried, they'd never be able to find Michael until after he turned eighteen, and he was legally out of their reach.

At least this way they couldn't manipulate him into returning to their house. I loved him too much to let him suffer through their cruelty and neglect.

CHAPTER 30

I had been feeling uneasy for some time. It felt like something bad would happen soon. I didn't know what or when it would happen. But I'd been feeling off since my father's attempt at questioning me a few weeks ago and barely being able to wave off his questions about my actions. I hoped he believed what I told him. But I knew that he wouldn't stop trying to find out what I was doing.

I needed to be more careful about my actions and make sure there were no tracking spells on me or that there was no one following me. The result, me on edge constantly for weeks, making me more irritable. Which was probably why visiting Michael today was a terrible idea. Did I listen to my brain? Nope.

I was going to see Michael. Even though I knew that I felt today was most likely going to lead to a massive blow up. But screw my feelings. I had a routine that I needed to follow. Besides, we'd been planning this trip for nearly two months. This was the only time we could both go to this museum. I couldn't postpone it, even though it would probably be the best thing for me to do. But when did I ever do the best thing for me?

We ended up taking a train into the nearest major city from the seaside town where Michael and I spent our time. It took us nearly two hours to get there, with all the different connections we needed to take. Poor Michael had to deal with my constant questions about the unfamiliar things that we saw along the way. Until now, my understanding of the human world was limited to the seaside town that Michael and I interacted in.

Upon arriving in the city, we didn't go straight to the museum like I thought we would but spent a few hours just exploring the city itself. We went around seeing various musicians performing in the streets, dancing to the music, seeing the most amazing pieces of art and marble statues. We did so much before going to the museum; I ignored my feelings as we entered the building despite it setting my nerves on edge.

It was fine at first. The museum was as interesting as I thought it would be. Learning about the different things that happened in the human world, about the unique cultures and how things had changed so quickly in their world but hardly anything had changed in Zoara-Bela. This thought made me wonder why very little had changed since the fall.

Even though the curse changed us into merfolk and suppressed emotions, it shouldn't have stopped progress or made our society stagnate. We were very focused on logic not emotion, so why had nothing changed?

Even our fear of my grandfather shouldn't have stopped changes from occurring in our society. Even if things changed slowly because of how long-lived we were, there should still be some change in traditions or beliefs. But seriously, *nothing* had changed in thousands of years. The human world was more advanced in almost every way. Be it culture or art or language or rights or law. The human world had changed since the fall of our society to the depths of the sea, yet we hadn't.

I was constantly reminded of this as I moved throughout the

museum with Michael during the day. But I was confronted by a deep sense of wrongness when I came to an exhibit about slavery within the museum.

It talked about the Transatlantic Slave Trade. The tour guide explained that over four hundred years, between the 15th and 19th Centuries (the 1400s to 1800s), that between twelve and fifteen million people were forcibly trafficked to countries around the world for forced labour. They were taken away from everything they knew. Their language. Their culture. Their home. Their family. Everything was taken from them for profit and trade. They lost everything because of other humans' greed.

"They justified it by saying that because they were from Africa. Because they were black, they were lesser in their eyes. Sometimes, they were considered less than human. And because the people who did this didn't see them as human, it meant they could keep them in the most horrible of conditions and subject them to the most horrifying treatment imaginable without reprimand or punishment. They were innocent men, women and children who were killed for greed. Despite slavery being abolished in 1807 in Europe, the illegal trade continued for at least another sixty years, mainly to sugar plantations in Cuba and Brazil. Even though officially slavery has been made illegal and is heavily punished by the law in the overwhelming majority of countries, more people are living in slavery today than at any other point in history," explained the tour guide.

I slowly raised my hand to ask about this topic, "What made them change their minds about slavery in the first place? I mean, what happened that made them change their minds or pushed them to consider abolishing it officially? And why do you think it still happens?"

You could practically hear crickets in the background despite being indoors.

'Well, this is awkward. Maybe I shouldn't have asked?' I thought to myself.

Eventually, she answered, "It didn't happen overnight. It took time. A lot of time to get people to change their minds about slavery. Specifically, the minds of those in power and those with a connection to people in power. Because the slaves wanted freedom but because of their enslavement the powerful silenced their voices. There were attempts to abolish slavery across the world long before the end of the Transatlantic Slave Trade. King Louis the tenth of France abolished it in 1315 within France itself. He passed a law to abolish it in their colonies long before the Transatlantic Slave Trade happened, but it wasn't passed in the largest colonial states, therefore not enforced."

She took a breath before continuing, "The Catholic Church officially condemned slavery in 1839. But the overall Abolitionist movement and shift in the minds of people happened more slowly as they questioned the morality of the action. It got to the point where most people were against slavery and believed that all people were born free. Despite this, some people still supported slavery and the money that it brought."

She paused again for emphasis, "Australia used slavery in the form of convict labour and the forced labour of their Indigenous peoples but also through the manipulation of people from small islands in the Pacific like Vanuatu. This ended as late as the 1970s, regarding Aboriginal forced labour. Often they were unpaid pastoral labourers or called indentured servants. This is despite slavery being illegal since 1948 under the *Universal Declaration of Human Rights*, which Australia was a signatory of. Things like protests, 'walking off the job', petitions, and demonstrations in mass numbers led to individuals and eventually governments changing their minds."

She seemed almost uncomfortable now as she finished her

explanation as my questions threw her through the loop, "Regarding your last question, I think slavery still happens because people are greedy or because they desire to harm other or just because they think it will bring in the most money. They don't think about the people but their wallets. Some organisations are raising awareness of modern-day slavery and the push to end it in the modern world. But like all things, it takes time. I hope that answers your question."

I wanted to ask some more questions like was slavery ever used as a punishment. But she moved on and ignored questions beyond basic ones specific to the exhibit.

It was on our return to Michael's home town that my uneasy feeling returned. We were sitting in our private carriage when Michael asked me, "Why were you so interested in how slavery ended so much?"

I stared out the window twirling my hair as I replied, "Because there are slaves in Zoara-Bela. That are made up of people who are descended from those enslaved before our curse. Outsiders who were punished or individuals after our fall whose punishment was enslavement. I just didn't know that humans had slavery too, or that it was illegal in your world."

"Wait. There are slaves in Zoara-Bela. Why haven't you freed them? I mean you talk about your city as being so advanced, but you still practice slavery. That is barbaric."

"Barbaric. Look at your world. The people enslaved by humans are abused, tortured and treated horribly. Those in Zoara-Bela are never harmed. We've never harmed them physically or emotionally. They are not overworked. We give them breaks and days off. Food and shelter are supplied, maybe not the most expensive. But their needs are met. Those who harm their slaves are severely punished, and the slave compensated. We can declare them free if they volunteer to work for the royal guard or their owners give them freedom and some money as a reward for hard work. It's rare, but it happens," I said despite not truly believing my words.

I was repeating back to Michael what they taught me. It was all I knew.

'You've never liked slavery,' I thought before telling my brain to shut up.

"Seriously. You think because you don't abuse them it's ok to make people work against their will. How is that right? Just how backwards are you people?" shouted Michael.

"Backwards. We're one of the most advanced civilisations on the planet. Our technology is far beyond what you are capable of," I said while raising my voice.

"Seriously. You think because your technology is advanced that your society is better than humanity. Look at your country. You're terrified of your family finding out about our friendship or you learning magic. You've got to do this in secret or you could get executed. You practically have no rights. Your people consider you barely above a slave in terms of rights."

He paused, looking as if he wanted to reach for my hand, "At least the slaves can eventually earn their freedom in your society. But you, as a woman, you're the property of the males in your family. The freedoms you have are those that your father gives you. And they can be taken away from you at any moment. Moriah, you've talked about how the way they treat the poor or women is wrong and how it needs to change. So you have to see how slavery is wrong," Michael said while attempting to reason with me.

"It's ... It's not the same thing. Besides ... even if I wanted to get rid of slavery. I'm just one person. I have no power in our society as you *oh so helpfully pointed out.*"

Tears welled up in my eyes as I shouted, "I'm practically voiceless. In under two years, the only thing I've been able to change is the way the grocer and merchants treat their female workers or making sure that the poor get food. Practically nothing has changed in Zoara-Bela. Nothing will ever change as long as my grandfather is on the throne!" I shouted back at him, not because I was angry but because my frustration overwhelmed me.

"Moriah. One person is all it takes to start a movement. Your people trust you. Listen to you. You have power where it matters. If enough people support your ideas then—"

"Then what, huh? What exactly do you think will happen? Hmm... That everyone will say you know what I think ending slavery or giving everyone rights is a brilliant idea, let's do it now. And we'll all hold hands. Seriously. Is that what you think? Do you know what will happen? War. A civil war will break out in Zoara-Bela. Thousands will die. Many more would be tortured in the futile attempt to change this law. More rights would be taken away. More restrictions placed on all of us."

I was shaking, my nail cut into my palm, "You've never seen a fight between users of magic. The damage a pair of fighters could do in a rage is bad. But thousands at the same time trying to take down the other side constantly will eventually affect the human world. Earthquakes, tsunamis, whirlpools, storms. Many humans will die. How do you expect the humans in the nearby continents to react to what they believe to be natural disasters?"

I took a breath, my voice became more desperate and frustrated, "Many of the nearby human settlements are poor in health supplies and their economy is very poor. How do you expect them to pay for it? To recover from the disasters we brought upon them? How can you ask me to be responsible for that?"

"There has to be a way for these changes to happen without violence. Maybe your father can advocate for changes to happen. He's a prince, and I assume trusted by the king. And from what you've told me about him, he's not supportive of the way they run the city."

"Right. I drag my father into this and reveal that I am

potentially plotting treason. What am I supposed to say? *Hi Dad! I just wanted to ask if you could risk your life by talking with Grandfather, you know the king and supreme leader that dictates everything in our city, and ask if he could pretty please give mermaids more rights and also free the slaves while at it. Thanks Dad, hope you don't die.* Seriously. I'm more likely to end up facing the executioner's axe after being charged with treason. My father follows the law to the very letter. He will never help me do this. And if I'm executed, *nothing* will ever change," I said.

Michael rolled his eyes, "Obviously not like that. Maybe talk to him. Ask him about his feelings on the issue. He could surprise you. If you have his support, he could begin pushing through some changes."

"He'll never listen to me. Firstly, I'm a mermaid. Secondly, I'm not an adult yet. Besides, why would he ever go against his father."

"You'll never know if you don't ask Moriah. Just ask him. Talk to him. Because your society needs a serious wake-up call."

"I don't want to lose his trust or contentment with me."

"Don't you mean love?"

"No. He may have loved my mother, but losing her broke him. I doubt that there is any room in his heart left for love. He cares about me, but I doubt its love. Besides, merfolk as a whole are emotionless because of the curse suppressing our emotions. Especially the positive ones."

"Unconditional love and acceptance come from the heart. If his treatment is conditional on you following the rules, he set down for you, then he doesn't care about you."

I froze for a moment at the thought my father didn't care about me before replying, "He cares about me. He's always cared."

"Yeah. Then why haven't you told him about me? Why are you so terrified of him finding out if he cares about you?"

"Because who could care about a monster like me!" I shouted with tears in my eyes.

"Monster? You're not a monster, Moriah. You're kind and caring. A bit naïve and stubborn, but that doesn't make you a monster. You are beautiful regardless of what form you are in. Beauty is staring you right in the face. You just need to look in the mirror," he said.

Instead of reassuring me, he just pissed me off further, "Did you seriously tell me to look in a mirror? There is a reason I try to avoid reflective surfaces. Mermaids are hideous creatures that only look human in the vaguest sense. Look at my reflection, Michael. Look at it."

I pull up the blinds of the carriage to let him look at my reflection. I purposely avoided looking at it. I already knew that I was a monster. I didn't need to see it reflected back at me.

"I am looking, Moriah. You're beautiful."

"Beautiful. This is the soul of a monster. This is our curse!"

"That's not what I see. I saw your reflection the day we first talked on the beach. My first thought wasn't 'monster'. It was beautiful. I thought you were unique and interesting. I wanted to know more. The word monster never crossed my mind. You need to love yourself."

His eyes glistened with unshed tears, "Just open your heart to the possibility that someone loves and cares about you, thinks the world about you and leave your doubts behind you. Moriah, the fact that I know what you are and what your soul looks like and I still care about you and call you my friend means something. Isn't that better?"

"No. Michael. It's not. Because I'm still a freak that has to avoid mirrors and all reflective surfaces or cause mass hysteria."

"Moriah—"

"I'm just done, Michael. I don't want to talk anymore."

The fight seemed to have drained out of me as we spent the next hour in awkward silence. It was like we were strangers. A rift opened up between us. And I don't know how to fix it. Or if I should fix it. As I returned to the sea, my sense of unease and worry didn't disappear. This unease and worry became an extreme sense of fear bordering on paranoia. Something far worse was to come. And my actions would come back to bite me on the arse.

CHAPTER 31

I spent a week after our argument avoiding Michael. But by the end of the week, my grandfather ordered me to attend court. Apparently, I was ready for more responsibilities regarding the royal duties. Traditionally, members of royalty were introduced to the court slowly from the age of eighteen onwards until they were declared responsible enough to work completely independently without being constantly checked on by nobles who worked within the court—or in my case, under the direction of my father.

This was most unusual. Even more unusual was that my grandfather wants me to observe how he ruled and dealt with matters at court despite being female. Despite his constant dismissal of me because of that. He had a hidden agenda. It was not as simple as 'you're old enough to learn how the court works'. I was supposed to begin this within my fathers' court, not his. He wanted something from me. I didn't know what it was but it couldn't be good.

The unease and fear that I'd been experiencing for the past few weeks went into overdrive with this announcement. Whatever happened today would not be good. At all. In fact, it would be worse.

I had spent all morning in my grandfather's throne room listening to complaints, resources, progress on city works, potential law bills, etc. But eventually, it moved on to crimes and the punishment given when judgment has been passed by my grandfather. And he surprised me. He was fair with the punishment he gave. Fines for those who breached laws to do with trade or committed minor infringements. A week in the dungeons with minimal food for those who continued starting fights. I took an interest in the proceedings, thinking I may have misjudged my grandfather.

Nope! Turned out that my original belief about him was still right. Because I forgot one convenient insignificant thing. Just one. All of those who were judged so far and received a fair punishment were men. Not women. I had gotten used to seeing fair judgments from him by this point that I did not expect this from him when a young mermaid was brought before him for punishment.

"My lord. This woman was caught discussing a motion to change the law and traditions surrounding the lower caste. She wished to protest against you and your rule and the treatment of the lower caste," the guard said, before pushing the woman to her tail joint.

He pulled her head back by her hair. Her face was heavily bruised but still recognisable. It was Ariel. A woman from the merchant class that helped Jedidiah feed the poor alongside me. Who the hell turned her in?

Abaddon rose from his seat in fury, banging his trident against the orichalcum floor, "She dare question my rule despite her privilege within the merchant class!"

"My lord, I wasn't questioning your laws or rule. I just wanted to improve the living conditions of the low caste to increase productivity. I'd noticed that they were slacking off, so

I was trying to work out a way to motivate them. I'd never—"
they cut her off before she could finish her plea.

"Silence, wench! You have no right to speak to me. Be
thankful I do not take your head for your insolence. Who
brought forth this charge?"

"Her husband, my lord. He said he caught her gossiping.
Turned her in this morning. I spent the past hour interrogating
her before bringing her to you. Your majesty," said the guard.

"You are satisfied by the evidence gathered?"

"Yes, your majesty. I am certain of her guilt," replied the
guard.

"Very well. You have left me no choice. Ariel, lion of god, you
are declared guilty of plotting reason."

'Wait. What?' I thought as he continued to drone on.

*'That's it? He didn't question her or use any spells to ensure she
told the truth. He didn't even ask if the husband's story was verified by
other witnesses or even ask to talk to other witnesses. Nothing. What
the hell?'* I thought to myself before my grandfather's
pronouncement of her punishment.

"Ariel, your punishment is that you'll be stripped of your
status of the merchant class. I will give you to Ambriel as a slave
to work in his mines until you die or you serve him for ten
years. If you should survive the ten years, you will be brought
before the court again and Ambriel will give evidence of your
repentance or your continued treason. If found guilty of treason
again, you'll be sentenced to immediate execution. Take her
away to her new position," he said, slamming his trident against
the floor.

I was frozen. They would enslave one of my allies for just
talking about improving the living conditions for the poor.

*'How is this just? How is this fair? What am I going to do? What
should I do?'* I thought.

I knew women were punished more harshly than men, but
the punishment didn't fit the crime. There was no evidence to

prove that she was conspiring to commit treason. She only complained that the women weren't treated fairly. She had done nothing wrong. Guilt crept into my heart.

'*This is my fault,*' I thought.

It was as they were dragging her away I shouted without thinking, "Stop!"

Everyone in the room froze. I couldn't let this stand.

"What did you say!" shouted Abaddon.

"I said stop, Grandfather. This punishment doesn't fit the crime. You also didn't question the witnesses or use a truth spell to confirm or disprove the occurrence of Ariel's crime. Please, Grandfather, I ask you to reconsider the punishment until you confirm the validity of the witness statements. If true, then I only ask that you reduce it to five years in Ambriel's mine as the charge itself isn't treason but the potential plotting of it. I'm sure she will rethink doing something like this," I spoke quickly without breathing in my nervousness.

He looked at me coldly before replying, "Very well. Take her to the dungeons until I get around to questioning the witnesses. Now take her away."

"Yes, my lord." replied the guard as he returned her to the dungeons.

"Thank you, Grandfather, for taking my idea into consideration," I said.

He ignored me before announcing to the court, "My granddaughter, Moriah, has been arranged to marry Zachariel. My most trusted lord. This marriage will take place next week once we sign the contract. My congratulations on your choice of husband, Moriah."

It shocked me. He must've been planning this for some time. He wanted an excuse to punish me. To limit me. My father was standing to the side with his head bowed. Silent. He wasn't even attempting to stop my grandfather or argue against his decision. He's clapping along with the other lords.

Why? Why was he just standing there? He'd promised that if I ever had to marry, I could choose. So why do this to me? Why let Grandfather marry me off to one of the oldest, vilest and cruel of the lords? Why him?

My horrified thoughts were interrupted when Zachariel stood in front of me with a horrible grin. As he grabbed my hand to pull me close, he said, "I look forward to the wedding. Don't you?"

His laugh as he pushed me back before leaving to talk to the other lords left me horrified and disgusted. I didn't know what I would do. What I knew was that I refused to marry that bastard.

The clapping and laughter of the lords echoed in my brain long after they made the announcement. It followed me throughout the day, trapping me within my horror and fear. But this was only the beginning of the horror to come.

CHAPTER 32

M y grandfather's announcement that I was to marry the
foul Zachariel echoed throughout my brain. I couldn't
believe it. He was going to make me marry that cretin. And
father did nothing. He just stood there. He ignored my pleas to
reconsider. No one was willing to do anything. So, I did the
only thing that I could. Swim away.

With tears in my eyes that could not fall as the water washed
them away, I packed. I grabbed my travel case, the one I had
enchanted to keep my human clothes and other belongings. In
my anger, frustration and panic I ignored every instinct that
screamed at me to stop packing and just get out of there. I
couldn't stay here. I'd find a way to survive in the human world.
Michael, he might let me stay with him, just for the night at
least. He was right. So long as I remained a mermaid, I'd never
be free.

Then I heard my father calling my name softly "Moriah?
What are you doing?"

"What do you think? I can't stay here! You heard him! He
will make me marry that foul, loathsome worm of a merman.
Why? Because I told him to spare that *poor* woman—"

"Moriah!"

"What, Father? If you think I will obey you because ... because you're a merman, think again. I'm through with following orders ... with being silent. I'd rather be human ... as human as possible for our kind. Because humans are *so* much better than us."

My father made a noise as if to interrupt. But I ignored him. I refused to give him the chance to force me to stay.

"Humans ... they grow, they change and they create. They create so much that is beautiful. Above all, they are kind, more kind than grandfather ... than that ... monster Zachariel. They've taught me so much. I refuse to ignore what they taught me. I refuse to give up my freedom—"

"I know Moriah. I'm not asking you to because you're right."

"My rights—What did you say?"

"You're right, my daughter. But there is something you need to know. About Zoara-Bela. About your sisters and your mother."

"Sisters? What sisters? I don't have any siblings. And what do you mean, my mother? You told me she died. A human ship killed her."

I was confused. I was an only child. I grew up wishing that I had a sister, not a brother, because a brother according to our laws would have more value than me, more freedom. But a sister, a sister I could talk to. I could share my hopes and dreams.

Why? Why did he hide this from me? I heard him tell me to sit on my shell so he could explain. In my confusion and shock, I sat unthinkingly. The story he told me was unbelievable.

As I sat frozen, I almost missed what he was saying. Catching the word, "... human."

"What?"

"Your mother wasn't Andromeda. Her name was Zevachya Mowriyha. She was human. So wonderfully human. She loved me. I didn't understand how or why. But she loved me with all her heart. And I loved her. She taught me how to love. How to be kind. How to treat others with kindness. I learnt that from her. It's because of what she taught me. What I learnt from the human world. That I raised you with more freedom and kindness than other mermaids in Zoara-Bela."

My anger built but then deflated as I saw his face. The grooves etched into his skin looked deeper, making him look old and worn thin. I had almost forgotten how old he was. He was there from the very beginning. His expression looked almost like sorrow.

"What happened?"

"Let me show you."

"How?"

"You're not the only one who can use the ancient arts. I'll be using a memory orb to show you what I know about the curse, your mother and what happened to her and your sisters."

Memory orb. He was going to use a memory orb. I would see, hear, feel and experience everything as he did. There was no way to hide or lie with the orb.

"Moriah?"

I nodded in reply. I agreed to use the orb containing his memories despite the risk.

CHAPTER 33

There was a reason most merfolk were reluctant to use memory orbs, despite being an effective tool for identifying the truth. The sensation that accompanied the activation of a memory orb was impossible to forget for one simple reason; it hurt more than anything else in existence.

Being pulled out of your own mind and thrown into the mind of another through the use of a memory orb was excruciating. My father was so much older than I was, his magic more mature and powerful—if I wasn't careful, his memories would shred my mind. The memory orb used by father didn't just contain his memories but his very experience.

I wanted to scream in pain, but at this point, my mind wasn't attached to my body. The memories felt like molten lava had been poured directly into my mind before being thrown into a whirlpool to be shredded. I thought I would die, trapped in my mind and his memories.

I didn't want to die. Not like this. It took every ounce of my will and magic to separate my mind from my father's memories. If I wasn't trained in magic by Amari (and my own reckless self-study), using the memory orb would have damaged my mind beyond repair. My brain would be a little better than mush. It took me what felt like hours to focus enough to receive the memories contained within the orb.

When my mind had finally focused, I realised that I was in the king's throne room. The orichalcum in the throne room glowed and shimmered in a beautiful teal tinged with gold, silver and pearl. The great big columns that held up the roof of the palace had jade carvings stretched around the pillars with pearls and silver etchings threaded throughout it. The throne room of my time seemed darker, colder and harsher than in my father's memories. Looking upwards, I noticed silver etchings that contained a prayer of love, honour, sacrifice and piety towards our mother creator.

It was only when I heard my father's voice announcing himself that I focused on the throne. I wouldn't have recognised Grandfather if it wasn't for Father's thoughts identifying him as Abaddon. The king's face was like carved marble, beautiful but emotionless, as he sat on his throne loosely holding his trident. Abaddon was always cold and emotionless in my memories, but there was something present in his eyes now that had been drained out of him since. I didn't understand what it was until his expression changed, his face lit up with joy upon hearing his son's voice.

Abaddon looked at his son kindly as he spoke, "My son, you have made good time. Have you enjoyed your break from your duties?"

"Yes, Father."

"Good, good. Come, take a seat, son. You will need to learn how to run the court and how to judge the crimes that our people bring before us. Specifically, the most horrific crimes are the ones who come before us. The others are dealt with by the magistrates in charge of specific areas unless they cannot effectively judge and sentence the criminal. Then we deal with those crimes," Abaddon said.

"What crime has this man committed?" Abdiel asked.

"The criminal Gadreel has been brought to me because he has committed one of the worst crimes any person of our city could commit against the people in his charge. As a lord, he has servants who attend him and assist in the management of his lands and home. However, in return for their service, he abused them. Many were beaten, heavily abused and tormented by himself and other members of his household. He denied them their rightful pay. Made them work in horrid conditions."

Abaddon paused for a moment before continuing, "I have seen nothing like this occur within our city before. It is more akin to the treatment the individuals who escaped slavery from our neighbours tell of their treatment. For that is how he has treated his workers, fellow free men and women. He treated them like slaves. I have already heard the evidence from witnesses to this abuse and his former servants. What do you think the punishment should be?"

To my surprise, Abaddon was furious with the actions of Gadreel, when he was known for keeping people enslaved. What made him so cruel? It was like Grandfather was a different man in this memory. He was giving the prisoner a fair trial when he punished me for asking him to give Ariel a fair trial. Before I could think on this further, I felt Father's emotions change from curiosity to horror as he looked at the pregnant young woman in the room.

She was thin, her face gaunt with pale and translucent skin, her veins visible. The clothes she wore looked like rags that hung loosely on her frame. Her light brown hair covered her eyes and most of her face as her head was bowed. She looked like the poor that I would help feed. It was like she had given up on anyone caring about what happened to her.

Father stood in front of her as he asked, "Is it all right if I move your hair to have a look at your face?"

I looked closely at her, trying to work out how I knew her because she seemed familiar. She gave a brief nod. Father gently moved the hair from her face. On her cheek, some bruises were a sickly green colour with mottled purple that had a deep cut that looked like it could have been made by a knife or possibly a ring if someone hit her hard enough with a backhand.

It looked like it may have been infected. Just before he was about to turn to Abaddon to suggest a punishment for the man, I felt his mind beginning to focus on something was on her neck. It wasn't obvious at first glance, especially not from where Abaddon was sitting.

To my horror, there was a collar on her neck that had etchings of entrapment, silence, subjugation and suppression. I could feel my father scanning the magic within the collar which was heavily infused with dark magic. I could practically taste the magic on the collar to the point I wanted to throw up, but could only gag at the sensation of the dark magic crawling over my skin.

I was nearly overcome by the magic of the memory orb that threatened to pull me under my father's mind. I'm only feeling this second hand, thousands of years after it happened, for my father to remain calm despite the desire to rip apart Gadreel was amazing. My father's emotions increased in intensity as examined the way the magic was infused with the collar. Gadreel didn't just turn this young woman into a slave. He stripped her of her voice, suppressed her will and ensured that she could not leave the borders of his property unless he gave her permission or he was nearby. But by using subjugation runes, he made her into a puppet that would follow every command as her mind rebelled against him. If he ordered her to kiss his boots, she would and if ordered her to kill or steal, she would without hesitation.

I wished that I could scream or cry, but the memories weren't mine; I was merely a spectator in my father's memories. I could only watch as my father wove his magic through the collar, safely disabling the enchantments, breaking the lock, keeping the collar closed around her neck, freeing her.

Abaddon turned to the criminal in anger, "This was beyond cruelty and greed. This goes against everything we believe. Against our very culture and traditions. Crown Prince Abdiel, I order you to destroy it."

I could feel my father's glee as his powerful magic shattered the enchantments placed on the collar. Eroding the poisonous green magic of Gadreel caused the metal to melt and drip through his fingers onto the floor. I could feel my father's fear as the young woman collapsed with tears falling down her face and gasping for air, believing that he missed a trigger hidden within the magic.

He knelt down beside her, checking her vitals, trying to see if both her and her child were harmed by a trigger hidden by the collar, when she leapt forward, wrapping her arms around him in a hug. I could feel a tingle of happiness within my father as he realised that she was unharmed.

I could feel her tears as she cried into his shoulder, which wasn't allowed as he was a prince, but I could sense that Father didn't care about the rules. She suddenly pulled away as she realised what she was doing. Father seemed disappointed as she stopped hugging him. Before she could apologise, he asked, "What is your name?"

"Andromeda, my lord. My name is Andromeda. Meaning to be aware of man."

"Andromeda. What a beautiful name. I wish that we met in better circumstances. I am Abdiel. My name means servant of God," he said with a smile on his face.

To my horror, the young woman was my mother, the woman that I grew up thinking of as my mother. I knew logically that my birth mother was Zevachya, but I still thought of Andromeda as my mother, I probably always would. How could anyone treat her like this?

I knew that she wasn't a noble or princess, but I didn't think she was a slave. But then I realised why she wanted to learn magic from Amari. She learnt magic for the same reason I did—power. She never wanted to be powerless again. She wanted the power to take control of her own life.

I was so lost within my own thoughts that I didn't realise that the king heard evidence from my mother until the king asked my father about how he believed Gadreel should be sentenced.

Abdiel said, "This criminal should be stripped of his name. He shall no longer be known as Gadreel, meaning wall of god. To lack a name is to lack peace in the afterlife. His lands and his titles should be taken from him. Members of his bloodline— children, siblings, wives, cousins—should only be given an insignificant portion of his estate, enough to live on but not enough to be called noble."

He paused before continuing, "This is only if they are free of guilt and had either no knowledge of the crime or did not participate in this monstrosity. Regarding this monster, he should be whipped and tortured in the main square before being publicly executed in the most painful way possible. His body should be cremated and ashes scattered at sea to further ensure that he knows no peace. May Charon and Thanatos send him to Tartarus without trial in the underworld."

To my shock and joy, Abaddon said, "I agree with the punishment laid out by the Crown Prince."

Time seemed to move quickly as the king ordered people to carry out an investigation into Gadreel's household. I could sense my father's attention was focused on my mother only, as he asked, "May I escort the fair Andromeda to a set of quarters within the palace to receive medical treatment and ensure that she is safe and comfortable before doing so?"

In response, Abaddon's lips gently curved into a smile before nodding in reply. Andromeda entranced my father as I could sense his attraction, what felt like the beginnings of love as he escorted her to the family wing of the palace.

I felt like throwing up as the memory shifted, but I could not as I lacked a physical form within these memories. I was in the throne room again, only this time there were very few guards in the room and none of them were next to the king. Abaddon was standing next to a beautiful woman with blonde hair that curled gently around her face and sky-blue eyes that seemed slightly off. She was obviously not from Zoara-Bela with her light peach skin and light blue tunic and head covering, trimmed in gold. None of the people in the memories so far looked or dressed like her.

Something seemed strange about her mannerisms, and there was a look in her eye I distrusted. I could sense my father's distrust of the woman the moment his eyes met hers. There was something about her that neither of us trusted.

Abaddon was smiling as he introduced the woman, "Abdiel this is my bride to be. The beautiful Eurydice from Eretria. My beautiful Eurydice, meet my oldest son, Abdiel. I hope that you'll be able to get to know each other well as you work together in your duties to this kingdom."

Grandfather seemed besotted by Eurydice. He looked gentle and kind as he looked at her with adoration.

Reluctantly, Abdiel bowed before Eurydice despite his distrust.

'*She is planning something. Something that will lead to our downfall,*' I heard Father think to himself.

"Princess Eurydice, I am curious to know the meaning of your name. It's something that we ask traditionally, it's part of our culture, you see. Normally, we introduce ourselves with our name and its meaning. I am Crown Prince Abdiel; my name means 'servant of God'."

He motioned at her with his hand to do the same. She looked at the king who smiled indulgently at her and told her to do the same.

"I am Eurydice. My name means broad fairness," she said, curtsying.

Her smile was false and cold in her greeting. She spoke reluctantly and curtly. I could tell that she wanted to be anywhere besides here. The way she looked at my father was strange. She looked at him as if he was an insect that stood in her way.

He bowed and reached to kiss her hand "Your name suits you. For you are beautiful."

"Thank you, my lord. I hope that we will get to know each other better as time goes on," she said.

The memory blurred as I caught glimpses of moments that increased Abdiel's suspicions about Eurydice. He caught her in the armoury which contained the city's best weapons and poisons, multiple times throughout the day. He became more suspicious of her every time he saw her in the armoury as she was from Eretria, a Greek city-state similar to Athens, where women could never learn magic or how to fight as they were expected to look after the household—meaning she should have no interest in the armoury. He had her followed, only to find out that she had bought enough poison to kill multiple men.

I watched in horror as Abaddon dismissed Abdiel's evidence and concerns about Eurydice. His love for Eurydice blinded him as he accused my father of attempting to sabotage his happiness because he believed Abdiel to be jealous of his happiness. Israfil, my father's younger brother, practically begged the king to listen to Abdiel's plan. It was only because of Israfil's insistence that the king even agreed to allow Abdiel to prove Eurydice's treason through a minor trick that would make her believe that she was the queen.

Horror and fear consumed my father as he realised that Abaddon's stubbornness and reluctance would doom us all.

CHAPTER 34

The shift to this new memory seemed more violent than the last, because of the strength of the emotions in these memories. Abdiel was sitting in what looked like a study as Abaddon declared the wedding would go ahead despite his warnings. What was Grandfather thinking? He was the one always telling us that even the suggestion of assassination was worthy of death. The king was normally the first person to interrogate a person suspected of treason. Those who committed treason were made an example of in Zoara-Bela. How could he be so irrational?

Even after Grandfather stormed off, Israfil, my uncle, remained sitting next to Abdiel, trying to calm him down. My brain felt like an axe was stuck in my skull and I felt my father beginning to panic. His fear and anxiety were so strong, it felt like I was stuck in one of my meltdowns, so strong that I lost sight of who I was for a moment. Israfil looked so young in this memory, younger than me.

'He's too young to deal with problems like this. He's only fourteen summers old. He doesn't have the training or experience needed to deal with this situation. Father has been over protective because he was

sickly as an infant. He shouldn't have to argue with Father on my behalf. He's too young,' thought Abdiel.

I could feel my father's overwhelming love and fear wash over me as I looked at my uncle. Every inch of his being was soft and kind. He had golden blonde hair, light bronze skin and sapphire blue eyes that sparkled with joy and mischief. He looked like Michael, in those brief moments of joy and playfulness.

As soon as the sensation that I normally felt during a meltdown passed I heard my father ask, "Israfil, why did you intervene in my argument with Father?"

"Because it was the right thing to do. Even if the information given to you by the merchant ends up being false, it is better to exercise caution than to ignore it. This isn't some mere attempt to spy on us from an outsider. This was a confession to plotting the murder of our king, our father. We cannot take this lightly. If this information is true then we have saved a life and stopped a madwoman from ending up on the throne," Israfil said, sounding older than his fourteen years.

I could see Abdiel's eyes soften as he spoke, "You are too young to be concerned with something like this. But I thank you anyway. You were aptly named brother; the angel who will blow the trumpet to reveal the darkness beneath."

"Thank you, brother."

"No. Thank you for doing this. Just—"

"Just what?"

"Just ... promise me something," Abdiel said reluctantly.

"What?"

"Promise me you'll be careful at the ceremonial dinner tonight. I won't be there as I need to check the security and ensure that there are no other traitors within the palace."

"I'm always careful, brother. Besides, she doesn't want me dead. It's our father she wants killed."

"We don't know that for sure. She only mentioned to the

merchant she desired father's death, but she purchased enough poison to kill multiple men. She may want us out of the way as well, but she hid that thought and desire better. We only know that she wants the throne. That she will kill for it. But we are still a threat to her rule. The people will not accept her as queen. She doesn't have their loyalty or love. We do. Her wanting us dead as well is not unreasonable. So, I need you to promise me you will pretend to eat and drink at dinner tonight."

"Come on, isn't that a little paranoid?"

"It's not paranoia if they are out to get you. Please, just for my peace of mind, don't eat or drink anything."

"Fine. I promise," Israfil said while rolling his eyes.

I could only smile as Abdiel kissed his brother's forehead. Israfil tried to rub the mark of his brother's lips from his forehead like a child before chasing him down the corridor as Abdiel laughed despite the dread that he felt in the pit of his stomach.

The memory shifted again as I found myself in the kitchens, watching my father supervise the servant. My father was just about to leave when he noticed a young apprentice cook about his brother's age who was being yelled at because he kept dropping the cookware.

I looked closely. His movements were jerky and the young boy's eyes were dilated unevenly. The boy attempted to speak when he collapsed onto the floor as was overcome with seizures and coughing blood. The dread he felt earlier returned as he ran to the young boy, turning him onto his side so he wouldn't choke on his tongue.

My father shouted at the cook, "What was this boy doing earlier? He is experiencing the symptoms of the poison that a traitor suspected of planning to assassinate the king purchased last night. Where was he? What was he doing?"

"M-my lord he was setting the cutlery in the dining room where the celebratory dinner is being held. When he came back, he mentioned the new queen Eurydice was in the room and that she made him uncomfortable. When he returned, he said the tables were already prepared—"

"M-my l-l-lord ... q-queen poi-soned c-cutlery ..." said the young boy as he struggled to breathe.

"What do you mean, boy?"

"N-no s-servant prepared table. O-only her in—room. N-no one else. J-just her. S-saw her put s-something on k-kings cutlery. I s-swapped it out with—clean set—distracted. Tried-tried to warn k-king. Wouldn't listen—"

I could only watch in horror as the young boy's lips had turned blue.

'Where the hell is the healer? I told him to prepare the cure,' thought Abdiel.

"I d-did the right thing?" asked the boy.

"Yes. Yes, you did. I will let your family know what you did today."

Just as the healer ran in with the cure the young boy's eyes closed shut with a final wheeze.

Abdiel turned to the cook and asked, "What was his name?"

"Uriel, God's light, my lord," replied the cook.

Abdiel turned toward one guard, "Ensure that his family is contacted. They will be provided for by the crown for the rest of their lives."

My father's face darkened as his anger rose. His anger felt like a whirlpool, spinning rapidly out of control.

"The rest of you follow me. We are to arrest Eurydice and throw her in the dungeon until sentencing," he shouted at the guards.

'Wait, she was alone until Uriel came to set the table. He caught

her putting poison on father's cutlery. Uriel only swapped out father's
for the clean set but not—' he thought as his fears were realised.

"Israfil! She must have also poisoned Israfil! Healer! You
come with us now!"

∽

The sound of plates and vases falling to the floor and shattering,
the thump of a body falling to the floor and the king's voice
shouting in panic could be heard through the door. I could hear
a cold, cruel laugh filled with malice, Eurydice was laughing in
joy as her plan succeeded. Fear, horror, guilt, shame and anger
had consumed my father as he attempted to break through the
magic used to keep the door closed.

The emotions were so intense that I struggled to concentrate
on the memory being shown to me. As the door splintered
through the forced Abdiel applied to it, the king was already on
the floor in tears, holding Israfil's shaking body close.

"He's just a child. Israfil is just a boy. Please spare him. Give
him the antidote," Abaddon begged.

Abaddon never begged, he only forced others to beg. But as I
watched, I could only hope that Eurydice showed mercy
towards Israfil.

"I refuse. He will die with you. I will take no chances."

"Why? Why do this? I love you," Abaddon replied with tears
falling down his face.

She laughed, "I know. And that's what made it so easy."

Abdiel interrupted her gloating "Eurydice, you are a traitor
to the crown. We will take you to the dungeons to await
sentencing. Healer, attend to my brother and administer the
cure."

I wanted to shout at them, warn them she was about to cast
the blasting spell, but I could only watch as they were all
thrown back into the wall. The necks of the guards close to her

snapped and their backs breaking as she threw them into the stone walls.

Abdiel laid on the floor, dazed and confused as he saw the healer kneel before Eurydice.

The healer began speaking, "My lady. I have done what you have asked of me. You are now the queen of Zoara-Bela. We now have the power necessary to subdue Sparta and all of our enemies."

"Good. Now remove your disguise, Perses."

With that, the healer changed into a man that claimed to be a slave of the outside nations.

Groaning, Abdiel staggered to his feet, "We sheltered you. Protected you from slavers. And this is how you repay our kindness!"

Before the false healer could reply, Eurydice's hand glowed with magic as it twisted, snapping Perses' neck.

Before Abdiel could react, she used her magic to throw him into another stone pillar, pinning him there. Her hands continued to glow as she made a motion that looked to be squeezing something. Abdiel choked and coughed out blood as her magic was squeezing his organs.

"I will enjoy this. I will make sure you survive this so I can have you executed in the morning as a traitor. The only people you told of your suspicions are the people in this room. And they are dead. And you ... you will be the traitor who murdered your father and younger brother and my attempted murderer. They will turn against you. Just as I turned your father against you. You will be dead and I will be queen."

Her hands continued squeezing his insides, causing him to scream.

I tried to scream, to beg her to stop hurting my father, but I was voiceless as this was only a memory.

"You are not the queen. You were never crowned. The throne will not go to you but to a lord in our court."

"So I kill one more man. No matter," she replied coldly.

"You ... You enchanted the door to suppress my magic."

"Well, I couldn't give you the chance to defeat me."

Blood dripped from Abdiel's eyes and ears as he began blacking out from the pain. His eyes blurred when his body collapsed to the floor. Eurydice's magic had let go of him.

The memory had blurred as Abdiel came closer to death, but through his unsteady sight, I could see Abaddon pushing his sword through Eurydice's chest. Tears continued falling from Abaddon's eyes as he killed the woman he loved to save his son. As the memory turned to black, I could only hope that Israfil would be saved.

My mind was consumed with pain as my father woke up in the healing chambers, attempting to sit up on his own. Abaddon's eyes were red from crying as he helped his son sit up.

My father was consumed with desperation and grief as he said to Abaddon, "It wasn't a dream. Was it?"

"No. I should've listened to you about Eurydice and cancelled the wedding. If I did then ... then my little Israfil would still be alive," he said before bursting into tears again.

My father attempted to reassure him, "It's not your fault. You didn't know that she would kill Israfil. We thought she was going to directly poison the food and drink."

Abaddon wrapped his arms around his only surviving son and cried into his shoulder. Looking at Abaddon in this moment, I didn't see the cruel king of my time, but a father who lost his child.

Abdiel, consumed by his own grief, barely realised that Israfil's death left a hole in Abaddon's heart that became filled with cruelty and vengeance.

My sympathy disappeared the moment I watched him

execute members of Eurydice's party, those who came with her, as spies and traitors. There were children as young as Israfil was among them. I could only watch in horror as the Abaddon in my father's memories changed into the monster I recognised.

My father could only watch in horror as everyone connected to Eurydice was either hanged or burnt alive and screaming.

The pyre of corpses burnt for three days and nights. The fire, smoke and ash could be seen from the mainland. The smell of their burnt corpses lingered in the air for the days that followed. I wanted to gag as I could practically taste the ash from the bodies on my tongue, just like he could in the memory.

Abdiel could only watch as Abaddon screamed and cursed Gaea for Israfil's death as Eurydice was the legacy of Kronos, son of Gaea. As the memory faded to black, all I could think was that Israfil was aptly named, he who blows the trumpet signifying the end of all things.

As I realised that it was his death that was the catalyst for the change that would overcome Abaddon and the people of Zoara-Bela. This was his first step into the darkness that would lead to the fall of a great nation.

"Clever. A misdirection ward designed to make the person feel uneasy and want to avoid the area and make others ignore its existence. It's not invisible, just unnoticeable. Brilliant," Abdiel said while examining the magic.

My brain struggled to focus on the fresh memory in front of me. It took me a few minutes before I realised that I was in front of Amari's tower. Why would my father be there?

"Thank you for the compliment," Amari said in a high-pitched voice. She rolled her eyes at his silence "Well, dearie. Are you going to come inside or just stare at my tower the entire night?"

He took a deep breath before speaking, "I came to ask you something."

"Of course you did, dearie. No one comes here without a reason. They all want something. Andromeda is probably the only one who genuinely comes for the company. The magic was just a bonus. So what did you want?"

"I want to ask if you could ensure that Zoara-Bela has a chance at surviving our patron and mother creator's wrath."

Why would he ask Amari that? Gaea was the one who cursed Zoara-Bela.

She laughed hysterically before replying, "What makes you think I have the power to petition the titans and ask for leniency?"

"I know who you are."

"Oh really. Who am I then? Hmm."

"Gaea."

She laughed cruelly, "You seem to believe me to be more powerful than I am. If I was her, why would I live peacefully among you?"

"But you don't. You live here on the edge of our country in a tower with potent magics upon it to dissuade others from coming near it."

"I don't like visitors. Especially nosy ones like you. You would look good as a toad dearie."

"And yet you let the princess, my wife, visit and learn magic from you. Magic that baffles most of our scholars. Magic that only the primordial gods and other deities can perform. The only exceptions are halflings and legacies to a lesser extent, as they are born with a fraction of the energy that deities are made of. And for my wife to be capable of those magics, the magic of the titans and primordial beings, there are only two options: either she is a halfling, or she has the blessing of a deity."

"What makes you think she isn't a halfling or that I am not?"

"You're too powerful. Your true form leaks through you in

moments of high emotion. And besides, I already tested my wife's blood. She is nearly completely human. There is only a mere speck of ichor in her veins, just enough that she can use magic but not enough to access such powerful magics that only the gods are capable of. For her to be strong enough to cast the spells you teach her, she needs the blessing of a deity. And based on the nature of her magic, it has to be someone with a talent for earth magics. Your blessing."

Amari looked angrier than I'd ever seen her as she glowed, transforming back into her preferred goddess form. I closed my eyes as even legacies of the gods couldn't see the true form of a goddess without turning to ash. I didn't want to see if that happens in a memory.

Once fully transformed I looked at Amari's lilac eyes, which held a glimpse of a barely constrained madness and cruelty. My fear, my father's terror increased as we saw her lips curl into a cruel smile as she spoke while clapping slowly, "Well, well, well. It seems you have a brain in that head of yours. How long have you known?"

"A few years now. You spoke of a son that had failed to uphold his promise to free his siblings. The story you told me was the same as the story of Kronos' betrayal of Gaea. I never planned on revealing my knowledge to you as you seemed to enjoy living among the humans, with your garden and teaching your magics to Andromeda," he said gently.

"Then why did you confront me?"

"Because I am desperate. I can see what my people's actions will lead to. Soon we will anger a deity and our city will be destroyed in return."

"What makes you think I won't?"

"Because of Andromeda. Because our city was the last thing you truly put your heart into. You created us. Created this land we live on so we could live in peace, without fear of being hunted. We were once beings that the other humans, in their ignorance, labelled Nephilim, and they were hunting us down. But you heard our cries and saved us. You only asked that we give you our love and worship through sacrifice and uphold the sacred laws of hospitality and the few laws you asked us to follow. You cared about us once. Cared enough to defy your father Chaos to protect us. I know that our people have become twisted but there is still some good in us. Please. Grant us mercy."

"Why should I?" she asked, head held high.

"Because there are still innocents within our walls. Andromeda and Cassiopeia are two of them."

She sighed, "Very well. I will give Zoara-Bela a chance—"

"Thank you, my lady."

"I'm not finished yet. There are some conditions. A price."

"What do you want in exchange?"

Her smile became cruel as if she delighted in his suffering.

"I will test you. Test the people of your city. I will send a priestess, a favoured one, to Zoara-Bela to test you. I will not tell you who. Nor will I tell you when. They will relay all they see and hear to me about their treatment. So long as one person, who is not yourself, stands up against the cruelty to protect my priestess and defend them, then your kingdom will be spared. Should none stand up against the cruelty or none protect her, then your kingdom will fall. Your people transformed into monsters and your island sunk to the bottom of the ocean for eternity."

She paused before continuing, "That is just the basic punishment. The worse the cruelty given upon my priestess, the worse my curse. However, should that occur, out of love for Andromeda and Cassiopeia, I will ensure a caveat is built into the curse. The method of breaking it will be woven into the curse should your people fail the test."

Why would she say that? Curses were designed to break. There would always be a caveat built into the curse. Why act like she was doing this out of love? You don't do this to people you love. Father couldn't agree to this. This deal wasn't worth it.

I could hear a hint of desperation in his voice as he said, "I agree to your deal."

With that, she unrolled the contract for him to sign. I wanted to beg him to reconsider, but there was nothing I could do as I watched him sign his name on the contract.

My mind felt like it was being shredded as it shifted to a new memory. I thought I was drowning as my father's horror and desperation made the memory blurry. I could only see my father running through the palace, his mind screaming that he needed to rescue Chava, the priestess that was sentenced on false charges.

When he arrived at his destination, I could see him push past the crowd, demanding that they move out of his way. He shouted that he was overruling his father's sentencing and judgement in this case as he had evidence that proved her innocence.

As I looked at Chava through my father's eyes I noticed that her eyes were dull, it was like she was the living dead. He kneeled beside her and covered her with his cloak before helping her to her feet.

I could feel his hope that he had done enough to save his city as he attempted to take her to the medical wing to make sure she received treatment for her injuries before helping her escape the city.

As I looked back into Chava's eyes I realised that she didn't understand that he had saved her. I could only watch in horror as he began leading her away and, in her desperation, she stole his sword and killed herself with it.

And in doing so she doomed Zoara-Bela.

CHAPTER 35

From the moment this memory began I knew that there was something different about it. It was only as I watched my father's interactions with Andromeda and his children that I realised that the emotions I was receiving from the memory were dull. He didn't feel love anymore when he looked at his children or his wife. However, regret for his inability to love them coated the memory.

I hardly recognised him in this memory, he was so different from the merman that I called Father. He raised my sisters to act like the perfect maidens; beautiful and voiceless. He never harmed them but there must have been some glimmer of care as I watched him stand up to the king by refusing to marry them off. I was lucky; Father allowed me to have a voice and granted me freedoms that I watched my sisters being denied.

The tone of the memory changed. The emotions were still dull, but they were stronger than anything else I'd observed so far. Boredom and curiosity drove him to swim to the surface and become human. Why show me this memory?

I suddenly found my eyes being drawn to a young woman dancing in the city square to the buskers' music against the firelight. As she twirled to the music her copper hair glowed bright like the fire, she was dancing in front of. Her eyes were a beautiful golden-brown, complimenting her warm olive skin. As I looked at her through his eyes, the way he was drawn to her, it was as if I was meeting Michael for the first time.

He looked at her sheer joy at listening and moving to the music; it created a sense of longing within his heart. A small part of him wished to feel the joy that she did in a simple action like dancing.

In a moment of distraction, the young woman approached him at his table and placed a light blue scarf around his neck before sitting on his lap, "Are you just going to sit there watching me dance? Or are you going to join me?"

I laughed as my father began blushing at her daring question and movements. He stammered, "I—I don't know how to dance. It's been a lifetime since I danced."

"That's okay. Luckily for you, you have an excellent teacher. Just follow my lead," said the woman as she held out her hand.

He had to make the same choice that I did, ignore her or take her hand. He placed his shaking hand in hers and let her pull him gently to the dance floor. The intrigue, joy and hope that I felt when Michael took my hand filled my father's heart. Her expression as she guided him through the steps of the various dances was soft and kind.

Like Michael had guided me, she guided him through the steps of the dance. She never made him feel stupid from his lack of knowledge. In what seemed like no time at all, he was smiling and laughing as they twirled along the dance floor.

When they finished dancing, they sat on the edge of the water feature within the centre and talked. They didn't know each other's names, but it felt like they knew each other for years.

He wanted to stay with her because with her he actually felt something more than regret or comfort, but he knew that staying with her wasn't possible.

She finally introduced herself as they were about to part ways, "Zevachya."

"What?" asked Abdiel.

"My name. It's Zevachya Mowriyha. What's yours?"

He knew that he should probably give her a false name and avoid coming back to this city again for a few more centuries. But something pushed that thought out of his head.

"Abdiel. My name is Abdiel."

"No last name?"

"Uh … no … we don't use them where I come from. We only have them for paperwork. Nothing else."

She bit her lip nervously and looked between him and the path leading to her home before saying, "Will I see you again?"

But before making his choice he asked her, "Do you want to?"

She smiled "Yes. Yes, I do. I had more fun today than I've had in years. And honestly, you interest me."

"What? Why?"

"I don't know. But … there is … something different about you. And I want a chance to get to know you more."

"I look forward to it, Zevachya."

I knew that this would end in pain. That seeing her again would leave him broken and hollow. I wished that he wouldn't have to experience the loss that would come from building a relationship with her. But then I thought about Michael; if someone told me before we met that our friendship would only end in heartbreak, would I stop myself from seeing him? No, I wouldn't change it for anything. I was a better person because of him. And I knew Father would think the same about Zevachya.

∾

He had tears in his eyes as he held my infant body in his arms. I could feel his tears, full of love and joy, dripping down his face. I knew that he cared about me, but I didn't know that he loved me so much. I could only watch as they couldn't decide what my name should be. They wanted to give me the perfect name.

I could feel my heart shatter as I realised that he named me after my mother; he gave me her last name because he wanted me to have something of her even if I never knew that I was half-human. His love and joy at my birth was visible for all to see. He loved me so much that holding in his emotions, as expected of merfolk, was impossible.

His sheer love and joy made him forget the danger of the situation he was in. He ignored every instinct that told him something was coming because he wanted to live in the moment. My heart broke at the realisation that his love for me, for Zevachya, made him reckless enough to ignore the possibility of being caught.

The memory shifted again, and I became overwhelmed with grief. It was like his heart had disappeared, leaving a hollow feeling in his chest, that spread throughout the body like a wave dragging away from the shore in a storm. I had to remind myself that I was in my father's mind, not my own when it felt like the air was being ripped from my lungs.

My father's tears became my own as his screams combined with magic when he saw my mother's broken body on the sand. As a merman, even in human form, his voice had the power to pull others in but he lost control causing many of the humans who heard him nearby into a spiral of depression that seeing her body caused in him. He held her body close, believing that she was dead before he felt a puff of breath against his cheek.

He paused in his screams and tears, hoping against all hope as he said, "Zevachya you're alive. Thank god. I'll get someone to send for help."

Her hand reached upwards to touch his cheek as he turned

around to call for help, stopping him in his tracks. She spoke slowly, gasping and choking on her blood as it filled her lungs, "Wait … Abdiel … even if they call … for an ambulance … they won't get here in time."

"No. You'll be fine. I can try some magic to heal you," Abdiel cried out in desperation.

"It won't work … Abdiel … Remember … healing is the one magic you cannot do properly … you only know enough to heal basic cuts and bruises. I'm too injured for you to heal. It's too late for me. But our daughter … she's still alive … I was able to hide her in time. She's in the bush… I hid her using that pendant you gave me … the one that makes me unnoticeable for those who wish me harm. He never saw her—" she said before coughing.

"Who did this to you, Zeva?"

"I didn't know his name, but he used magic to pretend to be you. He tried to trick me. But I … saw through it. I barely had time to hide her … please … keep her safe," she continued coughing, growing weaker every moment.

"Who was he?"

"He said … that … he was … your father … please … look after our daughter … I have no … relatives alive that could take her in … you need to take her with you."

"She won't be safe under the sea. She looks human. We don't even know if she can breathe underwater. Please don't go Zeva. I … I love you. Please stay with me," he said with tears in his eyes.

"And I love you … always … look after our daughter," she said as her eyes closed for the last time.

Tears continued falling from his eyes as he bent down to kiss her cold lips. Hoping against hope that he could save her with his declaration of love. But life wasn't a fairy tale. There were hardly ever any happy endings in real life.

And I knew that Grandfather has done something to ensure

this, as the magic from the curse breaking should have been enough to heal her.

~

I was left feeling hollow after my mother's body was taken away. I didn't know what to think as my father stood in front of the ocean holding my infant self in his arms. I could sense the magic coming from the ocean as he cast a summoning spell. There was only one being that had the power to make it so I could blend in with the other merfolk. I focused on the ocean as it glowed and bubbled.

Amari appeared slowly from the crest of sea foam, floating on the surface with a bright glow. She took human form for the first time in centuries. Her golden blonde hair was perfectly curled, contrasting against tan skin and lilac eyes. Like always, she wore a pink ancient Grecian dress. Her expression was like carved marble, beautiful but heartless.

"Why have you summoned me, Abdiel?"

He took a deep breath, "Because I need your help."

"And you've come to me for help? What makes you think I would help you?"

"Because you are the only one who could help. I can't ask anyone else. You're her only chance."

"Whose?"

"My daughter," said Abdiel as he slightly uncovered the bundle in his arms.

Amari moved closer to look at the baby in his arms before replying, "Well ... someone's been naughty ... cheating on your wife. But I don't know what this has to do with me?"

"She's mostly human based on what we observed. We didn't know if she could breathe underwater or if she inherited any mermaid traits. That's why I summoned you. I need to hide her as a mermaid and for that, she needs to survive underwater. Which is why I need your help."

She stared at him in surprise "She's half-human. What the hell did she even see in you?"

"I don't know. But she knew who I was. What I was. What I've done. And she accepted me anyway. I knew that I loved her. And she loved me. Losing her … is worse than dying. I don't feel different. I feel worse. Did the curse break?"

"It must have. If you truly loved her and she accepted and loved you in return, then the curse should've broken."

She raised her glowing hand and hovered it above me to see if I could survive in the ocean.

"As she is right now, she could survive in the ocean. She inherited your magic as a merman which will allow her to survive in the ocean. However, it will be hard for her to blend in, as her base form is that of a human. When she is older, she could learn to turn into a mermaid. But as she is right now, there is no reason why you couldn't take her into the sea."

"Is there any way that you turn her into a mermaid now?"

"Yes, there is. But there will be consequences for her."

"As long as it doesn't kill or physically harm her, do it."

"Abdiel, I will transform her body into a form that isn't natural for her. She will have no control over it. It will make her feel dysphoric. Out of place. She will look at her reflection and feel that something is wrong with her. And there will be something wrong with her as long as the spell is in place. Which is why I will enchant a bracelet that will anchor the transformation, keep her in her mermaid form and it will also grow with her."

Taking a deep breath, she continued, "Until she is about six years old the bracelet cannot be removed by anyone but after that age, she can remove it herself. Which is why you need to make sure you teach her to transform between human and mermaid form so she can remove the bracelet and hold the transformation herself. However, until she masters the spell, you need to make sure she doesn't take off the bracelet otherwise she'll turn back into her human form."

"Thank you. But what is your price? Everything comes with a price with you," he asked.

She smirked back at him "Nothing so sinister. I just want you to answer one question. Just one. And you must answer it. Honestly. You can't avoid it. Deal?"

"Deal. Now, what's the question?"

"What is the child's name?"

"That's it?"

I looked at Amari in horror. There was a reason why the meaning of a name was important in our culture—it gave others a glimpse at your soul, your very being. I knew exactly why she wanted my name. Names have power. You could control, track, or even influence someone mentally with a name. I tried to shout, to tell my father not to give her my name.

"That's it."

Abdiel looked at his daughter, who reminded him of her mother. It took him a few moments before the perfect name came to mind, "Moriah. Her name is Moriah, after her mother."

"Moriah. What a lovely name," she replied.

"Amari, you will stay away from her from this moment forward. Understood?"

"Fine. I agree."

That was quick. Why would she agree to his demand so quickly? But then I realised that she didn't need to come near me as she had my name, she could manipulate the things around me, leading me to her. I would do the work for her. She wouldn't be breaking her deal with my father as it would be my choice to go to her.

Father may not have given her the meaning of my name, but I did. I told the meaning of my name to an old maid who I later learned was Amari. I gave her the ability to manipulate the events of that day by planting enough information for me to be curious about the sea-witch, leading me to her. She planned this.

With a wave of her hand the bracelet she enchanted appeared upon baby Moriah's wrist and said, "As soon as you enter the water for the first time to return to Zoara-Bela the enchantment will take hold and she will turn into a mermaid. Our deal is done. Never summon me again."

Not long after she disappeared into the ocean, my father followed her back to Zoara-Bela. I watched as my mother, the mermaid I called mother, screamed at Abdiel for his betrayal. He may not have loved her, but he should have told her about his affair sooner. Despite his betrayal, she still accepted me as her own. She took me in even though I was the evidence of her husband's betrayal.

The memories moved through my mind quickly, but I still caught glimpses of love in Andromeda's eyes as she raised me, protecting me from Grandfather. She protected all of us as best she could.

I glimpsed a second-hand memory of a young mermaid with fiery orange hair rescuing a young man who fell unconscious after being thrown from a boat during a storm. The same mermaid becoming human and dancing under the stars with the same young man. She seemed so happy with him.

The memory shifted, and I was in my father's office. The young woman was arguing with my father. He had caught her with the human. I didn't recognise her until she shouted, "Father! Please, you can't tell anyone!"

It was Cassiopeia, my sister. She was the mermaid who fell in love with a human in the story I told Michael. My heart broke as I realised what would happen to her.

"He's just a human. An unimportant human that will die within a few decades. A mere shrimp in the eyes of merfolk, simple and fleeting. Why should I help you hide him?"

"Please, if Grandfather finds out he'll kill him. Please, don't let James die!"

"Why should I? I took you in when I didn't have to. I protected you for millennia against the cruelty of the rest of our kind and this is how you repay me!"

The memories blurred together so much that I could only see small glimpses of what happened to Cassiopeia.

"Abdiel help her! Please do not let him do this to her. You cannot let him hurt her. Please! You swore to protect us. To protect her even if she was not your blood. You swore an oath!" Andromeda pleaded for Cassiopeia's life.

"Haven't I done enough! She broke the law Andromeda! I told her to be careful. To wait until I could safely hide both of them away. To completely hide them from his eyes by either turning her human or making him a merman. But she didn't listen. Now, both of them will pay the price. She asked me to protect him and I did. He is safe. He will live. He is hidden. That was what she wanted above all else, Andromeda."

"A human. I don't care about the human. I care about my daughter. You cannot let her die!"

"Andromeda, I will plead for a lesser sentence and do my best to ensure that they do not harm her but you know my father. He will be even more cruel to her because he doesn't see her as family."

Memories swirled past even faster as the magic of the orb weakened. By the time I could focus on the memory in front of me all I could hear was the screaming of Cassiopeia, after years of imprisonment, being sold to one of the oldest and cruellest of lords that lived outside the Citadel.

I could feel my father's desperation as he protested against the forced marriage. Abaddon ignored his pleas as he used magic to paralyse my father, stopping for interfering with the punishment of my sister.

"Father, help me!" she screamed in fear as a collar of enslavement and entrapment was placed around her neck, silencing her and draining her free will from her.

She belonged to him now. It would force her to follow the lord's demands without the ability to protest. Tears fell down Abdiel's face as he realised that she was a slave in all but name, just like our mother was. He cracked like a fragile piece of glass as his father committed the same crime that he would have fought against so long ago.

I could barely focus as flashes of Amina and Davida being caught attempting to save their sister Cassiopeia from the cruelty forced upon her by the king. Andromeda turned to dark magic as they took her daughters away from her, to destroy the king and save her children.

My father's horror as he watched the poisoning of his wife, unable to save her as Abaddon blocked all magic in the room that wasn't his, because she found out where her daughters were being held. Tears fell down his eyes as he held her body as it turned into sea foam. He may not have loved her like he loved Zevachya, but cared about her deeply.

The cracks in his heart were one blow away from shattering completely. Fury coursed through his veins as he began planning on a way to take down his father. The flashes grew brighter, my mind felt like I was struck by lightning, the pain overwhelmed me. My memories and his conflicted. I was seeing a memory that my mind refused to believe despite knowing the truth of the orb.

My father and Adalina were attacking Grandfather, trying to kill him so they could free my sisters. He was playing with them. He wanted them to believe they had a chance at winning. But his smile disappeared as my father began casting a ritual designed to drain the life from him.

"Father, what are you doing?" I heard the voice of my five-year-old self behind me.

I shouldn't be here. Why did I follow them here?

The ache in mind grew, it felt like I was being drowned in acid. I watched in horror as Abaddon sent a blast of pure magic towards my five-year-old self.

Suddenly, I was trapped in my memory as it paralysed me in fear and horror.

"Look out!" screamed Adalina as she dived in front of me.

A twirl of blonde hair as she twisted from the blast of magic. I could feel her body collapsing on top of mine. The light disappeared from her lilac eyes. All I could taste was the blood on my tongue turning to sea foam. It was my fault. Adalina was dead because of me.

There was no going back for any of us now. He needed to pay for what he'd done.

CHAPTER 36

The memory of my mother's beaten and broken body choking on her blood in my father's arms. The memory of Adalina's corpse lying on top of me as she tried to cover me with her body, to protect me even in death from my grandfather's rage. To protect me from him. He threw an energy wave purposely in my direction as I stood watching my father and sister fight him, knowing that either my father or sister would get in the way. My father's screams and an overwhelming sense of loss and grief as he lost everyone he loved and cared about, one after the other until I was the only one left.

His pain and desperation, the sheer agony of losing nearly everything, making him hold on tighter to the only thing he had left. Tears fell down my face as I gasped, overwhelmed by everything I felt and saw through the memory orb. His pain and loss echoed throughout my entire body causing me to collapse to the floor and grasp my heart to stop feeling what he felt and experienced as I was ejected from the memory orb.

I could feel my father's arms wrap around me, to comfort me when I should be comforting him. The tears were warm on my face as they fell from my eyes, before being swept away by the sea. I had never felt such grief or desperation before. For the first time in my life, I understood my father.

I understood why he kept such tight control over me, only giving me access to small freedoms, indoctrinating me, making me believe in the rules and behaviours of Zoara-Bela despite not believing in them himself. Never standing up for me. Letting me believe that my feelings of wrongness at my form that I expressed to him as a child was just my imagination. Letting me believe that I was crazy. What he did wasn't right. But it was the only thing that he could do to keep me safe.

He didn't want what happened to my mother Zevachya, stepmother Andromeda, or my four sisters to happen to me. He had lost everyone else. He couldn't bear to lose me. None of it was right. I would not excuse his actions or lack of. But I understood. But one thing I couldn't understand was why I didn't remember my sister who died for me.

"Father, why don't I remember Adalina? Why do I have no memory of her? Or my other sisters?"

His eyes remained closed as he spoke "You were very young when you lost Andromeda, Cassiopeia, Davida and Amina within months of each other. You asked for them constantly. Cried out for them in your sleep but eventually when they stopped being mentioned you forgot about them. But Adalina... Adalina you adored. You held onto her tightly because some part of you didn't want to lose her like you lost everyone else. You never left her alone with my father. A part of you knew that he couldn't be trusted or that he was responsible for your family disappearing. That's why you were there. You followed us as we went to confront him. To take him down."

"What happened?"

"A guard who listened in on our plan betrayed us. He was expecting us. They caught us off guard. And then you were there. We tried so hard to take him down, but without support from the other nobles, we were doomed to fail. Seeing your sister's body collapse on top of yours and feeling her body dissolve into sea foam … it traumatised you. You woke up screaming for months, calling out for her. Seeing my father sent you into hysterics. So he cast a spell to suppress your memory of Adalina completely."

"Why would he do that? I was just a child. Who would believe me?"

"He didn't want others to rebel against him. And they would've questioned him. It's one thing to push excessive punishments onto the commoners of Zoara-Bela. But to kill your kin? To kill your blood is the one sin that could cause even his most staunch supporters to turn against him. Kin slayers are hated by merfolk of all castes. Not just the rich. His reign would end and he couldn't let that happen."

"Why did you never tell people about him killing my sister? My mother? My stepmother? Why did you tell no one?"

"I tried. But no matter what I did. No matter who I tried to talk to. I couldn't say anything. He made sure I couldn't tell anyone."

"But you're telling me about it now. If he made it so you could tell anyone, how are you talking to me about it now?"

"Because you already know what happened. That was the only loophole I found. If someone already knows about it, I can talk to them about it and the spell he put on me doesn't take effect. It can't stop you from telling others. It took me so long to work out a loophole in the spell he cast. To find a way for you to learn about all this. To learn what he did to you. To all of us. And the memory orb was all I could find. I'm so sorry, Moriah. I'm sorry for everything. For not telling you the truth about your heritage. For making you believe that the discomfort you felt at your body was your imagination. I'm so sorry. I never meant to hurt you. Please … believe me. I never wanted you to be hurt," he said with tears in his eyes.

"But you did. You made me believe that I was crazy. That

there was something wrong with me. I felt like a freak. And it's your fault."

"I'm so sorry, my daughter. I'm sorry."

"And I hate you for it. But I understand. Even though it hurts to know that you did this to me. I understand. And even though I hate you … I still love you. I can't help it. You're still my dad. You still raised me. Took care of me the only way you knew how. I don't like it. But I understand. I can't forgive you just yet," I said as tears fell from my eyes before disappearing into the water.

He hugged me tighter before saying, "I know that I don't deserve your forgiveness. But I promise I'll do better. I have no intention of losing my last daughter to another cruel lord. I'll follow whatever you decide to do."

"What do you mean?"

"If you want to go to the human world. If you want to become human and hide from my father in their world, then I'll help you do it. It will be your choice. Whatever happens from now on is your decision."

I looked down at my hands quietly, remembering that most of my family was gone because they tried to take down the king or to punish my father for standing up to him. But then I remembered that he said that last time they didn't have the support of the nobles.

This thought didn't leave my mind, "What if I said … that I want to fight. To take down Grandfather. To remove him from the throne. What would you say then?"

"That's suicide. He's too powerful. I can't let you do that. He'd kill you."

"You said it was my choice. That you'd help me do it, whatever I decide to do, you said you help. Well, I'm asking you now. Will you help me take him down?"

"I can't … he won't just kill you. He'll drain every scrap of magic from you to keep this curse active. You'll cease to exist entirely."

I straightened my back and made myself sound more confident than I was, "Maybe. Maybe not. But it's my choice. I won't marry Zachariel. I refuse. And I won't run. Because then nothing … will ever change. And Zoara-Bela has suffered under his rule long enough."

"Moriah. Every time that I have gone up against him, I've lost. I am not strong enough. I don't have the support to take him down."

"No. But I do."

"What?"

"Over the past two or so years, I've been slowly changing the minds of the merchant class and gathering support amongst the nobles. We don't need an army. We just need help in ensuring that Abaddon is distracted long enough for either of us to take him down or to ensure that whatever is keeping the curse in place shatters completely. If that happens, every emotion will become unbound, they'll turn on him and realise that he let them suffer."

I paused, looking him in the eye, and said "We don't need to convince everyone, just a few, that even the commoners and lower caste trust. Get them on our side. And others will follow. If they disagree you can make sure they don't tell anyone by using a similar spell to what Grandfather used on you to keep you silent about the murder of your wife and daughter."

"You think it's that simple."

"It can be. You said that even the rich and noble castes hate kinslayers. Well, he's a kinslayer."

"It's not that simple. They won't believe us. There is no evidence. No other witness besides me. And I can't physically tell anyone with his spell in place."

"Maybe not. But you can show them."

"The memory orb is deeply personal. They'll feel and see everything."

"They may not have to. I know a spell that will create a record orb. I can transfer the memory you showed me of my mother's murder, of Andromeda's and Adalina's murder. They'll view it through the record orb like a historical record. The emotions won't transfer. Just the memory itself. I can swear a magical oath to confirm the validity of the memory. I can explain everything."

His eyes lit up for the first time in years "A record orb, I had forgotten about that. This could work."

"But I need time. We need time. Can you try to postpone the wedding by destroying the contract? Because if the contract isn't there, then they must start negotiations again. It must have taken him months to organise it. We need that time. Can you do it?"

"Yes. I can make it so every contract that mentions your name and Zachariel's in the same document and the phrase 'dowry' and 'marriage' are destroyed completely. There won't be a single scrap of it left. It will buy you four months. At worst, one month. So we need to work quickly. You can't see the human boy until we do this. Until we remove my father from power. It's too dangerous."

"But—"

"I'll go speak to him. Tell him what's happening and give him the watch orb. Explain how it works and give you its pair so you can at least talk with each other in private."

"Thank you."

"Moriah, you'll only be able to use the watch in your room. Nowhere else. I've made it so it's nearly impossible for someone to use listening spells here. But it's not a guarantee. You won't be able to talk for long or often. But it's better than nothing. Do you understand? If you are serious about taking down my father, you have to work with me in convincing the nobles and merchants to back me up. You can't run off to talk to your human friend or visit Amari—"

"How did you know about Amari?"

"She told me when I asked. Besides, you weren't very subtle in your visits to the human world. I could barely cover for you. You are a poor liar."

I winced "Sorry."

"Moriah. If you want to take my father down, you have to be active in ensuring that we have allies that can't betray us to him. Think you can do that?"

I nodded.

"Good. I'll destroy the contract and make sure my father is distracted. I want you to write the names of any noble, merchant or well-respected merfolk you think will sympathise with our cause. Write what you think could convince them to support us. Anything you think could help. We won't have much time."

"I know. Maybe we could save Cassiopeia, Davida and Amina too. Find out where they are."

He smiled "I'd like that. But we need to focus on taking my father down."

With that, the both of us quickly hurried in our tasks. For the first time in forever, I felt hope. I had hope that things could change in Zoara-Bela. We could no longer afford to be idle. We had to take action or nothing would change. I knew that it wouldn't be easy, but nothing worth having ever was.

CHAPTER 37

Our first attempt at meeting with some respected lords and merchants was worse than the last time I attempted to gather allies. This time they refused to meet with either me or Father. In fact, they sent a message to us claiming that while they were curious about our plans; they did not want to put their lives at risk. Especially since they knew that I'd been betrothed to Zachariel, a known supporter of my grandfather, meaning that supporting me in getting the king off the throne was too dangerous.

However, I knew that a law was going to be passed that would affect their lives in a way that would push them to at least consider supporting our ideas. Like most merfolk, those within the noble and merchant class were selfish and believed themselves untouchable. Until the king announced an extra tax that would only affect the wealthy lords and merchants of Zoara-Bela, they would be content to stand by as he oppressed merfolk.

To get them to even consider my ideas or the evidence that we have about the king's actions, I needed to hit them where it hurt—their purses. I waited a week before approaching them again to give the law enough time to affect their wealth. I knew that they wouldn't believe that law would affect them severely unless they had enough time for the loss of income to build up. A week was enough for me to present the calculated loss in a year, decade and century.

This allowed me to compose a recording that outlined the effects of the recent tax law in the long term, focusing on their losses, and hinting at further laws that were being planned that would affect their wealth even further. I laced the recording with mind magic that would make them more willing to listen to my ideas. It wouldn't force them to attend a meeting with me just to suggest that it would be an excellent idea to do so.

I ended up waiting hours in my room, pacing back and forth in the belief that the king's guards would burst into my rooms and take me away. I had packed, just in case the lords told the king of my betrayal and I had to make a quick escape to the surface, to distract myself. Just when I had given up hope, a message from Lord Nathaniel appeared in front of me saying, "We agree to meet with you. Send us the time and date."

Things were finally beginning to go our way.

CHAPTER 38

In the weeks following my grandfather's declaration of my marriage to the cruel lord Zachariel, my father was successful in delaying the deal from going through. Thankfully, he didn't blame my father but Zachariel because he had been arguing about one term in the contract.

In the time that my grandfather could barely negotiate the first term of the contract, setting the wedding back by at least three months (no complaints from me), my father and I could discreetly invite several sympathetic merfolk to our cause.

Our first attempt at this failed because of the lords being content with the king's rule. It was only when they were directly affected by Grandfather's decision that they were willing to listen. It wasn't easy. But we did it, eventually.

We knew that some lords and merchants that we invited would tell others so with my father's help I reinforced a chained geas that we invoked during our last attempt at organising a rebellion. It linked every merman to the same oath that the original merman agreed to when they accepted the invitation. I made it so that none could communicate to a guard or the king about the meeting that would take place.

And as a bonus, I included a memory deletion spell within the chained geas with the caveat that if they intended to inform the king of our plans, that it would be deleted from their minds. It was as foolproof as we could make it, but if someone wanted to get around it, they'd probably find a loophole as we had rushed the geas in some areas.

I nervously waited within the cave that my father and I had chosen for the meeting. We would be attempting to convince several powerful lords and merchants to support our frankly suicidal idea of taking down the king, one of the most powerful users of the ancient arts in existence. I swam back and forth within the cave, pacing, as my fears and nerves overwhelmed me.

'How the hell am I supposed to convince over thirty mermen to throw in their support to take down the king or failing that, to swear neutrality when we try to take him out? I'm just a mermaid. Why would they listen to me? Most of them grew up hearing that mermaids should be seen, not heard or other horrible things. How am I supposed to get the most stubborn merfolk who are deeply entrenched within the culture and traditions that dismiss mermaids? How? What the hell am I supposed to say?' These thoughts continued circling in my brain repeatedly.

My fear of being laughed at by these lords, of being dismissed just because I was a mermaid, terrified me and echoed in my mind, because if I failed here and now, then nothing would ever change. I'd never be free again. I'd be a fish in a tank. Trapped. I couldn't let this happen. I wouldn't let Grandfather use me to destroy my father. Losing me, whether it was to the human world or my grandfather's actions, would destroy him. It would break him completely. How could I let myself potentially be responsible for that?

"Maybe I should let my Father talk. Maybe that would be better. They'd listen to him. Not me. Damn it. What am I supposed to do?" I muttered looking upwards, hoping for some guidance from a higher power.

"Not panic, maybe," my father's voice called out from behind me.

"Father! When did you get here?"

"Oh, a few minutes ago. You were deep in thought. I couldn't let myself disturb you until you said something idiotic."

"Idiotic? How is letting you do the talking idiotic?"

My father's face was kind as he smiled gently at me, "Because they trust that you want what is best for our people. They've seen you over the past few years slowly change the way several stubborn merfolk think. They've seen the positive changes that you've made to their lives or that of their servants. No matter how small. You've made things better. And they trust you because of that. Not me. I was here from the beginning and I have nothing to help the plight of my people. Which is why you need to do the talking."

"All right, Father. But promise me you'll back me up."

"I promise."

I wanted to say more, but the entrance of the merfolk who came to the meeting distracted us. Several of the lords and merchants disliked each other and were quick to express their dislike. They began shouting, demanding to know why they were here.

My father attempted to calm them down and get them to give us their attention. The noise from them was too loud. I hoped that playing with my necklace would help me calm down. But the noise was just getting louder in my head, more painful, even if the actual shouting didn't increase in volume. I placed my hands over my ears, trying to drown out the noise. Nothing worked. Finally, I'd had enough and laced my voice with compulsive magic as I shouted, "Stop!"

They all froze before turning to face me in an eerie silence.

"Now that I have your attention ... You are some of the most respected lords and merchants of Zoara-Bela. Merfolk come to you for advice. For support. And you act like this, demanding the Crown Prince bow to your demands immediately by shouting like children. You should be ashamed of yourselves, squabbling like children. Where is your dignity? Your pride? Did you abandon it for the reasoning of a goldfish?"

They looked at each other in shame. Shame at their actions and the fact a mermaid had to remind them of their station.

"Now, are you ready to listen to why we've asked you to meet with us or not?"

They all looked to each other before a single merman swam forward to ask, "Why did you ask us here?"

"I bet you it's about that rebellion I heard about," muttered a merchant.

"They have no evidence that proves to us we should support them," muttered another.

I took a deep breath "Because we wanted to show you something. Something that the king has done. To all of us. Especially to my father. The king has committed a crime that even the common merfolk would condemn him for. He is guilty of killing his own kin."

The shouting began again as the lords denied my declaration. They knew the king was cruel, but they never believed him capable of killing his kin. One lord shouted, "Why should we believe you? You're just a mermaid. Mermaids lie."

I looked darkly at him, making him freeze in his tracks "Because I have proof. Because my claim has nothing to do with me being a mermaid, but with the king's actions. So I'd suggest you keep any comments about my gender to yourself."

"Well then, show us the proof," demanded a lord.

To silence them I held up a record orb and asked, "Does everyone know what this is?"

"A record orb? How is that proof?" laughed another lord.

I smiled darkly at them "Because it contains my father's

memory of the murder of his wife and one of his daughters by his father, the king. This memory is unaltered. Micah, you are a well-known scholar. You've used record orbs. You know how to confirm authenticity. Will you step forward and tell the rest of the gathering after you examine the orb whether or not it is authentic?"

My question startled Micah, but he had no choice but to confirm it to the other lords who would have pressured him to do so if I didn't ask. After a few moments of examining the orb, he said, "It's authentic."

"Activate it, Micah. Let all here see the proof."

Micah nodded in reply as he activated the orb.

All within the room were left horrified by the king's actions. Their horror became fury when they found out that the curse was meant to be broken by my birth, and Abaddon's sacrifice of Princess Andromeda and my sister Adalina had anchored the curse. The combination of blood sacrifice, kin slaying, and the anchoring of the curse pushed them off the edge.

The kin slaying was horrible in their minds, but the fact he did this to fuel the curse, to keep it in place angered them beyond all belief. Because if it wasn't for the king's actions, they'd be free from the darkness of the curse. But not all of them wanted to believe it. Not everyone wanted to believe the evidence before them.

A merchant shouted, "It's a lie. It has to be. Our king would never do this."

"He did this. He condemned us to the darkness of the curse. Besides, my father couldn't lie. He showed me this through a memory orb that was confirmed to be authentic. I had to experience my mother and my sister's murders first-hand through the memory orb. I felt everything my father did. I felt his pain. I felt his grief as everything he loved was taken away. It is real."

"Then why not tell us as soon as it happened? Why wait nearly eighteen years?" the merchant demanded.

"Because I couldn't. The king used a geas on me. He made it so I couldn't tell anyone. It took me nearly eighteen years to find the loophole that would allow me to show my daughter my memories of this. I could only talk about this with merfolk who already knew about it, which was only my father until now," said my father.

"Why didn't you do anything to stop him!"

"I could have stopped this in the beginning. Stopped him while we were still human or when we had just been transformed into this. But I ... I thought that maybe he could change. That seeing what our creator did to us because of the cruelty we forced upon others would snap him out of it. Instead, it made him worse. You saw in my memory what he was like long before the fall, so you can understand why I wanted to think the best of him. But that man is no longer there."

He took a breath, "The king that I knew as a child would be horrified at what he has done. But Abaddon feels no remorse for the lives he's destroyed. He needs to be put down. There is no other way for this to end. Which is why we came to you for your help."

"To do what exactly?"

"To take down King Abaddon and destroy his hold on Zoara-Bela," I replied.

"What? That's suicidal," a lord said.

"It's dangerous, but it's possible. His hold on the curse is weakening, which means the anchor for the curse is draining him more and more. If we act now, within the next two months at least, we can take him down for good. We can defeat him. But we need your help and support. It was the actions of the royal family that caused this, I know. But we want to fix this, and we need your help. Or at the very least your sworn neutrality enforced through a magical contract. We can't risk this getting back to the king."

A few minutes later, Micah swam forward and asked,

"Which contract do I sign if I want to help you take down the king?"

I held out the contract and the quill. He read it carefully before signing with a flourish and saying to the others, "There is nothing in the contract that could harm you. Just a standard silence contract. You can't tell others who don't know about this. It won't kill you if you attempt to break confidentiality but will wipe your memory of any plans. The contract is fair. The other one is the same, only it makes it so you can't go against our plans or tell the king. It enforces neutrality."

With that many lords agreed to sign at least one contract without a fuss. Many argued with us about the benefits or rewards for assisting us in rebelling against the king. They wanted to be in the best position regardless of who won the rebellion. Things were looking up for once.

CHAPTER 39

I t took a few weeks before our rebellion gained momentum. We spent most of those weeks in serious negotiations over what certain parties would receive for throwing in their support for my father and I.

One lord, Jophiel ('beauty of god'), who controlled one of the most profitable farms in Zoara-Bela, had been in negotiation with both of us for the most time as he would be impacted by the rebellion regardless of who won. He also had a small group of soldiers loyal to only him and connections to other lords that we needed.

To gain his support, we had to concede to most of his demands as we were running out of time to organise the rebellion. In return for his support and resources, he wanted us to reduce his tax by half and allow him to keep a larger percentage of the profits and goods farmed by him along with a few other demands.

We ended up conceding to several demands; in particular, we signed a contract allowing him to keep a larger percentage of the profit and goods and a ten per cent reduction of tax.

Nathaniel ('gift of the lord'), on the other hand, controlled one of the wealthiest mines in Zoara-Bela besides Ambriel. He was more respected and trusted among the merchant, noble and lower castes, as he was considered to be fairer in his dealings. He had access to a store of weapons through his connection to a blacksmith, and soldiers who gave loyalty to him because of the benefits they received in return.

One of his demands we agreed to instantly, which was the ability to train anyone who wished to work or operate a mine regardless of class. However, he also demanded that his tax be reduced by half, control over the price of the resources from his mines, and control of Ambriel's mine.

Ambriel ('energy of god') was loyal to the king. He couldn't be swayed, which was why Nathaniel had demanded control of his mine. Again, we had to concede to a few of his demands, such as a small tax reduction and control of Ambriel's mines as he was necessary for the rebellion.

I had very few moments to myself that I could spend talking with Michael, not about the rebellion but about how he was doing and just random things.

I wanted to forget that I was planning a rebellion, a civil war, for a few moments. Not that I could forget. I spent every waking moment organising and planning.

There were moments where I just wanted to run away, to leave Zoara-Bela. I didn't create this mess. Why should I be the one to clean it up? As that thought crossed my mind, I realised that I needed to do this because if I didn't then no one else would. No one else would have the political power and support to do this. If I didn't do this, then nothing would change.

While we spent nearly a month gaining allies and securing support, today our sole focus was planning as our initial plan had failed. We wanted to avoid a full-scale rebellion but someone had found a way around the geas, not enough to reveal us, but enough to endanger anyone who attempted to complete the initial plan.

We needed to work together with many merfolk of different classes and come up with strategies that would work cohesively with each other to achieve our aim. My father had been doing his best to divert attention from us and trying to get the most stubborn merfolk to listen to me and my ideas. It was painstakingly slow, but at least we were making progress.

My father looked at me before saying, "Moriah. It's your turn to explain what the primary group will be doing."

At that, I quickly activated the holographic map of the city and zoomed in on the east entrance of the Grandfathers' palace. I began explaining, "The east entrance of the king's palace is the weak point within the wards and in the guard rotations. If we enter through this section, we'll be able to take the early morning guard by surprise. We'll need at least one small team to take out the warning system ahead of time to ensure that we can enter without being noticed until it is too late."

"Where will you be?" Micah asked.

"I'll be with the second team containing a handful of soldiers. We will need to destroy the anchor long before King Abaddon reaches us. From the information we've been able to gather, the anchor is made of crystal that is encased in orichalcum. Magic like that leaves echoes that we can follow."

"So you don't know where it is. Great. We're just a distraction," complained Lord Nathaniel.

"We've been able to narrow it down to Abaddon's private throne room. It is where he hears private complaints and has clandestine meetings with other lords. It isn't far from the primary throne room, but it can be easily accessed through the north-east corridor quickly through the east entrance. Which is why we will enter through there."

I paused before continuing, "My father, however, will confront the king to delay him for as long as possible. He will need a team of soldiers as Grandfather always has a significant number of guards with him. Their job is to distract the king and his most loyal guards from our actions."

I took a breath, "But we need to keep in mind that the king is a powerful practitioner of the ancient arts. At any moment he could detect us and bring the fight to us. This might bring you to the attention of the king and his most loyal soldiers, which means you will need to refine and practice your skills."

I continued, "If you know magic, then practice your spells until you can cast them without a thought. If you are capable of healing or medicine, refresh your knowledge and skills. If you are a skilled warrior, then spar and improve your reaction times. We cannot afford to be idle."

The constant back and forth between the different lords and merchants who had pledged their support continued getting louder. I had to push back the pain and uncomfortable sensation created from the increasing noise levels.

My hands were clenched tightly, turning my knuckles white, and my nails began to painfully dig into my palms. If the noise continued at the level, it has been the past few minutes, with my senses going into overdrive, I would explode. Which was never a good idea when someone had magic, let alone trying to convince bull-headed individuals to support a rebellion. My exploding temper would doom us.

Luckily, my father recognised the signs of my oncoming meltdown and silenced the bickering lords and merchants long enough to wrap up the meeting. It took me what felt like hours to calm myself down.

My body felt like someone had strung me out, my muscles sore and aching even if I had done nothing strenuous. But I felt like this every time I got close to the edge of having or if I did have a meltdown; tired, aching and wanting to collapse. I just wanted my shell or even a human bed.

A human bed would be lovely. I wanted to sleep for eternity. Ignore my worries, my responsibilities. Just focus on myself for a while. The stress that I had been under the past three months had me on the verge of a meltdown, and the noise level of the bickering had my senses ramped up to eleven. I curled up in a corner of the cave, humming and rocking myself slightly to calm myself down.

My father slid down the cave wall beside me, "Everything will be okay. This rebellion is not all on your shoulders. You don't have to take everything on by yourself. I'm here. I'll be here until the end. You are not alone."

"I know that. It's just that … everything could go wrong. Seriously wrong. We could end up dead, Father. And my sisters … there is no way that he'll let them live if we fail. He'll want to make an example out of us. And the noise from all the bickering … it just pushed me over the ledge. I know I shouldn't break down like that, but—"

"But nothing. Sometimes even I want to break down from all the stress and grief and loss. I let it rule me completely until you broke me out of my haze. You're strong, Moriah. Stronger than me. Stronger than your mother. Stronger than my father. You don't let your fear rule you. You move forward."

"Michael helped with that."

"He may have given you some help, but you were the one who had to act and move forward yourself. He didn't do that. You did. Trust me. Everything will be fine. He has no idea what we're planning and Michael is safe. Okay? Just let yourself relax for a while. There's no harm in visiting your friend for an hour. Let yourself relax. You deserve it."

"Thank you, Father. I think I might take you up on that," I said with a slight smile on my face.

This was too good to last. My hope died as a hologram of my grandfather appeared within the cave, pulling me back into despair.

CHAPTER 40

Seeing his face, even if it was just a projection, a hologram, filled me with dread. I had only just begun recovering from my earlier meltdown. I still felt strung out and drained. And this just set me back further. I hyperventilated, my fear and panic sending me into a downward spiral. But that fear turned to horror as I heard my grandfather say, "I believe that I have something of yours, Moriah."

The projection moved to show a still body within a crystal. The body was uninjured, but he had a look of horror and fear upon his face. It was only when Grandfather zoomed in on the face, I realised exactly who was imprisoned within the crystal. It was Michael.

I attempted to strangle the gasp that tried to come from my throat by placing my hand over my mouth. I could feel my eyes tear up in response. I struggled to keep myself from screaming or making any sounds. I didn't know if it was a one-way projection or if he could hear or see me. I didn't want to show weakness. And emotions were a weakness in his eyes.

My grandfather continued, "Oh, Moriah. Did you really think you could hide something like this from me forever? Did think I was stupid? I know that you and my traitorous son are planning something."

'He knows. He knows about the rebellion. We need to warn every-one,' I thought to myself as I turned to face my father with a look of horror.

"I know that you are planning something. I know that you have convinced my fool of a son to help you plan some sort of rebellion. I thought Abdiel learnt his lesson after last time. Apparently not. I know all this. But what I don't know is who else you convinced to help you in this foolish quest. I don't know when you plan on doing this or how you even think you have any hope of winning."

'Wait. That's all he knows? Maybe we have a chance. If he still doesn't know this. But he has Michael. Why would he take him? What is he planning?' I thought.

"It is only because you are of my bloodline, my son's child, that I even offer this. Give up your foolish goal of rebelling against me and conform to the rules of Zoara-Bela by marrying Zachariel immediately. Do so and your precious human lives. He won't remember you. It will be as if you never existed. But he'll be alive," he said with a smirk.

'No. He can't be serious.'

"Or you continue with this notion that you have a chance at defeating me. You go ahead with the rebellion and I will kill Abdiel, your human and your sisters. I will destroy everything and everyone you care about. Then I'll rip out your magic. Piece by piece. Before I finally kill you."

I couldn't hold back my emotions anymore and I burst into tears. I was completely horrified by the choice he gave me. It wasn't a choice at all. I felt my father's arms wrap around me to console me. It didn't work. I still had to suffer by making the choice.

My grandfather's smug voice continued, "You have two choices. And I know that you care about this human. About your father. Dare I say, you love them. Merfolk are meant to be as beautiful and heartless as marble. And yet you let human ideas and emotions corrupt you. So, you decide what is more important to you: your human and family or your freedom. Your choice. You have three days to consider my generous offer. After that, well, I can't guarantee that your human will still be alive within the crystal. I'll see you soon."

The hologram disappeared just as quickly as it appeared. I sunk to the cave floor in grief and horror at the choice that lay before me. Love or freedom.

I had to choose between my love for my father, my innocent sisters and Michael, and the freedom of Zoara-Bela from Abaddon's tyranny. My body shook in fear.

'How can I choose between them? If I take his offer then nothing in Zoara-Bela will change. Our people will still suffer. The curse will still be intact, although it should have broken a long time ago. If I don't, then Michael will die. My first friend will die.'

"Damn it!" I shouted as I slammed my fists into the solid rock underneath me.

"It will be fine. We're nearly ready. We can take down my father, you need to have hope."

"How can I? He has my friend. Besides, by the time that we're ready to attack, Michael will be dead. He's innocent. He hurt no one. He doesn't deserve this. He shouldn't have to pay for my reckless decisions."

"Reckless? That is the last thing that you've been so far." My father sounded incredulous. "You have been the one urging caution with every step of the planning." He paused, and I looked at him. "I know you care about him. Look, we might be able to use this as a distraction so we can take him down. I can convince the others that starting the rebellion two or three days from now is the best idea. We can still do this."

"How? We still don't have enough support." I took a deep breath. "Some of our supporters aren't ready yet. We don't even have a way to breach the wards with an army or the exact location of the anchor or exactly what it looks like beyond crystal and orichalcum as its materials. We don't even have a way to hide our army from his sight long enough to attack."

I paused, trying to stop my panic attack. "I'm barely journeyman level. I don't have the knowledge or experience to cast such a spell. We had originally planned on attacking in a month at the earliest. In two months at best. Not less than three days."

"You might not have the knowledge or experience to cast such a spell. But I know someone who does. And they want my father dead and off his throne as much as we do."

"Who?"

"An old friend," he said with a slight smile on his face.

At his response, I felt hope that maybe I could have both love and freedom … if this friend of his was as powerful as he thought.

CHAPTER 41

I didn't realise until we reached the tower that Father's old friend was Amari. She wouldn't help without asking for something in return. What the hell was he thinking?

Upon entering the tower, I could feel my hope drain away. As soon as we entered the waiting room my father shouted, "Witch! Come out of the shadows!"

In response, I whacked him in the arm, "Father, you don't speak like that to a friend, let alone a person you want to ask help from. Don't be rude."

"Oh, he's always been rude, little fish. And I wouldn't say that he's a friend. An acquaintance, possibly. Someone I dislike, definitely," said Amari with a high-pitched giggle.

"Hello, Gaea," my father said.

Her face lost the slight trace of humour as she spoke, "So you've come back here despite my warnings, Abdiel. I hope that you have the information you promised me when you made your deal."

"What deal?" I asked.

Her smile was cruel "You know … the one where I cast a spell to mask Moriah's presence above the surface … hiding her from your father … making it so Abaddon wouldn't be able to discover her interactions with the human. You still owe me. So do you have what you promised me?"

"Wait, you made a deal to keep my friendship with Michael secret. Why?"

"Because … I didn't want you to suffer what I suffered. I didn't want you to lose the small piece of happiness that you found with him. I lost your mother, your sisters and my wife because of my father. I didn't want you to feel what I felt. And this was the only way I knew how to keep you safe and happy," he said.

"But … it didn't work … he found out about Michael anyway. And now he's trapped in some crystal that is barely keeping him alive underneath the sea." I turned to Amari to question her further "What happened? Why did the spell fail?"

She gasped and acted as if I shot her in the heart before replying, "My spells never fail. I promised that he would never find you above the surface. And he didn't. I said he wouldn't discover your relationship with your human when you were on the surface. And he didn't. He must have found out about the human through one of his spies or a watch orb if you used that to communicate with him while in Zoara-Bela. That is not my fault."

"Wait. How could he find it out from the watch orb? It's a secure method of conversation here in Zoara-Bela. How could he even access it? It's literally only connected to one other orb," I said.

I looked to my father who had an uncomfortable look on his face.

"Well … Abaddon was the one to create the system the watch orb runs on. He created it not long after the curse because we could no longer use paper to send letters. So … theoretically, if one guard told him you received a new watch orb, then he could hijack it so he could view any messages or recordings. But I thought I sealed the loophole as I personally made those watch orbs," he said.

"You probably sealed the loophole. But he could have found out about Michael another way," said Amari.

"Like you, for instance?" he retorted.

Amari gasped, placing her hand on her chest "Me? Now, why would I do that?"

"Who knows what goes through your mind? Maybe you thought it would be the push Moriah needed to force her to fight against my father."

"Maybe I did. Maybe I didn't. You have no proof. This accusation is based solely on your hatred of me," replied Amari with a cruel smile on her lips.

Did she really tell Grandfather about Michael? I knew that I couldn't completely trust her, but I never thought she would endanger a person I cared about!' I thought angrily.

"Did you tell him about Michael?" I demanded.

When she looked at me her face softened "No. I wouldn't risk coming into contact with him. But I knew that he had a spy within your household."

I took a deep breath and moved to hit her, but my father held me back.

She continued, "Now. We have lost sight of our original conversation. Abdiel. Do you have the information you promised?"

'I need to focus on the current problem. I'll deal with this later. There isn't much time left to save Michael,' I thought.

"Yes."

"Well."

"My father ... he, uh ... used an unwilling sacrifice to anchor the curse to something. Something that is made of orichalcum and some sort of crystal. We have a rough idea where it is," said Abdiel.

"An unwilling blood sacrifice ... for him to anchor the curse the way he has … it would have to be someone connected to the breaking of the curse. Who did he use?" Amari asked.

"Zevachya. He used Zevachya. If she didn't hide Moriah when she did he probably would have used her to anchor it. He didn't know about her. He's always believed that Moriah was Andromeda's daughter. He never believed that a human and merman could have a child together."

"What makes you think he would have used Moriah instead of her mother?"

"She's the product of that love. She was born as a bridge between who we used to be and to who we are now. She's a mix of land and sea. She has the blood of both people who were supposed to break the curse. If he used her, then the curse would be fully anchored. The spell wouldn't have broken down as it has because of that connection," he said.

Amari sat down. "That makes sense. There is magic in her blood connected to the curse and the earth. She's connected to my domain because of her mother. But it's not just that. Abaddon tried to kill Moriah before as a young child, even when he believed that she was Andromeda's. Children are inherently innocent. That innocence sacrificed would have been more powerful than Zevachya because of the blood connection to you. But that still doesn't explain why the curse didn't break fourteen or so years ago. Zevachya was an adult connected to the curse being broken, but he still would have felt his anchor weakening. Something else must have been done for it to still be intact after all this time."

I thought about it for a moment. Fourteen years ago. I was about four, nearly five years old. Then it hit me. I knew exactly what happened.

"Adalina."

"What?" Amari and my father spoke in unison at my sisters' name.

"Adalina. She was murdered fourteen years ago. She sacrificed her life for mine willingly. She is blood-related to both of us. I was hurt in the attack. Bleeding. My blood could have gone into her wound. Would the combination of a willing blood sacrifice and the loss of innocence through the shedding of blood and witnessing her death have been powerful enough for the curse's anchor to be strengthened?"

Amari seemed to freeze as the thought ran through her mind. "That must be it. It must also be why you are the only one that has pushed for change in Zoara-Bela. Your blood and innocence was the ingredient. And as you questioned the reality around you ... as you changed, and grew as a mermaid ... as you had doubts, the ingredient lost power."

"How the hell would that work?" asked my father.

"Moriah, remember my lesson on curses. All curses want to be broken. It's a flaw in that type of magic. Because curses aren't a natural part of the world... even if the curse was designed to be unbreakable, the unnaturalness of it would wear down the curse until it was weak enough to break with the right catalyst. Which is why I built a caveat in the curse when I cast it. I purposely designed it to break with the right catalyst from the beginning. Allowing it to last for millennia, even when curses like this would have weakened enough in a hundred years."

"Would he know that? Grandfather is a powerful user of magic."

"No. He knows how to use magic effectively. He knows powerful spells and rituals, but he isn't a master. He learnt it on his own through scrolls and the occasional demonstration, not through a teacher. He mastered none of it. He never paid attention to the warnings. Because if he did, he wouldn't have tried to keep the curse intact for all of eternity as it increased the risk of destroying Zoara-Bela completely. Thank you for upholding your end of the bargain. Now, why have you come here?"

"We need your help. Grandfather knows that we are planning on leading a rebellion against him. That we want to take him down. He's kidnapped Michael. He's holding him hostage. I only have three days before he kills him. We can't wait any longer to take him down. Which is why we need your help. You have the power to cast a spell to hide our allies as we storm the palace. To break through the wards. Will you help us?" I asked.

"Yes. I'll help so long as your father agrees to reveal the true history of Zoara-Bela to the entire nation and he does his utmost to reintroduce worship of me back into the people. I'll also ensure that your human won't drown when the spell keeping him trapped breaks when you defeat Abaddon. Do we have a deal?"

"Yes," my father and I replied in unison.

"Well then, you know what to do. Sign on the dotted line," she replied with a high-pitched giggle.

"What now?" I asked.

"Now you get your allies ready. In two days I'll help you storm the palace."

Although we had a goddess on our side, a feeling of dread welled up in me. The possibility of our plan failing was high.

CHAPTER 42

Despite knowing that we had the support of Amari, a goddess, I was still filled with dread. Amari, while powerful, had only promised to hide our allies, break through the king's wards and stop Michael from drowning—nothing else. And that was what worried me. It was up to us to stop Abaddon and his men and destroy the curse.

Grandfather was powerful both politically and magically. Amari didn't believe that he was powerful or skilled—he was to me. He had thousands of years to perfect every curse, spell and ritual he knew. Being self-taught didn't make him less of a threat or less powerful—it made him more dangerous.

Which was why I made my way to my stepmother's secret study, hidden behind the engraving of the fall in her garden. I had been coming here the past year or so to study the magic that she left behind. It helped accelerate my learning of the ancient arts, allowing me to pass Amari's test earlier than usual.

After my mistake with a jinx that could have become a curse, I only learnt the spells and theories connected to what I was learning with Amari. I didn't want to make the same mistake again.

But with Michael's life and my peoples' freedom at stake, I couldn't afford to be weak or careless. I only had three days left to save him.

I spent hours sifting through the many orichalcum sheets and orbs within the study, searching for something, anything that could help me take down the king. In my frustration and anger, I pushed the orichalcum sheets and other objects to the floor. With tears beginning to form in my eyes, I knelt on the floor next to the desk for a moment before punching the desk so hard that one drawer popped open.

I looked in the drawer and found a small chest that had spells to conceal the magic woven into it. I examined the warding of the chest for any harmful spells before I picked it up.

"There's something inscribed on the lid," I muttered to myself. "Lehassir et haatsaot (remove the algae)," I said.

To my darling daughters, simply say the name of the destroyer who brings ruin in his wake and it shall open.' It read. *'Destroyer? Who's the destroyer?'* I thought to myself before I realised exactly what the password was.

"Abaddon."

The chest opened to reveal a record orb, and some ingredients sealed in crystal. Upon activating the record orb, I realised why Andromeda had sealed this within a chest containing a password.

This wasn't a spell or ritual that could be found in any record that Grandfather had access to, because she had created this ritual herself. According to the record, she tested it on prisoners that were being held in Father's dungeons who were going to be executed.

They had killed her before she could gather all the ingredients needed to complete the ritual on Grandfather. Looking at the ingredients in the chest, I realised that only three ingredients were missing, which were all fairly easy to collect. For the first time since receiving Grandfather's threat, I had hope.

As I left to gather the remaining ingredients for the ritual, I felt a shiver of ice down my spine as I wondered if this was the right thing to do.

~

In the early hours of the morning while everyone else was still asleep I was in my stepmother's study preparing to cast a ritual that I barely knew in hopes of defeating my grandfather. To cast it properly I used orichalcum orbs that I found in Andromeda's desk with a barrier spell built into them.

This barrier spell pushed the water out of the space within it, leaving the area dry. As I entered the space, I unravelled the spell that I had subconsciously kept in place after I gave Amari the bracelet which kept me trapped in mermaid form.

I stood above the cauldron, in my true human form, staring at the ingredients and the spells that were laid out in front of me. I knew what each of the ingredients meant. I remembered Amari's warnings about curses, the damage it did to the soul.

This was black magic. I had avoided dark magic after my mistake with the bad luck jinx that would have become a curse. I'd never cast a curse like this before. My understanding of curses was mostly limited to the theories on unravelling them, not casting them.

I shouldn't be doing this. I wished there was another way, but there wasn't. If I didn't do this, then he would be too strong for us to beat when we attacked the palace. This went against everything Amari had taught me, against everything that I believed in.

But I had to believe that I was doing the right thing. Belief or a strong resolve was needed for every spell and ritual to be successful. If I wavered in my belief for a single moment, the ritual would backfire on me and my magic would be devoured, just like I was about to attempt to do to him.

The cauldron already contained boiling water above a fire, the ingredients were all prepared; I had memorised the chant. But why did I feel guilty and ashamed? Abaddon had destroyed countless lives and brought our city to ruin. He deserved this. The water behind the barrier reacted violently.

'I need to calm down. I can't be angry when I cast this,' I thought, before taking a deep breath. *'There was no turning back now,'* I began placing the ingredients into the cauldron.

Winter sweet flowers and fruit containing calycanthine, which could cause convulsions. A handful of castor seeds contained ricin, which could cause seizures among other symptoms. In magic, castor meant hex or curse. A handful of white baneberries, also known as doll's eyes, containing a sedative effect and causing hallucinations, were thrown into the cauldron. Ten strychnine seeds (can also cause convulsions) were put in the cauldron.

Where Andromeda found these ingredients, I did not know.

Crushed alexandrite meaning 'obsession and delusion', along with powdered astrophyllite meaning 'cause the dead to torment him' when used in black magics. Fossilised shark teeth for vulnerability in water. Garnet to draw energy and ruby for intent were also placed within the cauldron, among the many other ingredients.

As I stirred the cauldron, I chanted the spell to combine the ingredients in this potion.

"Hosheh, ani mezamen otekha (darkness, I summon you).
'Asseh tt hahats'ott sheli (do my bidding),
Roken et hakesem meatzamot elu (drain the magic from these bones),
Ta'afoh oto le-kassar onim (make him impotent).
Ta'afoh oto le-kassar kokhott (make him powerless).
Tigerom lo lehishtakavott elyy (make him bow to me).

Barega' shehadam noge'a bakhefets zeh (once the blood touches
this object)
Litroff ett hakessem shelo (devour his magic)."

I repeated the chant three times according to the instructions, as three was a powerful number in magic. Carefully, I
poured the completed potion on top of the wraith dolls, carved
in the rough image of a merman and inscribed with his name. I
let the wraith dolls absorb the potion for an hour.

Once fully absorbed it would be safe for me to touch, as all
of the poison and curse would be contained within the dolls and
not on the surface.

As I waited, I prepared a contract on a blank orichalcum
sheet. Basically, the contract stated that I would stop the rebellion and support his rule so long as Michael was returned safely
to the surface immediately, and he would never force me to
marry anyone, and he would cancel my betrothal with
Zachariel.

I knew that he would be interested in hearing the offer
within the contract, but he would never accept it because it gave
me more power than him. He wanted me broken and in his
complete control. Especially if what looked like a geas was cast
on it among other obvious spells.

He would throw it back in my face, which was what I was
counting on. He would be so focused on the geas and the
obvious that he wouldn't notice the concealed curse that would
activate as he handed it back to me. With a smile on my lips, I
tied the cursed contract to the curse on wraith dolls, which
would allow the last but most vital ingredient to be added to
curse.

Waving my hand above the cursed objects, I chanted, "Hasster ett zeh mikulam (conceal this from everyone)."

To further conceal the curses, I individually wrapped each
item in silk, which would trap dark magics within it, and then I

placed it within my beaded purse. This would allow me to walk into Grandfather's throne room without him detecting the curses on me.

The bell rang within my father's palace, signifying the start of the day. Before leaving the room, I checked my watch orb to see if Grandfather had accepted my request to meet tonight—which he had.

As I swam out the door to meet with my allies I thought, *'everything is going to plan. I just need to make sure I slip my enchantment into Lord Ambriel's food so he provides the distraction I need to attach the wraith to Grandfather's throne and shell.'*

I knew that curses usually drained magic from the caster to hold it in place. However, this curse had been designed to steadily drain the magic from its victim and with the punishment for the caster included within the curse.

The curse would leave multiple scars on my magic, and the darkness from these scars would infect my very being. As a side effect, I would most likely become more ruthless. Even if I cast a purifying spell, which I intended to do after placing Abaddon under the wraith curse, some darkness would remain. This was a risk I had to take to increase our chances of victory.

I was terrified that Father would find out what I was planning to do tonight. If he knew, he would try to stop me. This was dangerous. If they caught me cursing the king or using magic to control several lords, then I would be publicly executed alongside my father to stop the rebellion.

By doing this, I was putting everyone at risk. But this is the only way that we could win the rebellion. I was not powerful enough, physically or magically, to take on my grandfather in a fair fight. Which was why I didn't intend to fight fair. Amari once told me I was too honourable to stab someone in the back and that honour separated me from the king. But I stood by what I said. Honour had no place in battle. Lives were at stake. Michael's life was at stake.

'*Fighting honourably will get us all killed,*' I thought as I stared at the empty vial that once contained a confidence boosting potion—I needed all the confidence I could get for this plan to work.

Which was why, after I had checked that the compulsions and triggers contained within the enchantment that I placed in Lord Ambriel's food was active, I began making my way to the king's palace.

I had also slipped the same enchantment into Lord Zachariel's food through the compulsions on his servants as a backup. I connected these enchantments to the straw dolls that I carried with me, which would allow me to trigger either of them to distract the king. I couldn't leave the distractions up to chance, but their actions couldn't be out of character.

The distraction they'd make had to be realistic and true to them, otherwise it wouldn't work. But they also needed to be where I wanted them at the exact moment I needed them. Which was why I used compulsions and triggers rather than full mind control.

Upon arriving at Grandfather's palace, his servants escorted me to the throne room which he apparently had set up for dinner. The servant's eyes were blank and his voice monotone as he announced, "Princess Moriah has arrived for your meeting, sire."

"Excellent. You are dismissed. Moriah, take a seat," Abaddon said.

"How kind of you."

"Isn't it just? I didn't expect you to request an audience with me."

"I've come to negotiate a deal, one that benefits us both."

"I've already offered you a deal. I expect you to take it or leave it."

"You were the one who told me to always read the fine print and to never accept the first deal because it shows desperation and weakness. You would never accept the first offer, so why should I?"

His lips stretched into a cruel mockery of a smile before he said, "So you can learn after all? What makes you think I should even hear your attempts to negotiate a better deal?"

"Because you would find it entertaining. And who knows? Maybe the deal I offer will be better for your position as king."

"You're right, it would be entertaining to see you flounder as you attempt to negotiate. Very well, negotiations can happen after dinner. The servants should arrive with the food soon."

"Not until you swear an oath upon your magic that you will do nothing to harm me, be it physical or magical, while I am in the palace and after I leave it, until five in the morning."

"You didn't include emotional or mental harm in that statement. Why?"

"Would the oath even stop you from doing that?"

"Of course not."

"Which is why I didn't include it. Now your oath."

"You should make an oath too, Moriah."

I tilted my head slightly as I asked, "Do you honestly think I am in any way capable of harming *you* with magic or physically?"

"No."

"Then why bother, you would kill me before I even let off a spell."

"True but you want me to swear a binding oath to not harm you."

"Yes, but you can also include a caveat which will allow you to do that if you see me attempt to harm you."

"Very well. I, Abaddon, King of Zoara-Bela do swear upon

my magic that I will do nothing to harm Moriah, Princess of Zoara-Bela, physically or with magic until five o'clock in the morning tomorrow so long as she does not attack me during these negotiations. So mote it be."

There was a flash of white light, signifying the oath being bound by magic. I hadn't thought he would be that honest when swearing the oath upon his magic. The smirk that was on his face when casting the vow disappeared with the flash of white light. I realised that he didn't think magic would accept the oath. He would never admit that though, as it would make him look weak.

Before I could mention the offer, the servants placed a plate of kelp and squid ink salad alongside some fish in front of me. I looked at the king's meal, which was more extravagant; a minor snub against me but not worth commenting on.

"Well, after we finish our meals, we will begin our negotiations."

I nodded in agreement. He needed to believe that he had all the power in this. So we ate in silence. As we ate, I slowly poured small bits of magic into the straw dolls containing the enchantments on Lords Ambriel and Zachariel.

By slowly activating the enchantment, the magic blended in with the magic of the wards. Grandfather wouldn't be able to notice my enchantment. It also meant the timing of the distraction would be at the exact moment I needed it to be. Minutes seemed to pass like hours before we finished the meal. Luckily the confidence boosting potion lasted six hours, otherwise I would have broken down by now.

As soon as the last plate was cleared away, Grandfather rested his head upon his hand before demanding me to begin the negotiations. I started with an offer I knew he would never accept, causing the discussions to move back and forth before whittling my offer down to what was on the cursed contract I'd created. I knew that he would not accept the conditions on that contract as long as a lord interrupted our negotiations because it would make him seem weak in front of his allies.

I felt Lord Ambriel approaching through the straw doll containing the enchantment, so I handed the orichalcum sheet containing the terms of the contract to the king.

"So, you had a contract already prepared with the terms you wanted. So why not give me this at the start?"

"I was taught to always ask for more than what I was willing to settle for."

"Glad to see your education wasn't a complete waste. What are the terms?"

"You have the contract in your hand. Why not read it?"

"I want to hear it from you."

"I will stop the rebellion and support your rule in return, you send Michael back to the surface, alive and unharmed, and you will cancel my betrothal with Zachariel and never force me into a marriage agreement again. I will also give you the names and locations of a quarter of my supporters."

"Give me the names of all your supporters and I may consider this."

"Half of my supporters."

"Three-quarters of your supporters."

The servant had opened the door to announce Lord Ambriel's presence while we were negotiating. Lord Ambriel had heard the king reduce his demand from all of my supporters to three quarters. It was only when Lord Ambriel cleared his throat that Abaddon realised that he had shown weakness in front of one of his allies.

"Lord Ambriel, what do you want?"

"My lord, there has been an issue with mines."

"Can't it wait until tomorrow morning?"

"No, my lord."

"What is the problem? Well, Ambriel? Speak!"

'Why isn't he pulling Ambriel into the side chamber to discuss the

problem like he normally does? Does he suspect me?' I thought, trying to stop myself from shifting and twitching.

Lord Ambriel shifted uncomfortably before saying, "My lord ... it is connected to a state secret. But if you wish to discuss this here, then I will do so."

"Very well, we will speak in the side chamber."

He then turned towards me. He couldn't allow Lord Ambriel to believe that he would give in to the demands of a maiden.

He said to me, "I've had enough of this game. Listening to your pitiful attempts at negotiation has bored me. Your attempts to bind me with a geas through the signing of this contract was both obvious and doomed to fail. I will not accept this contract. You have until I finish addressing the matter Lord Ambriel wishes to discuss to decide if you wish to accept the deal I originally gave to you."

He threw the contract at me before leading Lord Ambriel to the side chamber. Once I noticed the door to the side chamber seal behind them, I muttered, "Lehasstir (conceal)."

I didn't have much time to act, so I took out the wraith dolls that were in my beaded bag and enacted the last part of the curse. He gave me the last ingredient, his blood, given willingly and without care. I could now bind him to the curse. The amount of magic involved in this is minuscule. He wouldn't be able to detect it. With my shaking hands above the dolls and the cursed contract, I cast the last part of the curse.

There was a slight quiver in my voice, "Leaged oto leklalah zo (bind him to this curse)."

The dolls glowed red once I bound his blood to the wraith dolls. I cast the curse concealment spell again over the dolls, "Hasster ett zeh mikulam."

I quickly rewrapped one doll and placed it back in my bag before I swam to Abaddon's throne. I quickly looked for an opening in his throne that I could use to place the wraith doll. I noticed that there was a slight gap in the arm of the throne and quickly placed the small doll within the gap. To hide the wraith doll further, I cast the curse concealment spell for the third time over this doll.

I could hear Abaddon beginning to move towards the door so I swam as fast as I could to the same spot that I was in when he left the room and cancelled the concealment spell on me.

"Good to see you can follow instructions. What have you decided?"

"I assume that you won't reconsider accepting my offer."

"That is correct."

"Then I must think further on your offer before accepting."

"You realise that you only have one day left before your human dies if you don't accept my offer."

"I know but I have until sunset tomorrow to decide. I'll let you know my decision by noon tomorrow."

"Ten in the morning at the latest, as payment for wasting my time tonight."

"Agreed."

"You're dismissed," he said before waving me off.

I bowed my head slightly before exiting the throne room. As soon as the doors closed, I hid in the shadowy crevice behind the pillar, casting the concealment spell on myself thrice. My heart felt like it would jump out of my chest as I waited for Abaddon and Lord Ambriel to leave the throne room.

Minutes went by slowly. Before I could move from my hiding spot to go to the king's chamber, both Abaddon and Ambriel exited the throne room discussing the treason of some of his workers. I stayed frozen in my hiding spot until I could no longer feel either of them within the palace.

It wasn't difficult to find Abaddon's bedroom nor pass the protections on the door as he never believed that any would be dumb enough or crazy enough to break into his chamber. His room, while decorated extravagantly, contained very little furniture. I examined his shell to find a weak spot for me to exploit because if I placed the wraith doll in the wrong place he might detect it and the plan would be ruined.

'Come on, think. Where could I put this doll?' I thought before I slapped my hand against my forehead.

'Underneath the pillow. There's a gap underneath the pillow joint to the mattress. He won't feel it when he sleeps,' I smiled as I lifted the mattress to place the wraith doll within the gap, casting the curse concealment spell for the third time on this doll.

Before I moved to leave, I noticed the chest where he most likely kept his crown at night. Without thinking, I wove a different magic draining spell into the chest that would slowly weave itself into the magic of the crown overnight, weakening him further.

With my plan completed, I left the palace still under the concealment spell with hope filling my heart as I finally believed that winning was possible.

It was nearing eleven o'clock at night as I laid on top of the mattress of the shell in my stepmother's study and stared up at the roof blankly. Curling up in a ball, I wrapped my arms around my tail joint with my eyes squeezed shut. My body was shaking and my eyes felt itchy. I didn't know if I wanted to sob in fear, disgust, horror or relief. I didn't know what I was supposed to feel.

How could I cast such a horrible curse on anyone? It wasn't right. What I did wasn't right. I knew it wasn't. But what else could I have done?

I'd told father and Amari that Grandfather had so much more magic than me, that he was stronger than me, that we had to do something, anything, to weaken him before we stormed the palace. Why couldn't Father or even Amari weaken Grandfather?

They both had so much more power and experience than me. Why didn't they listen to me? Why did it always have to be me that came up with the plans? Why was I the one that took all the risks?

I grabbed and tugged my hair as these thoughts echoed in my mind. Rocking back and forth, I couldn't stop the sound of my sobbing from escaping my mouth. Suddenly, I felt a tingling in my spine that strengthened into what felt like a bolt of lightning being stabbed into my spine. Gasping, I sat up straight in the shell.

"It worked. I can't believe it. It actually worked."

The wraith curse. It had fully activated and attached itself to Abaddon. I could feel his magic being drained by the curse. We could win this. We actually have a shot at winning this.

To ensure that neither Father nor Amari figured out what I'd done, I needed to cast the purification ritual to cleanse my magic. The barrier spell was still in place from earlier and the ingredients needed for the purification ritual had already been prepared. I knew that what I'd done was wrong but a necessary evil, so I entered the barrier in my true form.

I lit the fire underneath the cauldron and filled it up with water. As it boiled, I lit the Arabic Gum incense that I'd purchased in the human world. In magic, Arabic Gum was used to banish negativity and would purify evil from a space when burnt or added to a potion, which was why it was the first ingredient I put into the cauldron.

Three leaves from the adder's tongue fern for healing, crushed alkanet root for purification, and aloe for protection were added into the cauldron. The steam rose from the cauldron as the magic built up.

Anemone flower for health, protection and healing was placed into bubbling concoction whole. A spoonful of ground-up leaves from the ash tree for protection, health and sea rituals was added quickly into the mix. Seven bay leaves for protection, healing, purification and strength, and birch leaves for exorcism and cleansing.

Crushed amazonite to heal my aura, and a single stone of aquamarine was added to the cauldron. Aquamarine was the stone of the sea goddess and it represented cleansing, purification and the bringing of peace.

As soon as I added the last ingredient, I closed my eyes to chant, or rather pray, "Taher et nishmati hashekhorah (cleanse my blackened soul)."

I took a deep breath before continuing, "Selah li 'ki hatati (forgive me for I have sinned)."

I poured the potion into a cup carved from aquamarine as I repeated the spell six more times to strengthen the magic within the potion. With my hands shaking, I slowly drank the potion meant to purify my magic.

Once the last drop past my lips, the cup fell to the floor, cracking as I lost all control over my hands. I fell to the floor, my body convulsed, and the potion moved through my body rapidly like a storm. It felt like acid had been poured directly onto my bones. I tried to scream, but no sound came out of my mouth. My body was under the control of the potion. The wraith curse must have been darker than I thought it was for this to cause so much pain.

The pain of the purification ritual felt like it lasted hours, but in reality it was only ten minutes. I could barely move my fingers because of the pain, so getting up, turning back into a mermaid and going to my room was impossible at the moment.

I set my watch orb to wake me up an hour before we needed to leave to meet with our allies before storming the palace. As I fell asleep, I dreamt of blood in the water and hoped it wasn't mine.

CHAPTER 43

The sea was dark. The lights of the city had yet to be turned on as most of the city was still asleep. We chose to lead our attack on the palace and other places of strategic importance at least two hours before the official start of the workday. This was the safest time to attack as there would be fewer guards and servants on the grounds and in the palace, meaning fewer casualties and fewer enemies.

We based this on our initial information. It was highly likely that Grandfather altered the security protocols and increased the number of guards at the palace and nearby, especially considering my visit yesterday (which I still hadn't told my father about).

My group would still enter through the eastern entrance. Hopefully, the first group could disarm the warning system as we weren't far from the palace gates. I looked towards Amari, who was dressed in her finest armour. She would be in a defensive role only. She would not be fighting but focused on taking down the wards and spells surrounding the palace and healing the injured.

Time moved slowly. My armour felt too tight, the straps dug

into my skin, as fear took over again. Why me? Why did I have to be the one to destroy the anchor of the curse? Why not my father? He had the most experience with magic out of the two of us. He should be doing this. Not me.

Despite my whining, my fear, I knew that the anchor was tied to my blood. My blood strengthened it. And my blood would destroy it. I couldn't let my fear take control. If I did, I would lose everything. My father, Michael, my sisters, my freedom. He would kill us all for our actions, for trying to stop him.

"Moriah, you need to address your group. Make sure they know what they're doing," my father whispered to me.

I took a deep breath before turning to address our allies "As we enter through the eastern entrance, we must all be careful. We cannot afford to make mistakes or to draw attention to ourselves before we are all in position. The spell that Amari has cast over us will hold so long as we do not draw attention to ourselves. We enter quickly. Quietly. Sticking to the shadows."

I paused before continuing, "We won't have long before the king and his men arrive to investigate the breach within the wards. Team A has already moved in to disarm the early warning system. If they have failed, then the guards will be ready for us. Which means Team B, my father's team will need to focus on distracting the king only. Team C is with me. We need to get to the centre of the palace to reach the anchor that is holding us prisoner."

I took another breath. "I need you to watch my back. To keep me safe until I've destroyed the anchor and shattered the curse. Not all of us will make it out of this alive. But by the goddess, we will be free. For freedom! For Zoara-Bela," I shouted, raising my spear.

"For Freedom! For Zoara-Bela!"

'Hopefully, my silencing spell holds,' I thought.

"Move out!" I shouted.

It was as we moved towards the entrance that they spotted

us. The first group must have been caught when they went to disarm the warning system. We had to act quickly as lingering here was dangerous and foolish.

We couldn't turn back or try again. This was our only shot at taking down the king. If we failed, then we would die. Everyone we cared for would die.

Our people would perish whether it was in a hundred years or thousands of years from now. The curse will take us all down if it was not broken.

Many soldiers fell within the initial assault of the east entrance. It was supposed to be the least guarded, but with the early warning, it was now probably the most guarded.

The last thing I saw before the whirlwind battle for our freedom began was my father's back as he led the charge towards my grandfather. The adrenaline took over as I headed in the other direction, towards the anchor. I could feel the energy being let off by the magic they were casting at each other. The magic was hot against my skin. The screams of pain from both our allies and his guards echoed in the water, sounding like sirens that rippled outwards from the epicentre.

It was hard to tell which directions the sounds were coming from. The screams. The magic. They surrounded us. Blending in with each other. Each voice was indistinguishable from the next. The sounds seemed a lot louder to me than they were in reality as my fear, my stress and the pressure of the situation I was in made the sounds feel like sandpaper across my skin and in my ears.

While I learnt battle magic from Amari, most of the spells I used in the battle were passive magics and telekinesis that I twisted to suit the battle. I used the spear as a tool to keep the enemy away from me and to channel my magic more effectively. I had some weapons training over the past few months, but nothing complex. Just enough to keep me alive.

Which was why when a guard leapt out from behind a pillar

as the sound overwhelmed me, I didn't think about my actions. It was me or him. Later, I would think about this. About whether there was another way to defeat him. But that was later not now. At the moment with the sounds of battle in my ear, magic scraping across my skin like sandpaper, I raised my spear and channelled a blast of magic designed to reduce stone into dust.

One moment he was there. And the next, he was blood and matter in the water, turning the sea red for a moment, before turning into sea foam. I numbed myself as best I could to the reality around me. I hardly remembered the other lives that I took along the way to Grandfather's private throne room, towards the anchor. Their faces and screams were a blur in my mind.

In my battle haze, a palace guard used magic to blast me into an orichalcum pillar. I fell to the ground in a daze. I touched the back of my head, which ached from the blast, with a ringing in my ears. Blood. I probably had a concussion. I used a basic spell to heal some damage. But in my distraction, the guard attempted to blast me again, this time into pieces. I knew that I wouldn't be able to move out of the way as the concussion had slowed my reaction time.

Before I could comprehend this, I heard Micah scream in agony for a moment, before I felt a shock wave and tasted blood in the water. Micah was dead. He died for me. The guard looked in disbelief at what was once Micah before I leapt forward, stabbing him through the chest with my spear. Jedidiah didn't let me wallow in my pain.

He pulled me up from where Micah had died. I wanted to just scream and cry, but I knew that I couldn't. The longer I was here, the higher the risk of me dying. I needed to move forward. I needed to get to the private throne room. I needed to take down the anchor. I had to push past my anger, fear, my loss and pain to survive. To free us from my grandfather's hold.

Why did it ever come to this? Why couldn't we solve this peacefully? Without a war. Without committing treason. Why didn't he just listen to our concerns?

I'd never wanted this. I'd never wanted anyone to die for me. I'd never wanted merfolk blood spilt. I could feel the tears welling up, my emotions beginning to overcome me. I shook my head. I couldn't let anything or anyone distract me from my goal. I wouldn't let him win. I had too much to lose. We all did. I couldn't let their sacrifices be in vain.

I refused to let their deaths have no meaning. I was so close to the anchor. I could feel its magic as I got closer. It tasted of blood, fear and darkness. It was like an itch at the back of my throat that wouldn't go away, that was slowly progressing into the feel of sandpaper and then rocks as I got closer to my goal. I could taste it.

Jedidiah and I reached the door to the primary throne room which would lead us to our goal. We quickly entered the room, locking the door behind us before we heard the sounds of swords.

'You have got to be kidding me.'

The room was full of soldiers pointing their weapons at us. We looked at each other and readied our weapons before I said to him, "I take the left. You take the right."

"Why do I get the right? You're the one with magic. You fight the big guy. I fight the scrawny ones in that group on the left," whined Jedidiah playfully.

"Nah! Don't feel like it."

The guards in the room got more angrier at our playful banter before I said, "Let's do this."

There was blood in the water and it wasn't ours.

CHAPTER 44

Blood. The smell, the taste of it rested on my tongue as Jedidiah and I fought our way through the throng of soldiers within the chamber. With each death, for every drop of blood spilt by our hands as we fought to the best of our ability, was used against us. The blood we spilt further strengthened the enchantment that anchored the curse.

The anchor was built on unwilling sacrifice, strengthened by a willing sacrifice and the loss of innocence. Our murder of these men. And it was murder, even though they were standing in the way of our goal to freeing our people from the curse. The only reason that this hadn't broken me was because of that.

I couldn't let my emotions cloud my judgement. I hated the fact that I was spilling the blood of my people. Besides, most of the guards and soldiers these days didn't exactly have a choice in working for my grandfather. They were innocent to a degree and that just made the spell stronger.

The darkness and cruelty of the curse's anchor built until we were almost choking on it. Even the remaining soldiers within the room were being affected. I shouted to Jedidiah, "We can't go on much longer. The more blood that is shed. The stronger the curse's anchor will grow."

"I know. But what can we do? If we stop fighting we die. If we don't destroy the anchor holding the curse in place even after your father broke it, then the king will murder you! Just like he murdered your sister to fuel the damn thing!" he shouted back at me.

One general was paying attention to our shouting. He was a son of a lord, a relative of ours who was present at the fall. Besides my father, Judah was one of the handful left that remembered being human and not a merman.

"Stop! Everyone, I order you to halt the fighting!" shouted Judah.

"They're committing treason, General Judah! We were ordered to protect the throne room by the king!"

"Because we were lied to. They have information that we do not. And they will tell us or die," Judah said.

"Very well. Stand down all of you," replied his second in command.

Judah stepped forward and asked us, "Is what you said true? Did your father break the curse that damned us? And did the king knowingly kill your sister to ensure that the curse remained in place even if your father satisfied the requirements to break it? Do not lie to me."

I stepped forward even though Jedidiah tried to hold me back, to protect me. But this was important. If I could convince Judah, the oldest general, that the king was a kin slayer, that he was the reason we were still damned and trapped by an ancient curse, then maybe the fighting would stop.

No more blood would be shed. And he could get the other soldiers and guards in the palace to surrender to my father's rule. To change sides. Despite my hopes, though, I was not stupid enough to be within the reach of his weapon.

"I won't lie. I'll even swear upon my magic. Make an oath so you know that what I tell you is the truth. But in exchange I want you to swear to a truce, bound in magic, so I know that neither you nor your soldiers will attack myself or Jedidiah while I am explaining this to you."

"I agree. Cast the binding truce. Then talk."

As soon as I bound him to a temporary truce with magic, I briefly explained how my father broke the curse and how the king used my mother, my stepmother and Adalina's murders to strengthen the anchor of the curse. How the magic holding the curse in place was unnatural, and that if it was left in place much longer, it would destroy Zoara-Bela.

I could tell my desperation and fear was etched upon my face even though I tried to hide it. I hoped that I could convince him to let us destroy the anchor. I had enough blood on my hands. I didn't want more. Which was why I swore the most binding oath upon my magic to confirm it. I knew that everything I said was the truth. The brief flash of light from my oath merely confirmed that for him.

We waited in silence for Judah's response. To find out if we needed to continue fighting. After a few minutes, he nodded and said, "What do you need us to do to break this curse?"

I sighed in relief before replying, "I need you to open the private throne room and lead me to a crystal type ornament or monument within the room that is encased in or framed by orichalcum. That is what he is using to hold the magic in place. We also need the rest of your men to hold anyone who tries to stop us from destroying the anchor. We need them to buy us time. It won't be long before the king gets here. I can sense his magic getting closer."

"Very well. Men. You heard her. Form a perimeter. Ensure that no one enters the room before the curse is broken," shouted Judah.

"Sir, how will we know the curse is broken?"

"Trust me, you'll know. It will cause a shock wave."

"I wasn't asking you!"

"I know you weren't. But I replied because I'm the one who has studied magic," I replied before turning to Judah "Let's move."

The door to the private throne room was strengthened by magic. Just the standard avoidance and shock wards. Still, I didn't touch the door as I used my magic to find a loose thread within its protections, unravelling in its entirety before blasting it open. The crystal of the anchor was glowing an ominous crimson, growing darker every time blood was spilt.

I swam as close as possible to the anchor without touching it.

Judah asked, "Is that it? How do we destroy it?"

The screams of the other soldiers who were trying to distract Abaddon while I attempted to break the anchor echoed within my brain. But I stayed silent as I examined the most complex piece of magic that I had ever seen. I was not a master of the ancient arts. I was merely at the journeyman level.

I didn't know the specific way to break the curse without destroying us. Not yet. I knew the basics of breaking curses and unravelling wards. But this was more complex than anything that I've ever done.

"You know how to destroy it, right?"

"To a degree. But I've never broken a spell of this calibre. It is complex. He's combined multiple spells and rituals to create this. Making it harder to decipher. Not impossible, but harder. If I try to hurry the breaking of the anchor without knowing exactly which spells to undo first, I'll end up destroying the city."

The screams died off as Judah replied, "We don't have much time. Hurry!"

"The city could be destroyed if I do it wrong!"

"I know! But either way, we will be dead! Our people will be dead if it stays in place. I'll buy you time. Now hurry!"

"Thank you, Judah."

I circled the anchor, identifying the different threads that had been tied together to create the anchor. It took me a minute to find the weakest thread in the anchor. I closed my eyes to channel my magic into the weakness in the stone.

And through that weakness, I could loosen the ties that bind us. Making what was once like tightly woven chainmail into a sieve, letting the magic drain away. Weakening it further.

Bang! The door blasted open, sending Jedidiah and Judah flying into a pillar. My grandfather had found us. But I couldn't stop my magic. If I stopped concentrating on breaking the anchor, then the magic would backlash horribly against me.

"Oh, Moriah. You should have taken my offer and signed the contract I gave you at our last meeting," he said as he lifted his trident, the symbol of his power, to kill me.

But Jedidiah and Judah attempted to distract him. Grandfather was too powerful. His magic blasted them again and this time neither of them got up. My ears were ringing. My head was throbbing from my concussion.

My grandfather attacked me, blasting me away from the anchor that vibrated dangerously. I struggled to breathe as Grandfather's magic froze me in place, choking me, but I still didn't let go of the magic that I was using to unravel the anchor. But then I suddenly could move. The magic holding me in place was gone.

My father attacked Abaddon, distracting him for me. I swam closer to the anchor, stretching out my hand as if trying to physically grab hold of something, and then I pulled with all my might. I fully unravelled the magic holding the anchor in place before I threw my spear at the crystal, shouting, "Litroff (devour)."

This was the spell activating a stronger drain of Abaddon's magic. The crystal shattered it into a thousand pieces. The shards were thrown across the room along with the shockwave and the blinding flash of light that flowed outwards from the room as the curse broke.

My grandfather screamed as the backlash of the magic turned on him because of it breaking. His magic was no longer strong enough to fight the backlash as my wraith spell had drained his magic.

While it weakened him, my father took his trident and ran him through with it. Abaddon attempted to use his magic to kill his son, to take my father down with him. But I was quicker. Without thinking, I used enough force with my spear to sever his head from his shoulders. It floated for a moment in the water before turning into sea foam. He was the last body that would turn into sea foam, as this was his punishment for defying the rules of nature.

His arrogance and cruelty were his weakness. And now they were his doom.

CHAPTER 45

In the moments after the king's death, with the support of Judah, we forced the other soldiers to surrender. Most did without argument. But some genuinely supported and believed in what Grandfather preached. Unfortunately, they were sentenced to death once we used magic to confirm that they would never give allegiance to us. To my father. While he was busy ensuring that none who supported Grandfather and helped him keep the curse intact got free, Amari and I went to the dungeons.

It was there that we found my sister Amina, in chains that slowly drained her of magic, and Michael, who was encased in crystal. Amari worked on freeing Michael, as the spell was more complex and she was more experienced than I. I looked at my sister and she was almost unrecognisable.

She was completely covered in bruises with years of dirt, sand, and algae covering her skin and tail. The years of captivity had aged her physically, even though as a mermaid she shouldn't have aged. But she should recover in time. I stared at her blue eyes with a smile on my face as I gently placed my hand on her cheek. There were tears in my eyes.

"Hello, big sister," I said, "It is very nice to see you again."

She stared at me in confusion before her eyes cleared as she slowly recognised me.

"Moriah? Is that you?"

"Yes. It's me. I'm so glad I found you," I said as I hugged her.

"But … you can't be here. If Grandfather finds you, he'll kill you."

"You don't have to worry. Grandfather is dead. Father will be crowned in the next few weeks. You're free. Here, let me remove these chains."

The chains shattered as I unravelled the spells holding her in the cell before I helped her out of it. She clung to me in disbelief and wonder as she was free for the first time in years. As we made our way down the corridor towards Michael's cell, I could see him struggling to stand next to Amari. She'd found a way for him to breathe underwater without drowning. As soon as I saw his face I let go of my sister and tackled him, hugging him tightly.

"You're okay," I said to him with tears in my eyes.

"Yeah. Moriah. I'm sorry. I thought the message was from you. I didn't know until I got there that it was your grandfather. I tried to get away. I'm sorry," said Michael.

"Michael, you don't have to apologise. He was thousands of years old. He knew tricks that we didn't. I didn't know that the watch orb could be traced or hacked. If I did, I would have been more careful."

"Neither of you should be apologising. You both didn't have the information you needed, and that wasn't your fault. You were both as careful as possible. Besides, he may have found Michael anyway," Amari said.

"What do you mean?"

"There's a reason he can see through magic, especially through disguises, even though he's human. It's the same reason the spell to allow him to breathe beneath the sea even works on him. Moriah … he's Chava's descendant, my legacy. As my legacy, despite how distant, he has a unique magical signature that would have got stronger with every exposure to magic, whether he used it himself or not."

"He's the legacy of the woman my father accidentally killed."

"What do you mean accidentally? He murdered her."

"No. He didn't. She threw herself on his sword to escape the pain. He found out too late that Grandfather had sentenced her to death and that he gave her to the men of his court. By the time he reached her, she was broken mentally. He tried to take her away from there. But she thought he would prolong her suffering, so she killed herself. It wasn't his fault. He showed me the memory. You can get him to show you. But you shouldn't blame him."

"It won't happen overnight."

"I know."

"I'll try, but no promises."

"That's fine by me. Now let's go to the throne room and see my father."

I took Michael's hand and wrapped my other arm around my sister's shoulders as we made our way to my father. Upon entering the throne room, I saw my father and my other sisters. Bruised and battered, but smiling and free. They had executed the lords that were keeping Cassiopeia and Davida hostage. My family was almost whole for the first time in years.

None of us were all right, but we would be. All of us would need time to heal and process all that happened to us. Even Michael. Which was why, despite all that happened and all the responsibilities that fell upon my shoulders, I made sure that Michael received all the support he needed to recover. I didn't want him to feel forgotten, even though my family still needed to learn how to be with each other again, because he was important to me.

Which was why weeks later, when my father was to be

crowned king, I made sure that he had a seat next to my sisters and I. I wanted him to know how important he was to me. I wanted Zoara-Bela to know that he was the reason they now had freedom. My sisters and I were all declared to be the 'crown princesses' as we were his heirs. But to my surprise, Father made another announcement.

"Moriah. Step forward!"

I had no idea about what would happen.

My father continued, "Moriah. What can I say? You are the reason we are all here today. This wouldn't have been possible if you weren't brave enough to fight against Abaddon. You changed the hearts and minds of those around you. Inspired hope and determination. Encouraged freedom. Which is why I declare you my heir. You shall be queen after me. I will stay king until you are ready to take the throne. Come forward and kneel in front of me."

In shock, I did exactly as he asked. He tapped me on the shoulders with his trident before placing the crown that only the heirs wear in my hair. He then shouted, "Rise Moriah. Future Queen of Zoara-Bela."

He continued, "In honour of her and all those who died because of my father's cruelty, I make a proclamation. I declare that all merfolk are free. Slavery is now illegal. No mermaid or merman will be owned by another. Mermaids are no longer the property of their male relatives. They have minds and wills of their own. My daughter is the perfect example of why mermaids should be valued and treated as their own persons."

He paused for a moment to gather his thoughts, "All merfolk shall have equal rights in law and tradition regardless of class and wealth. We shall over the next few years ensure that all people within our nation receive education and support they need to succeed. We know that this will take time, but all things that are worth it take time. And this is worth it."

The party that ensued after the ceremony lasted well into

the next morning. Michael and I returned to the surface world to see the sunrise together for the first time since the rebellion. The sun was warm upon my skin. The sky was painted orange, yellow and purple with dashes of white and blue. We stood on the sand and in silence for what felt like hours before he asked, "What's going to happen? Where do we go from here?"

"I want to still be friends. To hang out with you. If you still want me," I ask nervously.

"Yes. Yes. I still want to be friends. I want you in my life," he said before gently grabbing my hand.

"Are you all right with everything that happened?"

"No, but I don't think anyone is all right. But I will be as long as you're with me."

I continued smiling as I looked at his face, framed with warm light.

We were not okay now, but we would be. That was all anyone could ask for. Maybe love would have a chance to grow between people from two unique worlds like Michael and I.

I didn't know for sure, but I looked forward to finding out.

CHAPTER 46

In the battle's aftermath and my being named as the primary heir to the throne, Michael and I began dating. In the beginning everything was perfect, but as time went on, maintaining a positive romantic relationship became more difficult. We both threw ourselves into a romantic relationship, so happy to be alive and together that we never gave ourselves time to heal from our trauma. I knew that it wasn't healthy, but I didn't care because I could finally be with him. So I ignored my trauma, pretended that battle didn't happen, and it worked for a while.

My moods became erratic, unpredictable, I could be happy one moment and furious the next. My meltdowns became more frequent, lasting longer and becoming harder to manage as even the smallest thing could trigger me. I tried so hard to be this perfect, normal person and ignored my health. I had planned on ignoring my problems for as long as I could.

At first, everything had been going well. Both of us were having fun until we went into the water together for the first time in months. I was the calmest I had been in months. But Michael, after a few minutes, had got jittery and started breathing erratically.

I looked at him in concern. "Michael, are you all right?"

He refused to look me in the eye. "I'm fine."

"Do you want to get out of the water?"

"I told you I'm fine."

As I looked at him I realised that he would not admit that something was wrong. So I lied. "I'm starting to get hungry. Why don't we go get out the water to get an early lunch?"

He looked relieved as he said, "Yeah. Let's go."

As we began swimming back to shore a wave crashed over us. It was only when I stood up that I realised that Michael was still underwater. He was thrashing erratically, struggling to break the surface despite the relative calmness of the water, so I pulled him up and kept his head above water. It was like he was trapped in a memory as he continued thrashing violently. If I was a normal human woman, I wouldn't have been able to pull him to shore as he fought against me. He kept on thrashing even though I had got the both of us to shore.

"Michael! Michael, it's all right. You're safe. We're not in the water anymore."

Minutes felt like hours as Michael was trapped within a memory. When he finally came out of the flashback, I sat with him as he began breathing in deeply, trying to calm himself.

"Are you all right?" I said as I attempted to place my hand on his shoulder.

He flinched, moving back, lightly hitting my hand away as he said, "I'm fine."

"No, you're not."

"I told you I'm fine."

"Michael, you just flinched when I went to touch your shoulder. You're not all right."

He looked horrified as he realised what he had done, "I'm sorry. I didn't realise ... I didn't mean to."

"I know you didn't. You just came out of a flashback, reacting like this is normal."

"Normal. Nothing about this is normal. A wave crashed over us and all I could think about was being trapped within that crystal, unable to move or breathe. How is that even remotely normal? You're my girlfriend and I can't even let you comfort me. What the hell is wrong with me?"

He looked like he would burst into tears at any moment as his shoulders began shaking.

"Look, why don't we both get changed and go to your apartment. I'll order some lunch and when we have both calmed down, we'll talk. Ok?"

He took in a deep breath before nodding. "Yeah."

As we started changing into our clothes, I realised that neither of us were all right.

After lunch we sat quietly on the sofa, refusing to look at each other's faces. I had fiddled with the bracelet that Michael had given me as a gift as I waited for him to speak.

"Well, this is awkward," he said.

We looked at each other for a moment before bursting out laughing at how ridiculous we were being. We used to talk to each other about everything—our fears, worries and hopes. We kept nothing secret. Now, look at us. We could barely talk about our day as we avoided thinking about our trauma.

"I'm sorry about earlier. I knew that you were looking forward to showing me the coral reef nearby. I didn't mean for it to happen."

"I know. You had a flashback, Michael. You can't control that."

"But I should have realised—"

"What?"

"That I would react like that. I should have known."

"We haven't been in the ocean since I was named the

primary heir to the throne, so how could you have known that it could trigger a flashback?"

"Still, I shouldn't have let it get to me. I used to go surfing for fun, for god's sake."

"Michael, it's not your fault you had a flashback. It's not something you can control."

"But I should've been able to snap myself out of it. It happened months ago, why can't I get over it? You've been able to."

I closed my eyes as I realised that my pretending to be all right made him feel like he couldn't talk to anyone about what happened to him, not even me.

I took a deep breath before I said, "I haven't got over it. I just got better at hiding it."

"What?"

"What happened to you terrified me. I keep thinking that one day you will disappear. And I know that Abaddon is gone. But I'm still terrified that one of his supporters will take you again, despite knowing that we were able to track down and get rid of most of them."

He looked startled. "I didn't know."

"I know. I didn't want you to know that I wasn't coping. And I should've told you that instead of throwing myself into a relationship that neither of us were ready for."

"I love you."

"I know. I love you too. But you have to admit that mentally neither of us were ready for a romantic relationship. We were so relieved that we no longer had to fear being caught with each other and that we could finally be together that we didn't deal with what happened to us."

"Moriah, what are you saying?"

"I'm saying that we both need help. And that may be taking a break in our relationship so we can get the help we need, might be a good idea."

It broke my heart to say that, but I knew it was the right thing to do. We couldn't go on like this. I didn't want us to end up hating each other, which I knew would happen if we continued ignoring our problems.

"I guess you're right."

"I wish I wasn't."

There were tears in his eyes as he said, "If I promise to go see a psychologist about my kidnapping, will you do the same?"

I placed my hand on top of his. "I promise."

"What happens now? With our relationship?"

"We can keep hanging out as friends. Just not going on dates. We both need time to heal. I'll start looking for a psychologist to help me with … well … my childhood, your kidnapping and the battle. Maybe convince my sisters to see a therapist of their own. Growing up the way we did damaged all of us. And when we're both ready, we could give our relationship another go."

"I'd like that. But do you even know how to find a psychologist?"

"I knew I forgot something."

We looked at each other for a moment before bursting out laughing. It felt good to laugh again. To my surprise, for the first time in months, we just talked with each other without pretending to be all right. We were damaged but finally willing to get the help we needed.

We were us again.

CHAPTER 47

Since pausing our relationship, both Michael and I had been seeing psychologists to help us heal from our trauma. However, he had better luck in finding a psychologist that he could stand. Me, not so much. So far, all my attempts at seeking therapy failed because the clinics continually scheduled sessions with male psychologists despite the fact that I asked for a female psychologist. Hopefully, today's session with my new psychologist would go better than my previous sessions, not that I had much hope about that.

My hands shook as I stood before the door proclaiming the various qualifications of Dr Valentina. I hated standing before doors like this one as it told me nothing about the person within the room. I straightened my back and took a deep breath as I raised my shaking fist to the door, knocking twice.

"Come in," said the doctor.

The door muffled their voice like every other session I've been to. I couldn't tell if the voice belonged to a man or woman because of it. Slowly, I turned the handle with my hand still shaking and opened the door.

To my surprise and relief, there was a woman in the room.

She had a smile on her face as she walked towards me. She had warm brown hair and eyes with tanned skin. There were slight lines around her mouth and eyes.

She appeared to be the same age as Michael's parents were. But she seemed much kinder than his parents. There was a genuine warmth in her eyes and I felt myself relax as she closed the door behind me.

"Miss Adel, I'm Dr Cara Valentina. Why don't you take a seat, make yourself comfortable before we get started?"

"Thank you," I said as I moved to sit on the grey couch.

The room was decorated in greys, whites and beige tones with small bursts of colour from small decorations.

"Here you go," she said as she placed a glass of water on the table in front of me.

"Thank you."

"Miss Adel—"

When people called me by my false last name, I sometimes didn't know who they were talking to, which was why I cut her off, "Moriah, please."

She nodded, "Before we start with the session, I will introduce myself and explain what to expect within these sessions should you go ahead with future sessions."

"Ok."

"Like I mentioned earlier, I am Dr Valentina. I'm a clinical psychologist, specialising in trauma. As a clinical psychologist, I focus on assessing, diagnosing and treating individuals with mental, behavioural and emotional issues, particularly relating to trauma which is my specialisation. If you continue with these sessions, I will work with you to create a management or treatment plan that suits you."

She paused before continuing, "The purpose of the plan is to create goals for your treatment, measurable objectives and a timeline for treatment progress. This will need to be constructed over multiple sessions, but it can also be reviewed and edited as we move forward, especially if goals change. Now, today's session is mainly focused on getting to know you before making a psychiatric evaluation, which will allow us to create a treatment plan. Do you have any questions?"

"No. Not at the moment."

"Let's begin with something simple."

"Like what?"

"Your favourite colour?"

"Sky blue."

"Why?"

I could feel myself beginning to smile as I remembered having a similar conversation with Michael. "Because the sky is freedom. No one can touch it or tell it what to do."

The questions asked were simple, things that I didn't mind talking about, but eventually she asked a question that made me pause. As a mermaid, there were things that I couldn't talk about as keeping our secret was our most important law.

I took a deep breath before saying, "What about my family?"

"Some basic information to start with. How about their names and what they're like?"

I ran my fingers through my hair and began twirling and tugging on my curls as I thought about my answer.

"I grew up with my father, Abdiel and my grandfather, Abaddon."

"What about your mother?"

"That's ... complicated."

"How so?"

"The woman I believed to be my mother was actually my stepmother, she took me in after my birth mother's murder, although I was proof that her husband wasn't loyal to her. She died when I was a toddler."

"What happened?"

"She was poisoned. My grandfather killed her because she

had enough evidence to get him arrested if she got my sisters and me away from the compound."

"Have you told the police?"

"What's the point? He's dead. He died about four months ago."

"What happened?"

My shoulders tensed as flashes of the battle and the blood in the water rose to the surface. I closed my eyes, took a deep breath and ignored the memory.

"I don't want to talk about it," I said sharply.

"We will have to talk about this eventually if you go ahead with future sessions."

"I know. But not today."

"All right, you mentioned sisters. What are they like?"

"I don't know. I was young when they disappeared. I didn't remember them, not even the one sister I was old enough to remember because I blocked it out."

"Blocked it out?"

"I was there when ... my grandfather murdered her."

"How old were you?" she said with a horrified look on her face.

"I was about five years old."

"What was her name?"

"Adalina."

"What about your other sisters?"

"We were able to find and rescue Cassiopeia, Davida and Amina about four months ago."

She was about to ask me something else when the timer went off, signalling the end of the session.

Just before I left, she asked, "If you feel comfortable, we can continue with another session next week. The receptionist at the front will book you in."

"I would like that," I said as I walked out the door.

CHAPTER 48

A few weeks after I had attended my counselling sessions with Dr Valentina, I kept thinking the same thing repeatedly—should I have asked my family to attend therapy sessions with me?

Dr Valentina had suggested a group therapy session with another doctor because despite having been free for months my relationship with my sisters was still non-existent. We didn't know how to speak to each other and when we were together so we pretended that our trauma didn't exist.

I didn't think they had even attempted anything beyond physical recovery. In fact, I knew they hadn't; Zora-Bela had nothing even remotely similar to the therapies available in the human world. If nothing was done, our inability to talk with each other and with our father would blow up in our faces.

I didn't think any of my sisters even knew about the treatments available in the human world that could help them deal with their problems, because they have been imprisoned or oppressed their entire lives. They needed help that neither my father nor I could give them.

I knew that before we could attend any group therapy

sessions that we needed to have more confidence in ourselves, and we needed to have made some progress in our own personal trauma before we could tackle our damaged relationships. I wasn't in a place, mentally, where I could attend a group therapy session with my sisters, let alone my father. But I couldn't stand to see my sisters suffer in silence without getting the help they needed. So, I asked my sisters to meet with me in our mother's garden.

"Moriah, why have you asked us to come here? There's nothing here that we haven't seen before," said Cassiopeia.

I just smiled as I asked them to follow me. I knew that part of the reason they had not built a relationship with me was because they were angry and jealous that our father had only interfered, only helped them because I was in danger. It was not my fault, but emotions weren't rational. I was doing the only thing that I could do to help them in some small way, which would hopefully give them the closure they needed regarding our mother's death.

Cassiopeia, Amina and Davida were demanding answers as I had opened the secret door leading to our mother's study. I said nothing because I didn't know what to say, so I kept silent until we entered the study.

Before they could demand more answers from me, I said, "This was Mother's study, Andromeda's study. She kept all her notes, all her spells in here. But when I was looking for a way to weaken Grandfather, I found a recording from her. She didn't just give me the spell I needed to defeat the king; she left a message for all of us. She made a whole new spell, a ritual, to save the three of you because she loved you more than anything. In all her notes, every recording, she thought of you and ways to save you. Before she died, she had created a plan to rescue all of you. She wanted to take all of us to the human world before taking down the king. She wanted us safe."

"What do you mean?" Davida said, looking at me with her red-rimmed sea-green eyes.

Before I could say anything, Cassiopeia swam towards the desk and touched the decorated box, tracing the decorations lightly with her oddly twisted fingers. The joints of her fingers were bent slightly out of shape, slightly swollen, as if they had been broken so many times that her body no longer remembered what her fingers were supposed to look like.

As I stared at her, I noticed that her blue eyes had dulled. They had a watery look to them as if she was holding back her tears. Her lips trembled and her hands shook as she opened the decorated box and, upon recognising the item within, she sobbed.

Amina and Davida moved forward to comfort our oldest sister, who was sobbing as she gently picked up our mother's crown.

"I remember her wearing this. She loved this crown … Father made this for her with his own hands … to show her he loved her and that he loved me even though I wasn't his by blood. Princes weren't supposed to give gifts to former servant girls or peasants," said Cassiopeia softly.

"I didn't know that."

"I'm not surprised. She stopped wearing this crown after they forced Cassiopeia to marry that monster because she fell in love with a human. She said that she wouldn't wear that crown again until Cassiopeia was free. Because if he really loved her, he wouldn't have let the king get away with selling Cassiopeia to that monster," Amina said as she placed her hand on Cassiopeia's shoulder.

I tried not to stare at Amina's wrists, which were heavily scarred from the manacles that kept her chained in the dungeon. I always felt guilty when I looked at the scars on my sisters' bodies because our father fought to keep me safe my entire life, but he did nothing to protect them. Amina had thin white scars across her spine, arms and teal dolphin-shaped tail, which was also missing several scales because of the removal of barnacles that had grown on her during her imprisonment in the dungeons.

The scarring on Cassiopeia and Davida's throats and mouths from being silenced and their twisted limbs that had healed wrongly reminded me of the fate I'd barely escaped.

I didn't know if the guilt I felt was mine or the echoes of my fathers' guilt from the memory orb. I knew from his memory that they were so much like me. Looking at Cassiopeia reminded me of how lucky I really was because I knew for a fact her story could have been mine. If I had been caught before I learnt enough magic to fight back. If Amari had refused to teach me. If Father refused to help me or if I had been caught planning a rebellion by the guards—I would have been her.

I didn't know what to say to my sisters to comfort them. I didn't think reaching out and placing my hand on their shoulders or trying to hug them would help. I swam behind the desk and opened the drawer containing the chest with the ritual I used to weaken the king.

My hands shook as I gave the chest to Davida who read the inscription carved into the chest, "To my darling daughters, simply say the name of the destroyer who brings ruin in his wake and it shall open."

Her fingers traced the individual letters carved into the chest with amazement as she said, "This is a mother's handwriting … as a child I would watch her carve letters into orichalcum sheets. She would have to use magic to engrave on orichalcum because every time she did it by hand the words were always a little tilted or wonky."

"What is this? What's inside?" Amina asked.

There was a brief smile on my face. "Why don't you open it and find out?" I nearly laughed as she looked at me with her eyebrows raised. "Davida read the inscription. You already know how to open it."

Davida's mouth opened slightly as she realised how to open the chest and said, "Abaddon."

"Besides the spell she created to weaken Grandfather, she left a message for all of us. I looked at the date on the recording. She made this only hours before she was killed. She left messages for the three of you, and Adalina and I. Would you like me to play it?"

They nodded as I activated the recording orb, skipping the details of the casting of the spell I used to weaken grandfather. Even though Amina was the only one besides me to have any real training in magic, I knew that they would all realise that the spell and ritual I used was black magic. I didn't want them to look at me like I was a monster, so I kept quiet about the details of the spell.

As the projection ended with our mother's smile, her image had just faded when I felt the shaking arms of all my sisters wrapped around me.

This was the first time they'd hugged me. I could feel the roughness of Amina's skin and tail on my left, her brown hair nearly indistinguishable from Davida's copper hair as they both tried to place their heads on my left shoulder.

Cassiopeia had practically tackled my right side as her head of fiery red hair rested against my other shoulder, her arms wrapped tight around my middle and her tail wrapping around mine. Her hair tickled my nose; Davida's and Amina's made my skin itch as they all sobbed against me.

I slowly placed my arms around my sisters and gently patted their shoulders to try comforting them. It was only when I felt them squeeze tighter that I finally relaxed, closing my eyes and letting myself be held.

We spent hours in the study cradling each other as we told stories about our mother and our childhood. When we finally ran out of stories, my sisters seemed lighter, happier than when they first entered the room. They weren't in any way healed from their trauma. Healing would take time. They wouldn't be able to do it on their own. I could be there for them, support them, but I couldn't help them heal.

Our connection as sisters was finally beginning to grow which was why I suggested, quietly, avoiding their eyes, "On the surface, there are humans who are trained to help people heal from their trauma. There are some who specialise in helping humans who were treated the same way you were or who went through situations similar to you. Maybe seeing one of these specialists might help you heal."

"Did they help you?" Amina said.

"Yes."

"But they're human. How can you talk to them when magic is such an enormous part of who you are?" Davida asked.

"I use human words to talk about what happened. Most of what I talk about with her can be explained without mentioning magic. If something involves magic, I either try to describe it using human technology or I just don't mention the magic. She will make assumptions based on her human knowledge."

"And that helps?"

"Yes. Talking with someone who wasn't involved helps. She helps me understand why I feel a certain way and how to deal with what I'm feeling."

They looked at each other silently before Cassiopeia said, "We would need to know more about the human world first. My knowledge is over sixteen years out of date."

CHAPTER 49

As I waited for Michael at our usual table, I thought about how Zoara-Bela was almost unrecognisable because of how fast things had changed in the past year. Father had been strictly enforcing the laws about slavery, the treatment of maidens and the poor. Sometimes when I saw him rule or make decisions in court, I was uncomfortably reminded of Grandfather. While the changes made in Zoara-Bela have been positive, mostly, the king's rule was absolute. Zoara-Bela wasn't perfect, but it was better than it was before.

I snapped out of my daze when I heard Michael call my name; turning towards him I smiled brightly. When he came closer, I hugged him tightly, kissing him on the cheek, before grabbing his hand and leading him to our usual table with a bounce in my step. Not long after we placed our order, we started talking excitedly about the courses we were doing at the local university—he was studying to be a counsellor. I had started a creative writing course because I adored the stories and poems that he would read to me so much that I wanted to create my own.

As he spoke, waving his arms with excitement, I noticed that his green eyes looked brighter and happier than I had ever seen before. He felt lighter somehow. The darkness that used to be in his eyes was more like a shade that had nearly been extinguished.

There was a slight pause in our conversation as Michael asked, "How's Zoara-Bela?"

"Things are better. It's not perfect, but it's better than what it was."

"What do you mean?"

"I mean that we have laws that guarantee rights for all citizens—not just powerful mermen."

"Like the Universal Declaration of Human Rights?"

"I actually copied it, changing a few words and phrases here and there to make it more suitable for Merfolk. Most of the clauses have been put into effect, a few are still being debated on because of the wording. It's taking time for these changes to actually influence the people but to be honest, I'm just happy that things are changing at all."

"What about your dad?"

"He's trying his best to help us deal with what happened to us but he's the king which means he doesn't have much time to spare. We could barely get him to agree to attend group counselling sessions with my sisters and me."

"Really? How'd they go?"

"Um ... They've got better."

"That bad, huh?"

"Yeah. There was a lot of yelling in the first few sessions. Usually, it was my sisters who did the yelling, mostly Cassiopeia—"

"And you."

"Ok, so I may have joined in on the yelling."

"May have?"

"Fine. Definitely joined in on the yelling. He deserved it."

Michael stared at me as he raised his eyebrow.

"You have to admit he had it coming. He literally did nothing to protect my sisters. And don't get me started on the lying and the brainwashing. Did I mention the brainwashing?" I said, waving my hands in the air.

Michael's lips twitched.

"What?" I asked.

I rolled my shoulders, huffing as I looked away. From the corner of my eye, I noticed Michael struggling to hold back his laughter at my reaction. Pouting as I turned back towards him I said, "What?"

He stayed silent, his shoulders shaking as I exaggerated my pout until he burst out laughing. His laughter was contagious as I laughed alongside him. It took a few minutes before we finally stopped laughing.

There was a slight giggle in Michael's voice as he asked, "How are your sisters?"

"Better. They've been seeing therapists individually, not just as a group with Father and I. Amina and Davida have been visiting the surface more often outside of their therapy sessions."

I paused for a moment as we both stood up to go to register to pay. As we walked towards the line in front of the cash register, I continued, "In fact, Cassiopeia's actually about to finish her session for the day. I'm planning on meeting her here before taking her to a concert in the city. She's never been to one before. Amina and Davida decided not to go at the last moment. I have two extra tickets. Would you like to come with us?"

Before he could reply Cassiopeia came bouncing towards us asking, "Are you ready to go?"

I laughed. "We still have plenty of time to get to the concert Cassiopeia. Besides, I want you to meet someone."

She tilted her head sideways, "Who?"

I smiled, "Cassiopeia, this is my friend Michael. Michael, this is my oldest sister Cassiopeia."

"Nice to meet you," he said with a smile on his face.

As I finished paying the cashier for our meal Cassiopeia turned towards me with a smile on her face. "I can see why you like him. She never stops talking about you, by the way."

"I … uh … Shut up!" I said as my cheeks warmed.

"Have you asked him to come with us to the concert yet? We have spare tickets, don't we?" she said walking backwards towards the exit.

There was still a still bounce in her step. How she hadn't lost her balance or bumped into anyone yet was a miracle.

I rolled my eyes before replying, "I have asked him. And I would have already known the answer if you didn't interrupt us."

"Oops! Sorry," she said while twirling around.

I looked at Michael who had an indulgent smile on his face as I asked, "So would you like to come with us to the concert?"

"I wouldn't want to interrupt your quality time with your sister."

Before I could reply I heard my sister yelp, "I'm so sorry. I wasn't looking at where I was going."

"I could tell," said the young man.

Michael and I turned to look at the young man who caught my sister. He had a smile on his face despite having a strange woman trip and literally fall into his arms. He looked older than Michael, close to the age of Cassiopeia's physical appearance. He had chocolate brown eyes, olive skin and light brown hair curled around his ears.

My sister kept on staring at his chocolate brown eyes and when he smiled at her before asking, "What made you so excited that you fell into my arms?"

I nearly laughed as she stammered and her cheeks became redder.

"I'm going to the concert in the city tonight," she said while twirling her bright red hair.

"The Nevermore fundraiser concert?"

"Yes."

"You really like the band that much?" he said with a slight laugh in his voice. I could see her blush and twirl her hair.

"Actually, I have never been to a concert before," Cassiopeia said.

"Really? Well, I'm going to the same concert. I could meet you at the Morningstar Restaurant before the concert and show you around the city if you want."

She chattered excitedly with the young man. I shook my head and turned back to Michael, "You wouldn't be interrupting."

"Sorry, what?"

"You wouldn't be interrupting my time with Cassiopeia. That is … if you want to come with us to the Nevermore concert."

"I would love to come."

"It's a date … that is if you want it to be a date?" I said slowly.

Just as he was about to answer Cassiopeia bounced back towards us. "He asked me to meet him at the Morningstar Restaurant before the concert."

"I know. I heard."

She was still twirling her hair as she said, "Is it ok if I stay here a bit longer to talk with him?"

"It's fine."

"Are you sure?"

"Yes. Seriously, you're thousands of years older than me. You don't have to ask for permission to talk with a man."

"I know. I just didn't want to leave you without asking, just in case you planned anything else."

I shook my head, "I planned nothing else. Talk with him. Just remember to meet me at the beach house by five o'clock so I can help you get ready for your date."

"It's not a date. Is it?"

"He asked you to meet him at a restaurant before the concert, most likely to have dinner. It's definitely a date."

"Really?" she said while glancing at the man she fell into.

"Yes. Now go talk to him."

"I will. See you Michael, it was nice meeting you."

"It was nice meeting you too," he replied.

"And I'll see you at the beach house at five o'clock, Moriah."

Before she left, I asked, "What's his name?"

"Raphael Marino," she said before twirling on the spot and going back towards Raphael.

"It looks like Cassiopeia isn't the only one with a date tonight," Michael said softly.

I turned towards him, "You mean it."

"Yeah. I'm ready to give our relationship another go. That is if you want the same thing?" he said as he held his hand out for me to take.

I slipped my hand into his, grasping it tightly, as I replied, "I'd like that."

I smiled as we walked out of the cafe, where my sister was still talking to Raphael, hand in hand. My sister was being given a second chance, not just to heal from her trauma but at finding love. A chance she literally tripped into.

As Michael and I walked down the street, I leaned against him, my head resting against his shoulder. It was nearing the end of winter; the sea breeze was no longer bitterly cold and the sun finally felt warm against my skin.

Spring had come early this year, bringing with it many new beginnings. I didn't know what would happen in the future. None of us did. But I look forward to finding out.

Don't you?

AFTERWORD

My inspiration for *Voiceless* came to me as I watched writing videos by my favourite authors on YouTube and listened to *Poor Unfortunate Souls* on repeat.

I always loved *The Little Mermaid* growing up. She was different, an outsider who sacrificed everything for love. She struggled with her identity and finding her place in a world that eventually silenced her. But there were things in both the original fairytale and the Disney version that made me uncomfortable as I grew older.

As I wrote *Voiceless*, I thought about the choices the little mermaid made in the original tale and knew that I wanted her to make different choices, to grow as a person rather than a damsel in distress. There were moments in both versions where the little mermaid stood up for herself and made choices of her own. I wanted my little mermaid to be more than a mermaid who fell in love with a human at first sight.

As a coming of age story, I explore and mention many serious issues that affect young people today through the eyes of Moriah as she discovers who she is and what she wants.

Throughout the novel, there are mentions of sexual assault,

abuse, forced marriage and suicidal thoughts. I also explore mental illness such as depression and PTSD directly connected to abuse and trauma.

Mental health is an important issue facing young people today. Approximately 1 in 5 young people between 15 and 19 years old meet the criteria for serious mental illness such as anxiety and depression. Suicide is the second leading cause of death for young people aged between 15 and 24.

If you or someone you know is struggling with their mental health or needs help, there are many support services available, most of them anonymous, in every country.

For those living in Australia:

1. **Headspace**: 1800 650 890
2. **Kids Help Line**: 1800 55 1800
3. **Beyond Blue**: 1300 224 636
4. **1800Respect:** 1800 737 732

These services provided online or by telephone are confidential, free and private.

REFERENCES:

Black Dog Institute 2020, 'Facts and Figures about Mental Health', Black Dog Institute, <https://www.blackdoginstitute. org.au/wp-content/uploads/2020/04/1-facts_figures.pdf>

ACKNOWLEDGMENTS

I would like to thank my family and friends who have supported me throughout my journey as both an author and teacher. They gave me the strength to continue pushing forward regardless of the obstacles in my way. They gave me hope for a better future. My parents, Silvia and Norman, and my brother Raymond have been my biggest supporters. Thank you so much for your help and support.

I would also like to thank my developmental editor Angela Traficante, my copy editor Ash Spring and my proofreader Kathy DC (Fiverr); and my cover designer Vishnu Remesh (99 Designs) for all their hard work in helping me produce this novel.

ABOUT THE AUTHOR

Anna Finch lives in Melbourne, Australia, where she works as a teacher of English and Humanities by day and as a writer by night. She holds a Bachelor of Arts in Legal Studies with a major in Literature and Law and a Master of Teaching secondary.

Voiceless is her Debut novel. After participating in NANOW-RIMO, she discovered she could write a novel and decided to just go for it—she hasn't looked back since. She hopes that her Young Adult Urban Fantasy novel will delight Coming of Age readers and adults alike. It is a subversion of the classic *The Little Mermaid* story. Prior to writing her novel, she had been a serial poet and short story writer. She hopes to thrill, inspire, and reinforce a love of reading in all who pick up her work.